...inventive and original....
--Austenesque Reviews

Praise for Maria Grace

"Grace has quickly become one of my favorite authors of Austen-inspired fiction. Her love of Austen's characters and the Regency era shine through in all of her novels." ***Diary of an Eccentric***

"Maria Grace is stunning and emotional, and readers will be blown away by the uniqueness of her plot and characterization" ***Savvy Verse and Wit***

"Maria Grace has once again brought to her readers a delightful, entertaining and sweetly romantic story while using Austen's characters as a launching point for the tale." ***Calico Critic***

I believe that this is what Maria Grace does best, blend old and new together to create a story that has the framework of Austen and her characters, but contains enough new and exciting content to keep me turning the pages. … Grace's style is not to be missed.. ***From the desk of Kimberly Denny-Ryder***

All the Appearance of Goodness

Maria Grace

White Soup Press

Published by: White Soup Press

All the Appearance of Goodness

For information, address
author.MariaGrace@gmail.com

ISBN: 061578870X
ISBN-13: 978-0615788708 (WhiteSoupr Press)

Author's Website: RandomBitsofFaascination.com
Email address: Author.MariaGrace@gmail.com

Dedication

For my husband and sons.
You have always believed in me.

Chapter 1

MOTHERS OF YOUNG LADIES universally agree. A great fault exists in the management of young men's education when one receives all the goodness while another, all the appearance of it.

Late Spring 1812

Darcy closed his book and peered through the carriage windows. They had made Meryton in good time, just before the heat of the day. From all indications, the temperatures would become considerably less comfortable as the morning wore into afternoon.

Bradley, his friend and vicar, craned his neck and looked out the side glass. "What a lovely, quaint, little place, just as Mr. Pierce described. I think his cottage is quite close to your new home, Bingley."

Darcy squirmed in his seat and tugged at his collar.

"I imagine the society is something savage." He snorted and returned his attention to his book.

Bingley clapped his shoulder. "Come now, Darcy! You must leave this stuffy attitude of yours behind."

"Must I?" Darcy rolled his eyes and folded his arms over his chest. "Mayhap I must send you out of my coach and back to your own where you may impose your improvements upon your sister and her maid."

Bingley laughed and stretched his long legs along the floorboards. "Louisa banished me here as she wanted to sleep on the way this morning. Besides, you no longer impress me with your 'Master of Pemberley' mask."

Bradley smiled his wry, paternal smile. "He is right. Your glare scares off a goodly number of people."

"I believe that is his intention." Bingley winked and grinned most annoyingly. "He dons this particular visage often enough, especially when he must mix with strangers."

"Bingley—" Darcy grumbled. His forehead knotted. Though his closest friend, Bingley played the role of a most annoying sibling quite effectively. Perhaps it was best Darcy had no younger brothers.

"Your glower no longer frightens me." Bingley brushed the idea aside. "I will not allow you an excuse for avoiding unfamiliar company." He nudged Darcy's foot with his.

Darcy crossed his legs and looked away. For Bradley's sake alone, he curbed the colorful words that danced on his tongue. "I am not fond of company."

"I would not be so fastidious for a king's fortune."

"I am not fastidious. Can you not allow for differences among people? I do not enjoy making small talk and milling about."

Bingley's eyes twinkled, tiny creases wrinkling their corners. "And what of dancing?"

"Tolerable enough, I suppose, when one knows his partner, but with a stranger…" Darcy suppressed a shudder.

"A half hour can feel like a very long time when forced to perform for company. It becomes an eternity for one struggling for conversation with someone unfamiliar." Bradley rubbed his jaw.

"Thank you." Darcy tipped his head.

This discussion had been repeated often enough, and on this point Bingley would not concede. He remained determined to make Darcy enjoy society.

Bingley leaned forward on his elbows. "Given your way, you would find a woman as fascinated by estate management as you. You could sit at tea and discuss seed drills and crop rotations! No small talk regarding the weather at meals or in the drawing room. Tenant disputes and the price of wheat will dominate your dinner table conversation."

"Pray tell, why am I wrong to prefer useful dialogue to mindless fluff?" Darcy huffed and slouched against the cushions.

Bradley flashed a quick glance at Bingley and reached across the coach to slap Darcy's shoulder. "No one says you are wrong."

Darcy sighed and tucked his chin to his chest.

Bingley wrinkled his nose. "Come now, you have nary a thing to worry about whilst you visit here. None know you, and once you leave, you will never encounter any of them again. I can think of no more perfect place for you to spread your wings and learn the gentle art of sociability."

"You cannot expect me to expose myself in such company." Darcy squirmed.

Bingley dropped back, hands laced behind his head. "Meeting agreeable people is not the same thing as exposing yourself. You will enjoy it."

That smug smile Bingley wore tried his patience. What had he been thinking when he agreed to this ridiculous adventure? Darcy pinched the bridge of his nose.

"I will help you the way I did at school. While I occupy Netherfield, Louisa and I will host dinners, parties, perhaps a ball. We will assist you in becoming acquainted with the neighborhood—"

"Already you talk of meeting the neighbors and hosting gatherings, and you have not yet seen the house? You put the cart before the horse." Darcy looked from Bingley to Bradley.

Bradley smiled and pressed his lips together tightly. His shoulders quivered slightly.

"I have every faith it will be as the solicitor described. I say, you need not be so gloomy." Bingley pushed hair away from his eyes.

"I am not gloomy. I am a realist."

"The difference hardly signifies." Bingley's lips creased into a small frown.

The coach lurched to a stop.

Bingley peered out the side glass. "The Green Swan—what a curious name for an inn."

"You are certain Bascombe told you to meet him here?" Darcy asked.

"How many establishments by the name of Green Swan can be in a town this size?" Bingley laughed and pushed the door open. "Are you coming?"

Darcy glanced at Bradley. "Not now. Get your sister settled. I will continue on to accompany Bradley to Pierce's. Expect me for dinner."

Bradley raised his eyebrow.

"Capital! With any luck, I will be able to talk with Bascombe and arrange a tour before you return." Bingley touched the brim of his hat and ducked out.

Darcy leaned out and instructed the driver. He shut the door and settled into his seat. Without Bingley's refreshing—albeit maddening—cheer, the afternoon's heat turned stifling.

Bradley slid the windows open. "You are troubled."

"Is it so clear?" Darcy rested his head against the seat.

"Tell me."

"I fear this trip is a mistake."

"How? The timing could not be better. Your sister stays with your aunt, and the spring planting is finished."

"You are well aware that is not the issue." Darcy squeezed his eyes shut and shook his head. "I am not fit for company. I never have been."

"Your friends in Derbyshire might disagree."

"I have known them all my life."

"Are not the Lackleys recently come to Derbyshire? If I recall correctly, he purchased the estate two years ago."

"It is not the same."

"No, it is not. You met them in Coopertons' home, surrounded by friends who eased the way for you to become acquainted."

"Neither Bingley nor I know anyone in Hertfordshire. What am I to do?"

Bradley extended an open hand. "Let Bingley assist

you. He will soon be introduced to everyone here and make certain you are as well."

"It was one thing at Cambridge, but we are no longer in school. It is not fitting for—"

"Someone of his social standing to assist you?"

"No—well, yes." Darcy raised his hands. "I am the one who should make introductions for him."

Bradley nodded and scratched a spot behind his left ear. "So, you are too proud to accept the help of someone beneath you."

Darcy harrumphed and retreated into the squabs. "I will see the house as I promised Bingley, then I will go home. Write me when you are ready to return, and I will—"

"You will do no such thing." Bradley slapped the seat beside him.

Darcy jumped.

"Stop behaving like a child. You have spent far too much time holed away on your estate. How can you ever find a wife—"

"A wife? Here in the quaint little village of Meryton, a wife? Surely you jest." Perhaps Lady Catherine was correct. He allowed his vicar too many liberties.

"I do not expect you to find a wife here. It is, though, a good place to practice those disciplines which will make you acceptable to young ladies of your circles. Do not look so offended! You say yourself you cannot manage small talk. Practice! You do not like to begin conversations with strangers. Polish those skills here. You complain you would rather not dance with ladies who are unfamiliar. Here is the place to become accustomed to the activity."

"You cannot be serious! It would be a punishment."

"A punishment for your improper pride?"

Darcy rubbed his temples and rolled his eyes. "You, of all people, know it is not pride."

"You are shy as was your father before you. I well understand."

"You sound unconvinced." Darcy glared at him.

How was it Bradley humbled him into a mere school boy with only a glance? He looked aside.

"I wonder if shyness is not in itself a form of pride."

Darcy grumbled and elbowed the seat back. "I do not comprehend your meaning."

"Shyness thinks of its comfort first and foremost. Is that not pride?"

Darcy shook his head sharply. Knots settled between his shoulders.

"Have you considered how uncomfortable others are in the presence of an aloof, arrogant man?"

"I am neither one of those things."

"Your father was regarded as a cold, distant, prideful man by those unacquainted with him. You will have the same reputation if you do not practice things that do not come easily to you." Bradley tapped his foot.

Darcy sagged and hid his face in his hands. "I will make a fool of myself."

"If that should happen, and I honestly cannot imagine how, you may leave. None of your circle will be the wiser. The company here is not the company you keep in London. I believe your reputation would be undamaged." Bradley clapped Darcy's shoulder. "The only way you learn to do something difficult—"

"Is through practice. You say it often enough." The corners of Darcy's lips turned up in spite of himself. How many years had Bradley been challenging him? Far too many to count. "You may be right, but I do not have to like it."

"Of course, you do not."

They laughed.

"I believe that is Mr. Pierce's home. He said he lived on the outskirts of Longbourn estate." Bradley pointed toward a neat cottage off the lane.

"It seems well kempt," Darcy mumbled. "Are you sure you will be comfortable staying with a veritable stranger? You are more than welcome to take rooms with Bingley and me at the inn."

"I appreciate your offer, and I will keep it in mind should the need arise. However, I can hardly suggest you do what I am unwilling to."

The coach slowed to a stop. Darcy pushed the door open and jumped down. He helped Bradley disembark.

"I will send your trunk along this evening." Darcy held Bradley's elbow until he gained his footing on the gravel path.

"Thank you. I fear you are spoiling me for traveling post!" Bradley shook Darcy's hand. He turned toward the man who approached. "Mr. Pierce, I trust?"

The man was tall and lean, simply but neatly dressed. He walked with easy assurance and a peaceful confidence so like Bradley—could the two men be related?

"I am indeed. Mr. Bradley?" He bowed. "Welcome to my home."

"Thank you kindly, sir." Bradley glanced back.

"Good day." Darcy tipped his head and returned to the waiting coach.

The carriage wheels crunched along the road. He gazed at the pastoral landscape and chewed his knuckle. Bradley's words still rang in his ears. Many had thought Father proud and distant. Now Bradley intimated he might bear the same reputation. Father had not been unduly proud. Those close to him understood him to be reserved and uncomfortable in company, as was his son.

Darcy's chest pinched and stomach roiled. He wrapped his arms around his waist. His friends were few. What did others see? Would they call him arrogant and unfeeling?

How did one breathe in such beastly heat? He rapped on the roof and jumped out as the coach stopped. "I have been confined too long today. Return to the inn. I will make my way on foot."

The driver turned to look at him. "Are you certain, sir? I can wait here while you refresh yourself."

"There is no need. Inform Mr. Bingley of my plans."

"Very good, sir." The driver slapped the reins, and the horses walked on.

Darcy gulped the fresh, cool air that tasted of youth and freedom. A small path into the woods caught his eyes. A walk was just the thing to clear his mind. He hurried along the tree-lined trail.

An old oak stretched out to cover the worn footpath and shook hands with elms on the other side. Matlock had a similar path. He cringed. The last time he had walked it was the day he had overheard Uncle Matlock defend Father to Aunt Catherine. She had called him a heartless, conceited man. Even the family mistook Father's true nature.

Perhaps Bradley was right.

His footsteps crunched through the deadfall. He threw his hands up and groaned. Of course, Bradley was right! When had that blasted man ever been wrong? He kicked a small stone.

A trio of birds burst from a clump of bushes. Raspberry bushes! He darted off the trail.

How long had it been since Mother took him to the berry patches near the stream? Father sometimes joined them on a picnic, and they would feast on berries after. Somehow, the fruit always tasted better by the riverbanks than from silver bowls on the dining table.

He plucked some raspberries and pricked his fingers. Their sweetness was worth the sting. Bradley often said the sweetness of righteousness was worth the sting of correction. Gah! He tossed his head. How could that man's words follow and torment him everywhere he turned? He cast about for a place to sit and settled himself on a fallen log.

Practice! Bradley said to practice. He combed sticky fingers through his hair. Did Bradley believe he might one day be like Bingley? He gazed at the clouds and cringed. Producing the volumes of empty conversation Bingley did would surely be the death of him. Perhaps, though, he could become recognized as a quiet man instead of a proud one. But how?

Enough woolgathering. Bingley was waiting for him. He needed to get back. His quest for berries had taken him off the path. Now the trail was nowhere in sight. Bloody foolish move! Even his footprints were lost in the undergrowth.

A sweet laugh rang through the woods, and a feminine voice broke out in song.

His heart pounded wildly. Could salvation be so

easy? "You there! Pray, excuse me!"

Branches rustled nearby.

"Who calls me?" the sweet voice cried.

"Here, please. I am in need of assistance." His cheeks burned. The Master of Pemberley lost in a stranger's woods? How humiliating!

"Have you a name, sir?" A face—a lovely one—appeared in the bushes, the girl herself a moment later.

Darcy gasped.

Her fine gown and the well woven basket she carried declared her a gentlewoman, and he without a proper introduction.

The burn in his cheeks crept along his jaw to his ears. He bowed. "Forgive me, madam. I am Fitzwilliam Darcy of Pemberley in Derbyshire." His coat caught on a thorny cane, and he fumbled to release it.

"I am pleased to meet you, Mr. Darcy of Pemberley." She curtsied. "I am Miss Elizabeth Bennet of Longbourn, the estate you trespass upon." Her eyes twinkled and lips turned up in a dainty little bow.

The last of the branches released him. He stumbled near her. "Please forgive my trespass."

"How have you come to be lost in my father's woods, so far from the main road?" Her teasing voice belied her arched brow.

Her smile cooled the heat in his face. "We arrived from Derbyshire this morning. I left my friend at the cottage not far from here to visit with—" He glanced over his shoulder.

"Mr. Pierce?"

"Yes, that was the name."

"He is our curate and my father's tenant. Is your friend the vicar from Derbyshire?"

"He is."

"How came you to be in these woods, sir?"

Her eyes held him, compelled him to keep her attention, though in the same moment, stealing away his powers of speech.

He shook his head sharply. "Ah, yes. I needed to stretch my legs, so I decided to walk to town and sent my driver ahead. A small path off the road caught my eye and I followed it." Already he had spoken to her more than to any young woman outside his circle in a year at least. Bradley would be impressed.

"You became distracted by the loveliness of our woods and, before you knew what you were about, you lost your way?"

He dug his toes into the soft dirt.

"I should laugh at your misfortune, but I strive to avoid hypocrisy. I will show you to the main road." She beckoned him to follow.

"I am quite in your debt. Usually, I am far more observant."

"Long hours in a carriage cause my mind to wander. I am most sympathetic." She pushed her basket through the bushes ahead of her.

Where had she traveled? She must be a most agreeable travel companion.

"Might I be of service, madam? May I carry that for you?" He reached for the large basket.

"An empty basket is hardly any trouble. If you desired to be truly gallant, you should have lost your way several hours ago." She laughed, but allowed him to take the hamper.

"This would hold a meal for quite a large family." He held it in front of him, turning it this way and that. Surely it must be the heat—what else could make him sound so much like Bingley?

"It did. I brought soup and other comforts to two of my father's tenants who are taken with colds."

She visited her father's tenants. His heart skipped a beat. Bingley would find this rich.

"I hope their ailments were mild. Only recently we lost our previous vicar to a cold that settled into his lungs."

"So, your friend has only recently become vicar?" She gazed at him. A little crease formed between her eyes.

What a delightful expression!

"Yes, he served as curate for almost all my life. We rely upon his wisdom regularly."

"He sounds like our Mr. Pierce."

"Does your curate deliver a good sermon?"

"That would depend upon whom you ask. He writes his own sermons. Many speculate during the week as to what he will speak about on Sundays."

Darcy snickered. "Forgive me. My aunt's ridiculous parson once waxed most philosophical on the sinful arrogance of a man who writes his own sermons. I imagine his sermons are also much discussed, though for different reasons. No one accuses him of dispensing wisdom to his parish. His flock is truly safe from those unsettling influences."

Miss Bennet's expression softened, and she laughed, the ring of gaily pealing bells in the morning sun.

"We have reached the main road, Mr. Darcy of Pemberley." She pointed through a break in the branches.

"I am in your debt, Miss Bennet of Longbourn." He forced his fingers to release the basket into her hands. "I hope to make your acquaintance again, so we may be properly introduced."

Her cheeks colored with a dainty blush. Should that make him smile so?

"Thank you for the compliment, sir. If your stay here will be of some duration, we will likely meet in town, or perhaps at one gathering or another."

It was still too soon to let her go. What else could he say? "The other friend I traveled with expects to take a lease on Netherfield Park. Is that property near your father's estate?"

"Netherfield is our nearest neighbor. My sisters and I will certainly call upon his wife—"

"His sister will keep house for him."

"Then we will pay her a call soon."

He would see her again! If his heart beat any louder, she would surely hear. Bingley must take Netherfield.

She pointed down the road. "A short walk will bring you into town."

"I am much obliged." He bowed and set off along the lane. What an asset a pair of fine eyes was in the face of a lovely young lady. Bradley did not need to know that, net yet. Darcy chuckled under his breath. Bradley would be satisfied that he planned to continue his stay in Hertfordshire.

Bingley handed Louisa down from the coach and scanned the street. A slight breeze rustled the skirts of a passing group of ladies. The Green Swan's sign swayed and creaked. The inn appeared agreeable enough, probably the best accommodations in town.

Several attractive offices and shops flanked the building, display windows filled with tempting offerings. Across the street, a chocolate house and confectioner sent tempting scents wafting on the breeze. Doubtless Caroline would declare the whole place frightful—all the more reason to find it charming.

He stared into Louisa's eyes. "Are you disappointed?"

The corners of her eyes drooped, but she smiled, just a little. "Not disappointed, only surprised. I did not expect Meryton to be so…quaint."

He sighed.

She touched his arm. "I like quaint. Do not look at me that way. I do."

"You are too kind to speak what you truly think. Be honest. Will you miss the diversions of London?"

"I am not certain." She gazed along the street, eyes flitting from one establishment to the next. "I am sure there are pleasant entertainments here as well."

"I did not ask you to be the mistress of my home only for you to be discontent."

"Please, Charles, if you do not take this house, I will have to return to London…with Caroline." She swallowed hard. "As it is, she expects to accompany Mr. Hurst and me on our honeymoon. I dare say she will ask to stay on in our home after that."

"I had no idea."

"Of course not." Louisa's voice thinned and sharpened. "You might object and interfere with her plans, and above all, she will have her way."

"You should have told me. I would…that is to say, I will find a way to stop her." He squeezed his temples.

"I understand you wish to, but we both know how

she is. This may be the only time I am able to…" She screwed her eyes shut.

"Live without her?"

"Yes." She turned a rock over in the road. A light breeze swirled bits of dust around her feet.

"So you will be happy here?"

She looked up at him. "Yes, I am sure of it. You and I, we are so similar, the house will be very peaceful. I will enjoy that very much. Better still, I shall relish the opportunities to make decisions without worrying about Caroline's disapproval. We might have our favorites for dinner every night and never see another fashionable French dish the entire time we are here."

He placed her hand in the crook of his arm and laughed softly. "I look forward to it more than I can say." A letter to Hurst was definitely in order. Her betrothed would be only too happy to help Louisa take a stronger stance with Caroline.

"You see, it will be a very pleasing opportunity." She offered a determined little smile.

"I expect the society here will suit us well." He directed them to the steps. "Shall we? I believe I have a new landlord to meet."

Bradley followed Pierce to the front parlor of the neat cottage. The bright windows offered a good view of the lane. The sun had faded the aged furniture, but, filled with bookcases and fluffy pillows, the room invited him in like an old friend.

Pierce took a tea tray from the housekeeper. She curtsied and shut the door behind her.

"You will have to forgive my lack of elegance." Pierce laughed as he served the tea. "I would just as soon do this myself than tempt my housekeeper to gossip."

Bradley lifted his eyebrows.

"Do not get the wrong idea of her. She is a lovely woman, and I have no complaints with her service. Still, it does not do to lay temptation in another's path—even if they are," Pierce cleared his throat, "merely a servant. Do you care for sugar?"

"No, thank you." Bradley stroked his cheek. How interesting to hear his opinions from the mouth of another. He took the teacup and drew a long sip. "You have an excellent situation here. Your vicar treats you well?"

"Yes, he does. Have you met Mr. Bell?"

"I do not believe I have had the pleasure."

"I will make sure you do as he is in Hertfordshire this month. He could have had me quite cheaply, you know." Pierce chuckled. "But, he believes the worker is worth his wage and is quite generous."

"He is away from here often? Where does he travel?"

"London mostly. Many believe he is soon to become a bishop. He spends much time with the church leadership." Pierce set his teacup down with a soft clink and settled into his threadbare chair.

Bradley tapped his lip with his knuckle. "How do you feel about your vicar becoming a bishop?"

"Does not the Good Book say that the eye is not a hand and the hand not a foot? Each should serve in the best way he can with the gifts he is given, without jealousy or envy." Pierce peered into Bradley's eyes. "Do you wish for me to criticize him? I am afraid I cannot oblige."

"Indeed?"

"He is a gifted man in those areas that will serve him well if he is made bishop. I will rejoice with him should he attain the post. I do not have those same gifts and do not pursue such an exalted rank."

Bradley nodded. "You are aware I—"

"I understand you seek a curate." Pierce drummed his fingers on the arm of his chair. "I still wonder why you are here, though. I already have a position. If you desire a recommendation, I know of several young men, newly japanned, who would appreciate the opportunity you offer."

"Thank you, but no. I suppose I am a peculiar fellow. I only just took the living myself, having served as curate to my parish for decades. I am rather...protective...of my flock."

"Interesting."

"I have more work to do than I can manage on my own."

"So, you are looking for someone to work alongside you, not in place of you?"

"Yes. The crux of the matter is I want a like-minded man whom I can raise up to take my place. When the Good Lord calls me to His bosom, I wish to depart this earthly vessel knowing my people will be well shepherded." Bradley eased back and crossed his legs.

"Do you own the advowson, or have you purchased the right of next presentation?"

"Neither."

"Then what is the point in this exercise?"

"My patron and I enjoy a unique relationship. He promised me the privilege of choosing my successor."

Pierce sat up a little straighter. "You believe he will do this?"

"I have known him all his life, and he is a man of his word."

"How singular!" Pierce rubbed a knuckle along his lips. "Intrigued as I am, I do not expect to be what you seek. Most find me…unconventional."

Bradley smiled broadly. He had never been a good card player. "Many call me that as well. What have you done to earn the distinction?"

"Any number of things, I suppose. Most recently, Sir William Lucas, our mayor, asked me why I should write my own sermons. After all, so many perfectly good ones are bound in the books on my shelves." Pierce pointed to the overflowing stacks.

"Pray tell, how did you answer him?"

"I told him it was far easier for me to write my own than to choose from amongst so many."

"A most politic response, I am impressed."

"What are you looking for?" Pierce cocked his head, brows drawn tight. "I do not wish you to waste your time."

"It is never a waste to take time to know a brother in the service of our Good Lord. I hesitate to tell you what I seek, though. A proud man would tell me he fits my description, even if he does not. A humble man would tell me he does not, even if he does."

"Quite the quandary, I suppose. How do you mean to resolve it?"

"Allow me to get to become acquainted with you."

"If you seek to know me, perhaps I should introduce you to the parish. One knows a man best by the fruit he bears." Pierce's small smile blossomed into a hearty laugh.

"You are much amused?"

"I find I am already reconsidering. Young Billy Thompson might not be a shining example of my influence."

"Really? I would like to hear this story." Elbows on his knees, Bradley leaned forward.

"Naturally." Pierce rolled his eyes, face coloring. He recounted how the Bennet sisters dealt fairly with Billy's thefts, while also keeping him from the magistrate. "As I said, perhaps not my most shining example—"

"I disagree. I find a man's character becomes clearest when he deals with the mistakes of others. I would like to meet the Bennets, and the Clays and Thompsons, if you are willing to make those introductions for me."

Pierce nodded. "If you decide I am what you seek, why should I consider your offer? Given I have the curacy here on easy terms, why would I be inclined to give that up?"

"A fair question, though I must ask you to wait on that answer. I do not want the knowledge to sway you one way or another."

"There is one other thing you should understand." Pierce's gaze wandered to the window, and he sighed softly. "I expect to be engaged very soon. She is one of the Bennet sisters. Her father is also my landlord."

"I see."

"You do not look as though you approve."

Bradley chewed his lip. "No, it is not that. I simply had not considered that you might bring a wife."

"Of course, few curates are able to afford to marry so young. If you cannot pay—"

"So, she does not bring with her a large fortune?"

"Her fortune is no concern of yours." Pierce jumped to his feet and paced. "Besides, my greatest interest is in her character, not her dowry."

"Once again, you prove yourself most unconventional." Bradley wagged a finger.

Pierce turned sharply. His expression relaxed as he caught Bradley's eye.

"Would you introduce me to your young lady? I should like to meet her."

Pierce threw his head back and laughed. "You are certainly an odd man, perhaps as eccentric as I. But, you intrigue me. I shall do all you ask. Will you allow me to know something of you in the meantime?"

"My patron is visiting Meryton with his friend. I will introduce you, and you may have his opinions of me." And he would have Darcy's opinions of Pierce.

"Fair enough."

"You write your own sermons, do you? Tell me of what you last preached." Bradley settled into his chair to enjoy pleasant conversation that lasted long into the night.

Chapter 2

TWO WEEKS LATER, Elizabeth perched on the footstool in her father's study, his latest correspondence open on her lap. The afternoon sun played over his handwriting, but it did not help the letter tell her more. His plans had changed, again. He and Uncle Gardiner were to return from their journey to Kent today, but without the guest he had previously talked about. Uncle Gardiner was most welcome, though he rarely visited without Aunt Gardiner and the children.

How strange this business! Papa was a man of few words, sometimes too few. He offered no explanation, no hints to help her read his meaning. She had little patience for puzzles. No sense in belaboring the point further. She would have no answers until he returned.

Best make certain the guestroom was ready for

Uncle Gardiner. She refolded the letter, tucked it into her pocket and took a final glance about the study. Papa's mail sat in a neat pile on the corner of his desk. His favorite tome, an elegant volume given him by Uncle Gardiner, occupied the center of the blotter. The book stacks on the floor had been dusted and the correct books restored to each stack. Papa would be pleased.

Two hours later, Elizabeth peeked out the window. Papa's coach trundled up the lane toward the house. She felt for the letter, her heart outpacing the carriage horses' hooves.

She dashed to the stairs. "Papa comes! Make haste. He and Uncle Gardiner come."

Her sisters followed her to the front steps.

"Perhaps he brought me something." Lydia bumped Kitty's shoulder with hers.

Mary and Elizabeth glared at her.

"La! Do not be so crotchety. It is not wrong to wonder." Lydia tossed her head and edged away from her elder sisters.

Elizabeth rolled her eyes. Only just this morning, Lydia had said something sensible and mature. Perhaps once a day was the best she could hope for.

Kitty whispered to Jane, who blushed and covered her face with her hand.

Why did the driver proceed so slowly? If only she could run to meet them, but Mama insisted ladies did not run.

The coach rolled to a stop, and the door creaked open. Papa emerged, stooped and stiff as newly starched cuffs. Uncle Gardiner slipped out and unfolded himself like a letter creased too long.

"Papa! Uncle Gardiner!" Elizabeth rushed toward

them. "We missed you so, Papa!" She threw her arms around his neck.

He pulled her close. "I am glad to be home, my dear. I missed you all."

She breathed deeply against his chest. She loved Papa's warm, mellow scent. How could a smell so calm her spirit and soothe the emptiness she had forced herself to ignore since his departure?

"We are glad you are come home, Papa," Jane said, peering over his shoulder. "We are glad you are come, Uncle Gardiner."

"How much you all have grown!" Uncle Gardiner grinned. "Sister!" He hurried up the stairs.

When had Mama joined them?

Papa released Elizabeth and rushed up the steps. "Mrs. Bennet!" He grasped her hand. "My dear, I cannot tell you how happy I am to see you!"

Misty eyed, Elizabeth took Jane's elbow. "I think Papa believed we overstated our reports of Mama's recovery."

"Perhaps the affair with Lydia was not so bad a thing," Jane whispered.

Elizabeth shook her head and tried not to roll her eyes. Only Jane could make such a remark and expect to be taken seriously. "I am glad Mama is well."

They followed their parents into the drawing room. Mama called for tea. The family settled in, each taking up their favorite spots. How Papa's empty seat had vexed her all these weeks!

Mama busied herself preparing tea. "Were your travels pleasant?"

Elizabeth worried her bottom lip. Mama usually carried the conversation. Her veritable silence itched like a woolen cloak.

"They were most interesting. Thank you." Gardiner took the teacup and drew a long sip. "Ahh, decent tea cannot be found at the coaching inns!"

"Were the roads bad?" Mary smoothed her dress. "We heard of fierce weather between Kent and London."

"Relentless storms dogged our entire journey. I thought perhaps we should have taken a ship." Papa chuckled. "It might have been faster to walk."

"Did you accomplish your business?" Elizabeth asked.

"Well enough." Papa's brows drew together.

Elizabeth clamped her jaw shut and dropped her eyes.

He raised his cup, breathed in the fragrance, and took a long sip. "How I longed for a decent cup of tea! Used tea leaves are truly dreadful stuff. The comforts of home can never be too much appreciated."

"Hill prepared your rooms, and bathwater is ready should you desire." Mama's eyes flickered up and back down.

"Those are temptations too great to ignore. I am so tired of road dust." Uncle Gardiner pushed himself up from his seat and groaned. "Perhaps a hot bath will loosen these old joints." He tipped his head and left.

"Tell me of all that has transpired since my departure." Papa looked directly at Lydia.

"The regiment left and Mrs. Forster has barely written me." Lydia wrapped her arms tightly over her chest and stuck out her lower lip.

"Indeed." Papa's shaggy eyebrow arched high.

Jane passed him a plate of biscuits.

He took several and crunched them as his gaze

moved from one daughter to the next.

Mary sipped her tea and cast a quick sidelong glance at Elizabeth. "We had some modicum of excitement when Mr. Thompson and Mr. Clay experienced a small dispute. Mr. Pierce assisted us in resolving it quickly and amicably."

Mama choked back an unhappy squeak.

Kitty bounced on the settee and clapped. "Oh, oh, I sewed the entire time you were gone and remade dresses for all my sisters. So many of our friends have noticed! The whole neighborhood is talking about them. Miss Long even asked me to come with her for her next fitting at the modiste."

"I still would prefer a new gown," Lydia muttered under her breath.

Papa chuckled. "And you, Jane? Have you missed the company of the Carvers?"

"Certainly not." Mama picked at her skirts. "What a terrible family! Not fit companions for my dear girls."

"Oh, there is some exciting news!" Kitty said. "Netherfield Park is to be let at last."

"What a fine thing for the community." Papa huffed and crossed his legs.

Kitty and Lydia launched into the gossip and speculation surrounding Netherfield's newest occupants.

Half an hour later, they exhausted all the neighborhood news as well as their tea and biscuits.

"I am for my bookroom. My favorite chair and a stack of mail call." Papa's joints popped as he rose. "Lizzy, you will attend me, please."

His voice contained the barest edge of rebuke. Was it for her? Elizabeth followed him to his study and held her breath as he settled into his chair.

He pointed to the footstool. "Sit, sit. Your mother is not here to fuss at your chosen seat."

She pulled the stool close and sat.

Papa threw his head back and closed his eyes. He exhaled heavily, the sound of a contented tomcat. "I have missed this, Lizzy. Now, no more stalling, tell me everything that occurred whilst I was gone—Lydia, the tenants, everything." He leaned forward and tapped his fingers together in front of his chest.

"Oh, Papa, I hardly know where to begin."

"At the beginning is the accepted convention." His lips drew into a wry smile.

She braced elbows on knees, chin on her fists and recounted all the events of his absence.

"No doubt, Jane thinks Lydia's mischief a blessing in disguise." He clutched his temples.

She snickered behind her hand.

He winked. "I confess, I welcome the change in your mother, whatever the reason."

She bit her lips shut.

"Yes, my dear," he sighed loudly, "your warnings before I left were correct. Fortunately, the nonsense came to nothing, and we can return to our quiet existence."

"Until the next new gentlemen enter the neighborhood, an event destined to take place quite soon. Papa, please—"

"Do not make yourself uneasy, dear." He patted her hand. "I will have some words with her."

She stared at him, but his jaw was set. They would have no further conversation on those concerns. She nodded and dropped her eyes. "Will you tell me of your trip? Was your business successful?"

"Worry not for that." His gaze drifted to the window, and his lips drooped.

"You do not seem pleased—"

"I have no wish to discuss the matter."

His sharp tone sliced through her. She jumped back and nearly lost her balance on the narrow stool. "Yes, sir." The words barely carried in the chill air. She ducked her head and pushed to her feet.

"Wait." He caught her hand.

She settled on the far side of the footstool, hands folded in her lap and stared at her fingernails.

"I need your help—with your mother."

What had he said? She lifted her head and peered at him. His eyes revealed nothing, much like his letter. The nagging, anxious knot returned to her left side, just between her ribs.

"You wonder why your Uncle Gardiner visits with us."

She nodded.

"I asked him to come to help with your mother, as I am asking you."

Her stomach clenched. "With what, Papa?"

"You know your mother dislikes overnight guests."

"Uncle and Aunt Gardiner are the only people I remember staying with us."

"Quite so." He pursed his lips and released a long slow breath. "Your mother…there are reasons for her reticence, reasons which need not be discussed, but sufficient that I have never challenged her on this issue. Until now."

Elizabeth chewed her lips. So many questions raced across the tip of her tongue, she might well climb out of her skin waiting for Papa to provide far too few answers.

"In a se'nnight, at most a fortnight, we shall receive a guest whom you have never met."

"Oh, my." She bit her knuckle.

"My cousin, Collins, upon whom Longbourn is entailed, wishes to view the estate and discuss certain…aspects of its management with me."

"He cannot take rooms at the Green Swan?" She covered her mouth with her hand. Why could she not control her tongue?

"No, he cannot."

At least his voice lost some, though not all, of its harshness.

"Collins will stay here." He scrubbed his face with his hands. "He is a polite, well-spoken young man. I visited him while in Kent. I do not expect he will be a troublesome guest—except for your mother's nerves."

"What do you wish me to do?"

"Until he arrives, assist your mother in dwelling on other things, rather than fretting his arrival. Once he comes, help her to recognize him for the amiable young man that he is. I believe he desires to make amends for his father's ways. I misjudged him earlier. I will try to explain to your mother, but I suspect she will need more than just my assurances." He pressed his forehead on his fingertips.

"How long is he to stay?" A thousand other questions jostled for the opportunity to be asked, but with Papa's current temper she dare ask only one.

"I do not know." He closed his eyes, brow knotted. "I will do everything I can to hasten him on his way."

She nodded and watched him. Perhaps he might divulge something more.

Or not.

"I will do my best to help Mama."

"Thank you." He hoisted himself out of his chair. "Now I must break the news to your mother."

What with Papa's strange behavior, her mother's nerves, an unfamiliar guest expected in their home, sleep proved elusive for Elizabeth. Papa's arrival should have set everything back to rights, not created more agitation. She sat up in bed and wrapped her arms around her knees. The moonlight played along the folds of her sheets, painting the hollows with shadow.

She wanted answers. Papa offered none. Patience. She needed that virtue which, for her, seemed always in short supply. If only there were a way, other than practice, to obtain it.

Perhaps caring for Mama might take her mind off her own frustration. She yawned and slid under the sheets, her eyelids finally heavy enough for sleep.

Elizabeth slept later than usual and hurried through her morning ablutions, concerned she might be too late to assist with Mama. She should not have worried. Mama's morning meeting with Hill lasted much longer than usual, so Jane and Elizabeth lingered over breakfast. Surely Mama would appear soon.

The kitchen door rattled.

"Girls," Mama's voice trembled, a breathy whisper. She leaned on the doorframe.

Jane rushed to her side. "Sit with us, Mama. We have tea and toast for you."

Elizabeth made the tea while Jane held Mama's hand and murmured encouraging things under her breath.

"Thank you, my dear." The cup rattled against the saucer as Mama took it from Elizabeth. "So many plans to be made! I…I…"

"Perhaps we might help." Jane scooped jam onto a slice of toast.

"I hardly know how to arrange the menus."

"He cannot expect us to be aware of his preferences." Jane passed her a plate.

Mama nibbled at the toast. "I should acquire a new gown." She glanced at her sleeves. "This one is dreadfully out of style. When shall I find the time to visit the modiste? She is frightfully slow. What will…he…think of me? Just look at these sleeves!"

"You should let Kitty attend to it. Did she show you my old sprigged muslin?" Elizabeth raised her brows at Jane. Much as she tried, she did not understand how a new dress could be so important right now.

"She showed me some of her projects a few days ago." Mama sighed and pushed her half-finished toast aside.

Jane straightened the lace on Mama's sleeve. "A new gown would be just the thing for when you visit our new neighbors at Netherfield."

"Oh, yes!" Mama's eyes widened, and the corners of her mouth turned up.

Of course, Jane would find the way to distract Mama. She always knew what to say.

"Hill said that a gentleman is taking Netherfield and his sister will be his hostess. He is unmarried, girls! Once your father visits him, you must take every opportunity…"

Elizabeth struggled not to roll her eyes. How profoundly unfair! Matchmaking would be the thing to divert Mama from her worries. Mary would tell her she should not find fault with her blessings, however small. But, Elizabeth doubted she could manage that.

"I already met her, Mama," Jane said.

Elizabeth gaped at her. "You have?"

"Indeed?" All traces of heaviness left Mama's countenance. She leaned toward them. "What sort of lady is she?"

"She is pretty, with a gentle disposition that you will like very well. Her betrothed is on the continent. She will keep house for her brother until he returns."

"How did you meet? Tell me more." Mama's color rose. "Was her brother with her? Was he a well-looking man? What of his fortune? Did you—"

"No, Mama, I did not meet him, nor could I have inquired after his fortune so early in our acquaintance."

"Well, never mind that." She patted Jane's forearm. "You did well to meet her already. Tell me of your meeting—you must stop dithering."

Tiny creases appeared on Jane's brow. So, even her patience had limits.

"The day before yesterday, I was in town, on my way out of Mr. Nash's shop, and she on her way in. We ran into each other in the doorway. I begged her forgiveness for the mishap. Sir William was there as well, and he introduced us. Her name is Miss Louisa Bingley. She told me of her brother's intentions and asked me to call upon her at the inn at my earliest convenience."

"Well, certainly you must visit her!" Mama

clapped.

Elizabeth cringed.

"The poor dear must be frightfully lonely with only her brother for company. Well-meaning though he might be, a brother is never as welcome as a sister or another woman."

Elizabeth stared at Mama. Could she have misheard?

"She was well-mannered and asked what shops I recommended. I think she is trying to find her place as mistress of Netherfield. I should like to know her better."

"Did she say when they would take possession?" Mama asked.

"They have not yet fixed on the date, but she expects it will be soon."

"What a fine thing! I will insist your father visit him as soon as may be managed. Perhaps even today! Then we may host a dinner for them to introduce them to the neighborhood. Oh, we must invite the Lucases and the Gouldings and the Longs…oh, I must go discuss this with Hill. You girls go to town and find out when I may fix upon a date for the dinner party. What a good plan this is!" She rose and dropped her napkin on the table. "Hill! Hill!" She disappeared down the hall.

Elizabeth scratched her temple. "I am not certain whether Mama is more excited about the matchmaking prospects or about a new lady in the neighborhood."

"I am willing to call it a blessing either way if it keeps her melancholy at bay." Jane laughed. "Miss Bingley is a dear girl, and you will not regret an acquaintance with her, no matter what her brother is like."

Elizabeth chuckled.

"Come, you will see. Let us go and pay a visit to my new friend."

"Very well, how can I resist the opportunity to give pleasure to so many, all at the same time?"

Their preparations to go into town attracted much notice. Soon all five sisters donned gloves and bonnets and headed out.

"I am off to the linen draper to find ribbons and lace and new patterns." Kitty skipped ahead, basket swinging at her side. She turned to face her sisters and walked backwards. "Mama asked me to attend to her gown—"

"What of mine?" Lydia folded her arms across her chest.

"I have done so many of yours already."

Lydia stomped. "You promised."

Kitty turned around. "It will be finished in time for the assembly."

"And the other one?"

"Lydia," Mary said firmly and wrapped her arm in Lydia's.

"You will tell me to be patient—but I do not want to be patient. I do not like patience!"

Elizabeth looked away. Lydia was not the only one who disliked patience.

"It is a necessary virtue." Mary smiled a lopsided smile and shrugged.

Kitty called over her shoulder. "I will sew as quickly as I can."

Lydia screwed her face into an ugly scowl.

Mary sighed.

"You will come with us to visit Miss Bingley, will

you not, Lydia?" Jane asked.

"Oh, yes! I have had no entertainment since the Miss Carvers and Mrs. Forester left." Lydia pulled away from Mary. "Oh, do not glare at me. I like to have fun, but I learned my lesson. Did you not notice that I did not ask if she has a brother? I do not care, so do not tell me."

Elizabeth hesitated and stared at Lydia. How had she neglected to note Lydia's failure to inquire after the possibility of eligible young men? She needed to pay more attention to her youngest sister.

"I think Miss Bingley might appreciate a bit of fun. It is difficult to come into a new place," Jane said.

"Well then, let us hurry." Kitty stepped up her pace for the last half block to the Green Swan Inn.

They paused at the base of the stairs to straighten their bonnets and brush the road dust from their skirts.

Jane led them into the parlor. The room was snug and neat, decorated in an older style. The furnishings were worn, but not worn out. Shelves along the far wall were populated with a few books that probably knew little use. Lydia would call it shabby, but Elizabeth found it cozy. Only three patrons occupied the space, two older men playing cards and a fashionably dressed young woman sitting in a sunny corner, focused on her needlework.

"There she is." Jane approached her. "Miss Bingley."

Miss Bingley jumped and looked over her shoulder. "Miss Bennet."

"I brought my sisters with me." Jane beckoned them nearer. "This is Elizabeth, Mary and Catherine—"

"Kitty if you please," she interjected with a quick curtsey.

"Certainly, Miss Kitty." Louisa stood and curtsied.

"And my youngest sister, Lydia."

"I am pleased to make your acquaintance. Will you not sit with me? The innkeeper will bring tea soon."

Jane looked over her shoulder. "Were you expecting other company? We do not want to intrude."

"It would be no trouble for us to return later, or on another day, if you like," Kitty added.

"No, no, not at all! It is only my brother and his friend. I am certain he would not want you to leave on his account. He is a great lover of company and has wanted to meet you since I first told him of you. Please stay."

Miss Bingley looked so lonely, only the coldest of hearts could have denied her.

They moved several chairs into a close group as the innkeeper arrived with the tea service.

Jane sat near Miss Bingley. "What do you think of Meryton?"

Miss Bingley handed her a cup. "I find it charming."

"It is nothing to the diversions of London, I suppose." Lydia sniffed.

"Oh, I meant no insult at all," Miss Bingley stammered. "I quite like the quietness of this place. The hurried pace in town is not what I prefer."

"We take no offense, Miss Bingley." Elizabeth flashed a brief scowl at Lydia. "Different places accommodate different tastes. I am pleased Meryton will suit you."

"Do you know when you will take the house?" Mary folded her hands in her lap.

"Not yet, but soon, I think. My brother meets with the landowner this evening to finalize the plans."

"What fun to keep your own house!" Kitty clapped softly. "Will you be allowed to decorate?"

"I hardly expect my brother to be interested in redecorating a place he only leases." Miss Bingley pressed her lips tightly.

Elizabeth suspected she struggled not to laugh.

"You shall get to do that when you are married, though," Lydia said.

"I hope to." Miss Bingley twisted the pearl ring on her left hand. "He is on the continent attending to business matters. I shall be here until he returns."

"How long you do expect that to be?" Mary's cheeks colored.

Miss Bingley gripped her hands. "His last letter suggested it might be as much as a year."

Kitty frowned slightly. "It must be difficult to be away from him for so long. If you do not mind my asking, what is his business?"

Miss Bingley caught her breath and bit her lip. "He inherited his father's estate—"

"I meant nothing untoward by my question. Please do not be offended!" Kitty stammered. "Our Uncle Gardiner in London is in trade, and I just wondered if Mr. Hurst's business might be similar."

The little creases at the corners of Miss Bingley's eyes disappeared. "I fear I am a bit sensitive. My sister objects to Mr. Hurst's connections in trade. I am sorry if I have offended."

"It is forgotten." Jane smiled.

"You have a sister?" Elizabeth asked. "Will she join you here?"

"No. She stays at my brother's house in London.

Country life holds little appeal for her."

"What a shame! She shall never know how jolly a country assembly can be." Kitty traded wide-eyed glances with Lydia.

"What are the assemblies like?"

Lydia giggled. "They are ever so much fun!"

"Well, that is a relief to hear!" A warm voice called from the doorway.

Two gentlemen stood just inside the parlor, and one looked very familiar.

"Charles!" Miss Bingley hurried to his side. "Please, allow me to present my brother, Mr. Bingley, and his friend, Mr. Darcy. May I present my friends? These are the Miss Bennets of Longbourn—Miss Jane Bennet, Miss Elizabeth, Miss Mary, Miss Kitty and Miss Lydia."

They rose and curtsied as Miss Bingley introduced them.

The men bowed and followed Miss Bingley in.

Mr. Bingley took a seat beside his sister. "How kind of you to call on Louisa!"

Mr. Darcy sat in the lone remaining chair, next to Elizabeth. Miss Bingley poured tea for the men, and soon the conversation resumed with Kitty and Lydia detailing the last assembly to a rapt audience.

Elizabeth felt Mr. Darcy's gaze on her. He stirred in his seat, hands laced together. Odd that he should have been quite glib in their earlier encounter, yet so aloof here. "Did you enjoy your share of my father's raspberries, sir?" she asked softly, eyes on her sisters.

"Of what do you accuse me, Miss Elizabeth?" He glanced at her. One corner of his lips drew up.

"The last time I saw you, you sported drops of berry juice on your fingers and on your chin. I fear you are a most ineffective thief." She arched an eyebrow.

He colored and looked aside. His brows drew together until a deep crease formed between. "I suppose I must practice more. Pray tell, does your father have another garden I may sample from? Preferably one not so far from the main road." He ran a finger along the edge of his cravat.

"I think not. He prefers to keep them well hidden from the likes of gentlemen such as yourself."

Mr. Darcy squirmed in his seat.

Guilt nipped at her heel. She should not tease.

Darcy snorted. His cheek twitched with the hint of a smile.

Then again, perhaps he was capable of enjoying a good joke after all.

Bingley regaled them with yet another amusing tale. What a contrast to his reserved, quiet friend.

"We meet tonight to finalize Bingley's plans for Netherfield. He and his sister will soon be your neighbors," Darcy whispered.

"And you, sir, now that his business is completed, will you stay on with him or return to your own estate?"

He studied her with piercing eyes.

What did he seek? Only her old music master had scrutinized her so. Mama had dismissed him for it, too. A tiny shudder raced down the back of her neck, though she was not certain why.

"I believe I will stay on for a few weeks at least."

"I pray you will find it pleasant. Though we cannot boast the sophistication of London, many find Meryton a welcome respite from better society."

"I am sure I will." He shuffled his feet and glanced

about the room. "Are you acquainted with Mr. Bascombe?"

"A little. Why do you ask?"

"I prefer to know the reputations of those with whom I do business. What sort of man do you find Mr. Bascombe to be? What is his reputation in the community?"

Elizabeth frowned. "I do not wish to be branded a gossip."

"So, your opinion of him is hardly positive." His eyebrow rose.

"What have your dealings with him suggested?"

Darcy pressed his lips together. His eyes drifted to the ceiling roses. "Netherfield is clearly in need of repairs. Either he does not keep up his property, or he is short of the capital needed to make them."

She dipped her head and blinked.

"The condition of the tenant farms, the cottages and outbuildings suggests a man who is neither interested in the details of management, nor in the lives of his tenants."

"My sisters and I regularly call upon several of his cottagers—"

"He does not attend to their needs, but allows others in the neighborhood to fulfill his responsibilities." Darcy's gaze held hers.

His eyes were striking—and expressive—startlingly so. She looked away.

"Would his tenants agree with me?" He leaned in closer.

"I do not believe they would disagree," she whispered, cheeks uncomfortably hot.

"I have heard his name spoken in several establishments in town, with little fondness."

"But neither with animosity. He is not a quarrelsome man."

"Nor is he a generous one."

She turned to focus on a carriage passing by the window. "He is a proper gentleman."

"Faint praise, indeed."

"It is the best praise I can offer. Please do not press me further in this matter."

"Of course, forgive me. I appreciate your assistance. What would you prefer to speak of?"

She bit her bottom lip and cocked her head. "Pray tell me, do you grow raspberries on your estate?"

He chuckled.

Several hours later, Darcy and Bingley waited in the best room of the public house nearest the Green Swan. The tables around them were filled with loud men, talking, laughing and eating. Smells of food and hard work mingled into something less than appealing. Darcy reached into his pocket and pulled out the leather case containing his silverware. The plates on the other tables appeared none too clean as it was—eating off the forks in this place was not to be borne. The serving girl dropped two pints in front of them.

"Not the service or the victuals to which you are accustomed." Bingley lifted his pint and took a long draw from the tankard.

"My preferences are not the relevant ones here." Darcy examined his mug. He pulled out his handkerchief and wiped the lip. "The real question is whether or not you are comfortable in these environs or will you pine for the refinements of London in a few short months? The society here may be too confined and unvarying for you. A lease on a house like this one is a serious commitment."

Bingley parked his tankard on the table. "Three times you repeated that today. Rest assured; I take your point. I find country manners charming and am never as at home as I am in the country."

"As long as you are certain. Bascombe has arrived."

"How did you know? You could not possibly have seen him." Bingley peered over Darcy's shoulder.

"His nasal whine." Darcy did not look up. "Listen, it carries to all points in the room."

Bingley paused and cocked his head. "So, it does." He laughed and waved to Bascombe.

"Good evening, gentlemen. I took the liberty to instruct the girl to bring three plates." Bascombe dropped into the chair with all the grace of a sack of chicken feed. He spilled over the edges of the seat. The wooden joints groaned under him.

"Capital." Bingley bowed from his shoulders.

Bascombe waved at a passing serving girl and pointed toward the pints already on the table.

She returned a moment later and bounced a third mug in front of him. Bascombe took a long drink and wiped his mouth on his coat sleeve.

Darcy turned his head and shielded his eyes with his hand.

"The neighborhood is to your liking?" Bascombe asked.

"Very much so! Several of the local ladies have already visited my sister to welcome her."

"I am not surprised. Meryton is renowned for its friendliness." Bascombe leaned forward on his elbows. "I should warn you, not all the families here may be suitable company for your sister."

The server appeared, balancing three plates along her food-stained sleeve. She dropped them and utensils on the table with a grunt and turned away before they could comment.

Bascombe crammed his napkin between collar and cravat and plucked a knife and fork from the center of the table.

Darcy unrolled his utensils and polished them with his handkerchief. He carefully slipped a napkin into his collar and watched Bingley do the same.

"Indeed?" Bingley asked.

Bascombe sawed at his meat. "Absolutely, every neighborhood has its families to avoid. We are no different. My advice, keep a wide berth between your sister and the Bennet family."

Darcy straightened in his seat and drummed his fingers along his leg. "Why?"

"You have not heard? Even they have supporters, I suppose." He rolled his eyes. "My previous tenant found them unsuitable companions for his young sisters, not that those girls were exactly proper themselves."

How ironic. Miss Elizabeth refused to speak of the man who so freely voiced his opinions of her. Darcy ground his teeth until they squeaked together.

"The eldest Bennet girl is quite lovely, I grant. Our curate pays the plain middle daughter a great deal of attention, though I cannot make out why. The younger girls," he flicked his hand, "are nigh unmanageable. The entire town knows that the youngest one attempted an elopement, stopped by the next eldest, no less, not above two months ago. Such a thing taints the whole family—"

Darcy struck the table with the flat of his hand. The tankards rattled. "We are here to discuss the house and the lease, not the neighbors."

Bingley nodded. "Quite."

Bascombe pulled back and placed his fork and knife along the plate. He rubbed his palms together. "As you say, sir." He eyed them narrowly. His brows rose, and he cocked his head. "You already met them and found a bit o' that sort o' muslin to your liking?" A lewd smile twisted his mouth.

"Enough!" Darcy growled. "I take umbrage at your vulgar insinuation. If you do not cease, this conversation is at an end."

"Forgive me, sir. I mistook your meaning. I meant no offense."

Darcy grunted. If he walked out now, he would be throwing Bingley to that wolf, Bascombe, to be fleeced. He could not permit that. Though it took all his patience, he would stay.

"Yes, to business then." Bascombe cleared his throat and made a show of turning toward Bingley. "You and your sister toured the house and grounds. What say you of my humble home?"

"The manor is certainly ample for our needs." Bingley sent a pleading look at Darcy.

"However…" Darcy leaned in on his elbows.

Bingley relaxed into his chair.

Though Bingley might be at home in a ballroom, he was utterly lost in business negotiations. Here, Darcy was at his ease. He suppressed a smile. "Several matters need to be addressed before my friend will consider letting the place." He removed a folded paper from his coat pocket.

"I see, sir." Bascombe pulled at his cravat. "I cannot imagine any impediment to a speedy settlement."

"As you say." Darcy unfolded the paper and smoothed it on the table.

"What? No need for such formality—" Bascombe covered the list with his meaty hand.

"Do not trifle with me." Darcy snatched the notes and glared. "You and I are both well aware of the shortcomings of Netherfield Park."

"Who are you? Bingley's solicitor?"

Darcy rolled his eyes.

"You are a candidate for his steward, then? Well, you are not needed. The lease does not include—"

Darcy shoved his chair back. The legs squealed against the floorboards. A man who resorted to insults was not one with whom he wished to deal. "We can discuss the terms I have here and come to an agreement, or we can leave now. The choice is yours."

"Mr. Bingley! This is highly irregular. I am not accustomed—"

"To treating clients with courtesy and respect?" Bingley pushed back from the table. "I asked my friend's advice in this matter. If you will not treat him with the consideration due a gentleman of his standing, our conversation is at an end."

Bingley was a quick study.

"Do not be so hasty, sir. Of course, I would welcome his interfere—ah—assistance." Bascombe took a deep draw of his pint.

"Let us begin with the matter of the roof…" Darcy tapped the list.

Two hours of heated negotiations followed. Bascombe argued, pounded the table, turned red in the face, and capitulated to Darcy's requirements. Finally, when only one other table of patrons remained, the papers were signed and Bascombe trundled off, muttering invectives under his breath.

"I must say that was prodigious good fun." Bingley drew on his gloves and dusted off his hat.

"I am glad you found it so rewarding." Darcy smirked and led the way outside. "Do you still find country manners charming?"

"Not his." Bingley sniggered.

The night air held lingering traces of the day's heat, mingled with reminders of the horse traffic along the main street. A full moon lit the street for the pedestrians.

"I am not sure I would choose him as an example of country manners, though," Bingley said. "I believe the Miss Bennets a much better standard of comparison."

"Indeed."

"What think you of the insinuations he made of their family?"

Darcy deftly avoided Bingley's gaze. An imprudent younger sister? What a hypocrite he would be to condemn another family for a misbehaved relation! The Bennet sisters' graciousness toward Miss Bingley—and the fact they did not throw themselves at Bingley and himself—spoke of their character much more than the foolish actions of one. He tugged his sleeves. "I believe Bradley would say it is best to judge them on their own merits, not on the prattle of a man like Bascombe."

"Sensible advice." Bingley straightened his cravat.

Bingley liked one of the sisters. Naturally, he found a new angel wherever he went. Which one? Or had he even decided yet? Darcy shook his head.

Bingley was free to like any of them he chose, except Miss Elizabeth.

The next morning, Darcy and Bingley left on an early ride. On their return, they found three of the Miss Bennets with Miss Bingley in the inn's parlor.

"Please come and join us." Miss Bingley beckoned them in

They removed their hats as the ladies rose.

"Good day." Bingley bowed.

Darcy did likewise.

"Good day." The ladies curtsied and returned to their seats.

Bingley settled between his sister and Miss Kitty. Darcy's cheeks heated as he sat beside Miss Elizabeth.

"I told them everything has been settled for the house." Miss Bingley beamed.

"We will take possession in a fortnight," Bingley added.

Miss Elizabeth glanced at her sisters. "If it is agreeable to you, our mother wishes to hold a dinner on your behalf. She thinks it a fitting way to welcome you to the neighborhood and be introduced among us."

"How very kind! We would be most delighted." Bingley sat a little straighter in his chair.

Miss Kitty clapped softly. "Mama hosts the most delightful dinners—everyone here will agree. We dine with four and twenty families! You must tell me your favorite dishes. She wants to make sure to serve them at dinner."

Darcy felt himself smile in spite of his best effort

not to. Miss Kitty's exuberance reminded him comfortably of Georgiana.

"You too, of course, Mr. Darcy, if you will be continuing on here for a while." Miss Kitty added.

Bingley turned to Darcy, eyebrow lifted. The ladies all looked at him.

A flush crept along Darcy's neck. "I…that is…yes, I will be staying for some time yet. Thank you."

"Excellent." Miss Elizabeth smiled.

Was her smile for him or mere politeness? Hopefully the former.

"Now, we must wait for our father to visit so we may officially begin our acquaintance." Miss Elizabeth's eyes twinkled.

Bingley laughed. "Rest assured, I will welcome him when he does."

After another quarter hour, the Bennet ladies left, and Darcy excused himself to attend to a stack of correspondence just arrived from Pemberley.

Upstairs, seated at an awkward little writing desk shoved in the corner near the sunny window, Darcy leafed through the packet of letters. He responded to several.

"Beastly hot window," he muttered under his breath and mopped his forehead with his handkerchief. Groaning, he stretched out the cramps in his legs.

If he could only walk in the cool woods now—as he had when Miss Elizabeth first appeared like a fairy-tale creature out of the woods.

He chuckled. Perhaps he had found the mythical creature of which his cousin Fitzwilliam spoke. What would Fitzwilliam think of the Bennets?

He pressed his pen to paper.

Fitzwilliam,
Come quickly. She has four sisters.

FD

Chapter 3

FOUR DAYS LATER, Pierce and Bradley ambled along the shady path toward Longbourn House. The fragrance of loam, punctuated by the perfume of distant blossoms, carried on the gentle breezes. Afternoon sun peeked through the branches, teasing with glimmers of warmth. In short, a perfect afternoon for a stroll.

"Mrs. Bennet is an amiable hostess and sets an excellent table, even for tea," Pierce said.

"Her invitation is most gracious. After hearing their tenants speak so highly of them, I am anxious to make the Bennets' acquaintance." The name *Bennet* sounded familiar. Bradley scratched his ear. If only he might remember why.

"The Clays and the Thompsons are grateful for the way they handled matters with young Billy." Pierce offered Bradley his arm as they approached

Longbourn's front steps.

Bradley leaned heavily on Pierce's arm. His knees complained in language that would offend a soldier. Stairs were doubtless an enemy more threatening than a French invasion.

The housekeeper showed them to a cheerful and sunny parlor. Too formal to welcome like Pierce's room, it still offered cozy hospitality. Two gentlemen sat in quiet conversation near the window.

"Mr. Bennet." Pierce bowed.

"I cannot believe my eyes!" Bradley rushed forward.

"Mr. Bradley?" Gardiner jumped to his feet.

"Gardiner? How many years has it been?" Bradley grinned.

Gardiner took his hand and pumped vigorously. "Far too long."

Pierce gaped at Bradley.

"And you are the Bennet I thought you might be." Bradley laughed heartily.

"I suppose I must be." Bennet offered his hand.

"I had planned to introduce my friend to you. It hardly seems necessary now." Pierce removed his hat and scratched his head.

A young woman appeared in the doorway. She wore a cloak of peace and good humor as subtle as the smile on her lips. From the corner of his eye, Bradley caught Pierce's expression. This was his—

"Mary, my dear, you must come." Gardiner waved her in. "This is the fabled Mr. Bradley of whom my wife has so often written."

Miss Mary's smile blossomed, and she dropped in a graceful curtsey. "What a pleasure to meet you, sir. I confess, I feel as though I already know you."

Bradley bowed and chuckled. "Your aunt has written of you and your sisters so much, the feeling is mutual."

Gardiner turned to Pierce. "Bradley was the curate in my wife's childhood parish. She grew up under his teaching. He performed our wedding."

Pierce glanced at Miss Mary and nodded.

"She tells our children the same stories you told her and her brother when they were growing up." Gardiner eased into his chair.

Bradley dipped his head. "Indeed! How is Miss Maddie?" He removed his handkerchief and wiped his eyes.

"She is well, though the children keep her busy. Silas, the youngest, is quite a handful these days."

Bennet sat and peered at his daughter. "Is Mrs. Bennet on her way?"

She bit her lower lip. "Jane and Lizzy are with her. I expect she shall be ready soon."

"I hope she is not ill." Pierce raised his brows at Miss Mary.

"I am well." Mrs. Bennet stood in the doorway, flanked by two girls, her eldest daughters, no doubt.

Bennet rushed to her side and offered his arm. "My dear, do you remember Mr. Bradley—"

"Of the Derbyshire parish?" Mrs. Bennet turned to Bradley. "I do, indeed. You are most welcome, sir." She curtsied.

Bradley bowed. Though her smile was genuine, her eyes were red and puffy, and the edges of her mouth drew into fine, tight creases.

She turned to the girls beside her. "May I present my eldest, Jane, and her next sister, Elizabeth?"

Like their younger sibling, they wore peace and

good humor, but by their posture and smiles, Miss Bennet possessed the greater share of the former and Miss Elizabeth the latter. "You are as lovely as your aunt says."

"Thank you, sir." Miss Bennet blushed.

Miss Elizabeth beamed. "You are very kind."

The housekeeper bustled in with the tea tray. Mrs. Bennet occupied herself serving her guests.

"What brings you all the way to Hertfordshire?" Gardiner accepted a cup and settled into his seat.

"I came to further my acquaintance with young Pierce." Bradley watched Miss Mary with a sidelong glance.

She took a quick glimpse at Pierce, eyebrows raised. He cocked his head and blinked. She bit her lip. When Bradley met her gaze, she dodged away.

"Your visit is a delightful surprise. One does not often have the opportunity to meet an old friend for the first time." Miss Bennet smiled and sipped her tea.

Miss Elizabeth licked her lips. "I do believe you are Mr. Pierce's first visitor—"

Mrs. Bennet gasped and pressed her fist to her mouth. She bowed her head and squeezed her eyes shut. Her ragged breaths filled the room.

Pierce pointed his chin toward Mrs. Bennet. Miss Mary nodded so slightly Bradley was not even certain it had happened.

"Your garden behind the house is in spectacular bloom." Pierce gestured to the window framing a resplendent rose bush, blossoms cascading from every cane. "Would you condescend to show me what you have done with your roses? Mine are frightfully leggy and unsightly. Yours are the talk of the neighborhood. I can think of no better tutor."

Mrs. Bennet's head snapped up, eyes bright. She opened her mouth, though her words lagged several breaths. "Of course, I would be most happy to show you. My mother taught me to manage roses. I always hoped to produce a garden as lovely as hers."

Pierce stood and offered his arm, though his eyes remained on Miss Mary. She hurried to her mother's other side. Mrs. Bennet took Pierce's arm, and the three ambled to the garden door.

Bradley's gaze followed them. Pierce and Miss Mary made an excellent team, though yet unmarried. Moreover, she was Miss Maddie's niece—the pious, sensible, reliable one, with a compassionate heart and gentle disposition. A girl could have no better recommendation. She would do well for Pierce and for the parish. Bradley approved, very much indeed.

"It would seem Providence made quick work to provide your desire, Gardiner." Bennet stared at his daughters and jerked his head toward the door.

They excused themselves.

Bradley took a biscuit.

"Before you arrived, I told my brother I wished we had time to write to you for advice in a rather delicate situation." Gardiner placed his teacup on the table.

"How interesting." Bradley brushed crumbs from his fingertips. "I suppose I am compelled to place myself at your service. I dare not interfere with the hand of Providence."

Pierce walked slowly with Mrs. Bennet leaning heavily on his arm. Heady perfume hung in the warm air, almost stifling in its sweetness. Petals cascaded with each step, veiling the path with velvet and silk. Normally spry and quick, her labored, deliberate footsteps cried out her distress.

She stopped at a bush, lush with pink blossoms. "These have always been my favorite. They were grown from a cutting taken from my mother's garden when Jane was born." She pressed her face into the blooms.

"They are most lovely, like your daughters." Pierce peered at Miss Mary over Mrs. Bennet's head.

Miss Mary blushed, the same color as her mother's roses.

"My girls have no thorns to protect them." Mrs. Bennet sniffled. She pulled a handkerchief from her sleeve and dabbed her eyes.

"You fear for their safety?"

A little sob caught in Mrs. Bennet's throat.

Pierce's forehead wrinkled. Why would she fear for them? What threat—his throat pinched. "You are afraid of visitors in the house?"

Mrs. Bennet turned and shuffled deeper into the garden.

Miss Mary's eyes widened, and she trotted several steps to catch up. "Mama?" She caught her mother's hand.

"You do not understand!" Mrs. Bennet yanked her hand away. "You do not understand the harm a…a man is capable of." She stared at Pierce, face florid.

Pierce approached slowly. "You were not protected."

Mrs. Bennet pitched forward. Her hands covered her face, shoulders heaving. Miss Mary slid her arm over her mother's shoulder, and held her until she calmed. Pierce led them to a bench in the shade.

"I do not understand why it happened. I cannot endure the thought that one of my girls…"

Miss Mary rubbed her mother's back.

"Mr. Bennet, he is aware of the…circumstances?" Pierce chewed his lip. What did one say in these situations? Thank Heaven for Miss Mary's presence.

"Yes." Mrs. Bennet sniffled.

"And your brother?"

"He, too."

"They are good men, who care for you and your girls deeply. They will take every precaution to protect all of you." He caught Mary's eyes.

She brushed her fingertips along his. How could a simple touch restore him so?

"I know they will. They are the best of men." Mrs. Bennet threw her head back and looked skyward. "You do not understand—"

"You are correct; I do not. I cannot. However, the Good Book says once we have done all we can do, we must stand in faith. Between your husband, your brother and the Good Lord, your girls will be safe."

"I wish to believe it will be as you say. But…but…" Mrs. Bennet hid her face in her hands.

Miss Mary's lips pursed into something neither frown nor smile. Her eyes did not mask her heart so easily. Oh, the depths of pain they spoke. How he longed to bring her ease!

A door clattered. Mrs. Bennet squinted toward the house. "I see Hill. I need her to make my tea. I must go." She trundled away.

Miss Mary and Pierce stared at one another. A breeze fluttered through the bushes, showering them with petals.

How improper! They should not be alone. There

was only one reason for a private interview. Bradley's offer remained contingent upon too many things. Still, Bradley knew her family, and the look in the vicar's eye declared approval. His cheeks prickled as though scoured by rose thorns. Could he? Dare he?

"Miss Mary," Pierce cleared his throat. "Can I convince you to take a turn with me about the garden? In your mother's absence, perhaps you may assist me with my questions." He offered his arm.

She slipped her hand into the crook of his elbow and peeked at him, cheeks flushed a deeper shade than the nearby roses. "I hope I have the answers you seek."

He breathed in their fragrance. Pink roses were indeed his favorite.

"You wish to know more about the roses?"

"Ah, yes." He pulled a spray of blossoms closer. "I must reveal my ignorance, but will you show where I might find the 'hips' of this plant?"

"Excuse me?" She cocked her head and glanced from Pierce to the roses and back.

"Rose hips, what are rose hips? Mr. Bradley's apothecary in Derbyshire recommended he drink a tea brewed from them every morning. I want to provide him with a fresh supply but have not the slightest notion of what they are or where to find them." He knit his brows, heart thundering so hard his hand shook. "Surely with so many roses here, there must be some you can show me."

She chuckled. "I comprehend your confusion. You shall find no 'hips' on these plants for quite some time, for they are the fruit that follows the blossoms. There will be none until autumn."

"Oh, I thought surely…" Pierce blushed and

threw up his hands. "It does not matter."

"You can ask Lady Lucas. I know she has a supply on hand as does the apothecary in town if you should prefer." She sighed and turned away.

"What is wrong?" Cold gripped his face and pinched his breath. "You are unhappy. Is there some trouble with the Lucases?"

"No, my friends are quite well, thank you."

He took a step closer to her. "What has affected you so?"

"It is true then." She bit her lip.

"What is?"

"He will take you from us."

"What do you mean?" He tried to catch her eyes, but she avoided him.

"Mr. Bradley has come to find his successor. You will follow him to Derbyshire," her voice dropped to a low whisper, "and we shall never see you again." She rubbed tears from her cheeks.

He took her elbow.

She stared up at him, eyes glittering, and pulled against his grasp. "No, no, there is no need. It is a good thing, and I am pleased for you."

His fingers tightened around her arm, and he led them to a stone bench. The rough seat scraped his coat. Would it be uncomfortable for her? He glanced heavenward. Oh, for the right words!

She lighted on the stone, hands braced, as one prepared to flee.

"Mr. Bradley seeks a man to be his successor, one he will mentor, so he may leave this life in peace, knowing his parish will be well tended. His patron agreed to this plan and promised to appoint Bradley's curate as vicar."

She blinked rapidly. "What a rare opportunity."

"He and I share similar views as to how a man should shepherd a flock. I would be a fool not to take the opportunity to learn from someone like him."

"Of course—"

"No offer has been made."

Her breath hitched.

"However, I must be honest. I expect one to be forthcoming."

She pressed her folded hands to her mouth. Eyes closed, she rocked slightly. "What a great honor. I am glad for you. I know how concerned he is for his parish. Mr. Bradley will be an excellent mentor and teacher."

"He is. I have enjoyed his company these weeks." He traced his fingertips along a small crack on the edge of the bench. Stupid, stupid man. Why could he not force himself to speak? Such significant things should not be said sitting down.

He rose, and helped her up. They walked toward a patch of pale yellow climbing roses that wound their way up an arch over the walkway.

"I am always amazed at the Good Lord's ingenuity." Pierce leaned into a blossom and breathed deeply. "Tucking so much sweetness into a tiny bloom—"

"Or healing properties into the hips a rose leaves behind?" She peeped at him through a curtain of petals, eyes shimmering in the filtered sun.

He laughed heartily. Several small birds launched in a flurry.

"Or such beauty in the eyes of a young woman." He stepped closer.

She gasped.

He took her hand. "I know it was not long ago I

asked permission to court you, Miss Mary..." Why would his tongue so stubbornly refuse to obey? He looked into the sky and rubbed his wooly tongue along the roof of his mouth. "How strange that I, who earn my keep through my weekly oratory, should now be at a loss for words." He shrugged.

She swallowed hard and met his gaze. The corners of her lips turned up just enough.

He held his breath. Dear, dear girl, she understood. Air rushed into his lungs so fast his vision fuzzed.

"I hardly think you can compare the two situations. As you do not read from someone else's sermons, do you not spend many hours studying and considering what you will say on Sunday mornings? You carry extensive notes with nearly every word you speak written before you."

"Quite so."

"You brought no notes with you now, no weighty journals, no tightly folded sheets." She raised her eyebrow. "What surprise is it that you stumble over your words? How can you be expected to speak without adequate preparations?"

He shook his head, unable to contain a smile so broad she must question his lucidity. Was it wrong to feel such elation that another should understand him better than he did himself? "I am not an impulsive man. In the future, I may try to think ahead and arrange a few compliments that are generally acceptable to ladies so as not to be caught tongue-tied again."

She giggled behind her hand.

He twined his fingers in hers and drew her hand to his lips. "You always seem to know what to say to set me at ease."

She looked down.

"It is true." He traced the side of her face with his fingertip. "And not just for me. How many times have you come with me to call upon the sick and known precisely how to ease the suffering of those around you? You are the embodiment of compassion and wisdom." He tipped her chin and gently met her eyes. "I rely upon your judgment, and I do not wish to ever be without it."

Her breath caught.

He licked his lips. "Please, Mary, dearest, sweet Mary, would you consent to become my wife?"

Tears streamed down her cheeks though she blinked furiously. "I would be most honored to be your wife…Ethan."

His name on her lips caressed his ears and sent prickles down the back of his neck. He kissed her open palm. "You have made me the happiest of men."

"And I the happiest of women." She sniffled and pressed her lips into a teary smile.

He pulled out his handkerchief and dabbed the tears from her cheeks. "I hate to see you cry, but these tears I will cherish." He folded the silk square and tucked it into his coat pocket.

"I do not understand."

He memorized her expression of wonder and love. "Those tears answered my prayers. I was a terrible coward and could not bear the thought you did not return my feelings. This handkerchief I will keep always, as a reminder of answered prayers."

Mary giggled, softly at first, then uncontrollably, and hid her face in her hands. She looked up, into his questioning eyes. "I must make you another, and I shall embroider it with…"

"Roses?"

"No," she winked, "rose hips."

Chapter 4

TWO DAYS LATER, Elizabeth sat at her dressing table, pinning her curls. Since the news of Mary's engagement, Mama required Jane's and Mattie's constant attention. Elizabeth did not mind seeing to her own hair, that was a small enough thing, but she did miss Jane's company.

Soft steps padded in the hall, not Jane's though. She turned in her seat.

Mary stood in the doorway. "Please, Lizzy, come downstairs with me. Mama called me to the drawing room and I cannot bear to face her on my own." She sagged against the doorframe. Her cheeks were drawn and dark circles shadowed her eyes.

Elizabeth beckoned. "Come in and close the door before anyone hears you."

Mary scurried in and shut the door with exaggerated care. She dropped on the bed and fell like a ragdoll along the headboard.

"Mama has been most attentive." Elizabeth sat beside her.

"Attentive is one thing. This is altogether another. Hand me your hairpins. Let me finish your hair for you."

"Do you mean to tell me you are not enjoying the role of Mama's favorite daughter?" Elizabeth handed her a small dish of hairpins.

Mary grimaced. "I never had any desire for such attentions, nor do I enjoy them." She picked up a pin and coaxed Elizabeth's hair into place. "I am not like you, Lizzy. You are so confident and always know what to say to make people smile and laugh. I…I do not like others to watch me, or pay attention to my hair, or my gown. I would much rather visit Mrs. Black with her cold." She wiped her eyes with the back of her hand.

Poor Mary never complained. Elizabeth squeezed her knee. "I am sorry. How may I help?"

"I do not imagine you can get yourself engaged to a wealthy man who will make Mr. Pierce and I look like poor relations?"

Elizabeth snickered. "I would do anything for you, but that seems quite impossible."

"Two possibilities reside in the neighborhood, you know, Mr. Bingley and his friend." Mary cocked her head.

Elizabeth rolled her eyes. "Be serious."

Mary scrubbed her face with her hands. "Help me persuade Mama that four weeks is sufficient time to carry off a wedding."

"So quickly?"

"Yes. The longer we wait, the more Mama insists

upon. I want the simplest of celebrations and need only a few wedding clothes."

"What of your wedding trip?"

"Mr. Bradley offered us his parsonage in Derbyshire. We will go there and meet his parishioners." Mary's cheeks flushed, and she turned aside.

Elizabeth cocked her head. "Meet the people of Mr. Bradley's parish? I do not understand. Mr. Pierce already has a curacy."

Mary sighed. "Please, do not tell Mama yet. Mr. Bradley is considering inviting Mr. Pierce to serve as his curate."

"Why Derbyshire? Is not our parish enough?"

"Mr. Bradley wants to train up Mr. Pierce as his successor."

"You will move away to Derbyshire?"

"I expect so." Mary wrung her hands.

A sharp breath tore from Elizabeth's chest. Her shoulders sagged, and she slumped into the mattress. "I did not anticipate…that is to say…" She squeezed her eyes shut. A cold, empty wind blew through her belly. "Oh, Mary, I will miss you."

Mary opened her arms, and they embraced. "You simply have to marry Mr. Darcy and move to Derbyshire, too."

Elizabeth choked on a laugh. "How can you say such a thing?"

"You never know. Perhaps he will come to like you."

"I think not. He walks in entirely different circles than we do. I am sure our acquaintance here will be but a fleeting one. When he returns to his grand estate, he will barely remember us in Meryton."

"You consider yourself far too meanly." Mary slid

the final hairpin into place.

"I do not think a mere country gentleman's daughter likely to be of great interest when there are so many spectacular matches to be made among the *ton*." Elizabeth shrugged. As much as she enjoyed her acquaintance with Mr. Darcy, raising her hopes to a man like him could hardly be wise. "Are you afraid to leave Meryton?"

Mary stared at the ceiling. "Yes, Derbyshire is so far away."

"Only one hundred miles of good road or so."

Mary rolled her eyes.

"You love him."

"I do."

"All will be well. I am certain." She squeezed Mary's hand. "Come, Mama will send Hill for us if we do not go down soon."

Elizabeth led the way to the drawing room.

Mama frowned as they walked in. "Mary, dear, why did you keep me waiting? Elizabeth, you should not be so inconsiderate as to divert her from me."

She dropped her eyes. "Yes, Mama." Only Mary's distress kept her from bolting. While Mary had increased in Mama's favor, the corresponding truth was she had fallen in her mother's sight to the same degree.

Mama patted the settee. "Sit, Mary. I started a list of all that must be accomplished before the wedding. We will need at least three months, I am sure."

"The wedding is in four weeks, Mama." Mary turned to Elizabeth.

"Elizabeth, help me." Mama shoved her journal at her. "Just look at this list. How can it be done before fall?"

She picked up the book and paged through list after carefully penned list. "You have included so many—"

"As I said! Listen, Mary, she agrees with me." Mama crossed her arms over her bosom and nodded sharply.

"Wait, wait." Elizabeth placed the ledger on the table. "I did not say that."

"What do you mean?" Mama's shrill voice sliced sharper than one of Cook's knives.

Elizabeth perched on the footstool. How was poor Mary to endure even four weeks of this? "I am not certain everything on your lists is necessary."

"Exactly, Mama." Mary clasped her hands tightly.

Mama whirled on Elizabeth. "And just how would you know what is necessary, Missy? What experience do you have with weddings or marriage? I have a far better notion of what—"

Loud footsteps—two sets—pounded down the stairs. Mama rose and peeked through the doorway.

"Are you working on wedding plans?" Lydia danced into the parlor and bounced onto the large chair near the settee. "We are ready to help." She folded her hands primly in her lap and settled in.

Bless Lydia's rude interruptions—anything to put mama's focus elsewhere!

Kitty handed Mary a quire of paper.

Elizabeth craned her neck to see. Drawings of gowns filled the sheets of foolscap. Kitty must have spent the better part of a day preparing them.

"I drew these for you. Please, let me make your gown. If none of these suits, I can do others." The words raced from Kitty's mouth as though to ensure neither Mama nor Lydia interrupted.

"They are lovely," Jane said.

Elizabeth jumped. When had Jane entered? How did a body move so silently all the time? Elizabeth made room for her on the footstool.

Kitty beamed and dragged a chair from the window to the settee. She balanced on the edge of the seat, toes still bouncing.

"Show them to me." Mama held out her hand.

Mary passed her the stack. "I like the topmost one."

"No, no, no, dear. A wedding dress needs more lace."

"I do not like lace."

Jane leaned into Elizabeth until their shoulders touched. "Do not be upset with Mama," she whispered. "I know she was unkind. She is most anxious—"

Elizabeth savored her sister's affection and support. Mama's sharpness was nothing new, but it still cut, just as it always had and probably always would. She swallowed hard.

"She does not mean to be harsh."

Elizabeth shrugged her shoulders and pressed her lips hard to prevent a frown. If Mama thought her scowling, she would be all the more cross.

"What if I added a touch of lace here and here?" Kitty tapped her sketch.

"No! Mama is right. A bride should be dripping in lace." Lydia pulled the stack of drawings into her lap and sorted through them. "This is what I would choose!" She handed the sketch to Jane.

Jane took the drawing and held it up to the light. "It is lovely, to be sure. When your turn comes, I am certain you can wear this. However, you are not to be the bride this time—"

Hill rapped on the doorframe. "Mrs. Bennet."

Everyone jumped.

"A carriage approaches. I think your visitor is come." She curtsied and scurried away.

"Oh, oh!" Mama shot to her feet, hands trembling in the air. "What are we to do?"

"Mama, he is a guest, not a French battalion." Elizabeth reached for her hand, but Mama slapped her away.

"You do not understand!" She hurried for the door. "Mr. Bennet! Mr. Bennet!"

Jane touched Kitty's shoulder and steered her toward the doorway. "Take your drawings upstairs. You do not want them damaged or mislaid."

"I will find Hill to make some of Mama's calming tea." Mary nodded at Elizabeth and left.

Jane, Elizabeth and Lydia followed Mama's shrill voice to the study. They lingered just outside until Papa caught Elizabeth's eye and waved them in.

Mama huddled in a chair near the fireplace, her face hidden in her handkerchief.

"Mr. Collins will be here in a few minutes." Deep creases furrowed Papa's forehead, matched by the lines beside his mouth and eyes.

"I will help Mama to her chamber," Jane whispered.

She took Mama's arm and encouraged her to her feet. Kitty supported her other arm, and they half led, half carried her from the room.

Elizabeth sidled toward the door, torn. They both needed her. Perhaps she should join her sisters helping Mama. Yet, Mama did not seem to desire her comfort right now, and her heart was not strong enough for another rebuff. Besides, Papa looked so forlorn.

Lydia peeked through the window. "La! I do not understand the fuss. People receive guests all the time. I cannot fathom why Mama should be at sixes and sevens."

Papa pinched the bridge of his nose and sighed. Elizabeth touched his arm. His shoulders fell, and his eyes aged a decade at least. Mama had Jane and Kitty. He should not have to manage Lydia and a guest by himself.

He puffed out a deep breath and tugged his coat. "I suppose we ought to meet him. We cannot delay the inevitable by hiding here." He nodded at Elizabeth.

She and Lydia followed and stood just behind him on the landing.

"La! I say his carriage is not fine at all." Lydia planted her hands on her hips and scowled. "With the fuss, I expected so much more. He has not nearly the consequence of our new neighbor or his friend."

"You cannot judge a man by his equipage," Elizabeth hissed.

Lydia flounced and snorted, the same silly girl as ever. She turned her back to them.

The modest carriage crunched over the last few feet of gravel and stopped near the front steps. A man was perched atop with the driver. Tall and broad shouldered, his wide brimmed hat shaded his features. He jumped down and thanked the driver in a deep, furry voice that made Elizabeth's skin prickle delightfully. She could not make out his face until he mounted the final step.

"Mr. Bennet, I presume? William Elliot Collins at

your service, sir." He bowed.

Elizabeth swallowed hard. With all Mama's nervous flutters, she expected nothing less than an ogre. This man had the face and form of a Grecian statue. His eyes sparkled with intelligence and wit. Oh, my!

"Mr. Collins." Papa bowed. "May I introduce my daughters, Elizabeth and Lydia?"

They curtsied. Elizabeth knew she should not, but she stared at his smile. From the corner of her eye, she caught Lydia's rapt expression. She chided herself for staring and forced her gaze away.

"I am honored to make your acquaintance. I appreciate the opportunity to visit with you and hope my presence will not be too much of a disruption on your good home." He tipped his head.

"I expect you are peckish from your travels. Hill will have a cold luncheon set out by now." Papa led them inside. "Would you care to see your room first?"

"That can wait, sir. I do not want to keep your repast waiting on me." Mr. Collins bowed from his shoulders.

"Very well." Papa ushered them into the parlor.

They served themselves from the cold plates and sat. Elizabeth bypassed her favorite footstool for the settee. Mama would be pleased.

"I fear Mrs. Bennet is indisposed at the moment. She will join us later for dinner." Papa muttered.

"I am sorry to hear she is unwell." Mr. Collins glanced at Elizabeth. "I pray I have not added to her distress."

Lydia shrugged. "It is just her nerves—"

"Lydia!" Elizabeth nudged her with her foot. "We are pleased you are come, Mr. Collins. You are most welcome here." She dared another glimpse at him and smiled.

The smile he gave her in return nearly tore the breath from her lungs. "Thank you, dear cousin, for your hospitality."

Lydia fluffed her skirt. "Well, I am glad you are here, too."

Papa rolled his eyes and cleared his throat. "Your last letter left me uncertain whether I should expect you today or two days from now. My dear wife found the ambiguity difficult to tolerate."

Mr. Collins's shoulders drooped, and he closed his eyes. "Please accept my deepest apologies. I am one afflicted." He raised his left hand. "I have, all my life, sought to overcome this thorn in my flesh. Alas, like the apostle Paul, the Good Lord has not seen fit to deliver me from it, so I muddle through as best I can."

"I see." Papa nodded. "Penmanship is a challenge for those who are left handed."

"Upon my honor, I penned that letter no less than three times in an effort to make it as legible as possible. It grieves me to cause your family difficulties through the weakness of my flesh." He folded his hands across his lap and bowed his head.

"You are gracious to take such efforts on our behalf." Elizabeth would have patted his hand if it had been proper. He would likely accept her comfort far more graciously than Mama.

Lydia snickered. "You never accepted that excuse before."

Elizabeth glared.

Lydia's eyes widened, and she clamped her mouth shut.

Papa cut a slice of meat to fit his bread. "Have you

fixed upon a length for your stay?"

A long visit would be most agreeable. Elizabeth's cheeks burned. Selfish, unfeeling girl thinking only of her own comfort and not Mama's. She bit her lip.

"I do not wish to upset your home, sir, so will strive to make my business here as brief as possible and myself as little trouble as I am able." Mr. Collins sipped his glass. He peeked at Elizabeth. His eyes twinkled above the rim.

Lydia tossed her head.

"Have you any siblings, sir?" Elizabeth struggled to maintain a proper expression. Lydia did not like to be laughed at.

"Two much younger sisters." His eyelid twitched in the barest of winks.

Papa coughed, but it sounded much like a snicker. "Your visit is no trouble at all. Consider yourself most welcome. Would you care to ride the estate tomorrow?" He laid a slice of cheese on his bread.

"If you find it convenient, I would appreciate a tour." Mr. Collins set his glass aside. "My father once said you were a great lover of books."

Papa's eyes narrowed, brow knotted. "From my cousin's lips, it was no compliment, to be sure."

"There has been a longstanding breach between our families. I cannot apologize enough for the transgressions of my father. I hope you will not hold his shortcomings against me. My sincerest desire is to repair the break and soothe prior misunderstandings. My father often spoke in haste, in words short and hurtful. Forgive me for bringing up bad memories." He sighed and looked away. "I meant a compliment. I am a prodigious reader myself, and my library is paltry at best. I hoped only to beg your indulgence and allow me access to your library whilst I am here."

Papa shifted in his seat and crossed his legs. "What do you prefer to read? I cannot offer you a vast collection of sermons."

Lydia laughed hard into her hands, punctuating it with an unladylike snort. Elizabeth shuddered.

Mr. Collins snickered and grinned. "I know relations between you and my late father were tense at best. You do share a familial sense of humor, though."

Elizabeth choked back a giggle. "What do you like to read?"

"Histories, poetry, the bard himself when I have the chance. I will tackle nearly anything in print, given the opportunity." He leaned a little closer to her.

Her heart did a flip and struggled to land in its rightful place. "Would your interest extend to the lowest form of literature, the novel?"

His voice dropped low. "On rare occasions, I do indulge in a gothic novel, just to better understand the young ladies who read them." He shot a quick glance at Lydia.

"Of course," Elizabeth whispered. He seemed to share the family sense of humor as well.

Lydia huffed.

Tongue in cheek, Papa guffawed. A wry smile crept across his face. "Would you like to visit your room now? We may tour the house and my library on the way." He pushed himself up.

"I would." Mr. Collins rose, bowed to his cousins, and followed Papa out.

"Oooh," Lydia hissed. She rubbed her upper arms briskly. "I do not like him, not at all."

Elizabeth glared, hands on her hips. "How can you

say that?"

"I do not like him. He is—icky."

"What are you talking about? He is well mannered, well spoken, well read—"

"And well-looking. I saw you stare at him. I must grant you, he is well favored. It does not signify though. I still do not like him." She rose and circled Elizabeth. "But, I think you do."

"You may keep both those opinions to yourself, Lydia. Neither one is fit to be spoken in company. You are put out because he did not pay you the attentions you believe you deserve."

"He was ignoring me, but that is not why I do not like him." Lydia tossed her head. "I just do not."

Elizabeth stood and shook out her skirts. "You should go attend Mama now. You always manage to cheer her." She strode away.

How strange Lydia should take such a dislike to the most eligible man either of them had ever met. Perhaps it was a blessing. Lydia would not be throwing herself at their cousin the way she did at the officers. Yes, it was a blessing, indeed.

Three days later, Bennet sank into his favorite chair in his bookroom. He puffed out a deep breath and rolled his eyes. That he should be reduced to sneaking around his own house to avoid company was intolerable. Collins was well-mannered, attentive and appreciative—everything proper and to be desired in a guest, yet too much more of Collins's solicitous presence would drive him to Bedlam. He liked Collins, far more than he ever expected. He did not resemble his odious father, quite the opposite in fact, a most amiable young man. Yet, Bennet was not a lover of company of any kind. He craved solitude, needing it like a drowning man needed air.

If not for his dearest Lizzy, Lord knows what he would have said. The sweet child knew him so well. Lizzy alone understood his peculiarities. She inserted herself between him and Collins regularly, allowing him repose when he most required it. He would have been overwhelmed by guilt for using her so, except that she did not appear to dislike Collins. In fact, she gave the impression that she enjoyed his company and shared many of the same tastes.

He pressed his head into his chair and rubbed his forehead. Pricks of guilt still plagued him. How many times in recent days had he been short with her? Far too many. Yet she remained patient and faithful to him. He did not deserve her solicitude. Once life returned to normal, he would make it up to her. How, he did not know, but he would.

For now though, he still needed to bring Collins to his way of thinking. A mortgage was the only means by which to improve the estate and increase his income so he could provide properly for the girls. He shifted in his seat. How many hours had they spent riding the estate over the last two days? The pain in his back and legs attested to far too many. Any reasonable man could see how the improvements he wanted would prove to be a smart investment for the future.

Heavy footfalls resounded on the stairs. Not yet! He had barely gotten his equilibrium back. What dratted bad luck! Lizzy had already left with her sister, leaving him to face Collins alone. He could not be rude to such a pleasant guest. Blast it all!

A polite rapping at the door ended his reverie. He grumbled and picked up the nearest book, opened it at random and dropped it into his lap. "Come in."

The door opened, and Collins stepped in, immaculately groomed and smiling pleasantly. Was it possible for him to be in an ill-humor, ever?

"Good morning, Mr. Bennet." Collins nodded and slipped into the chair opposite Bennet's.

"Might I do something for you this morning? Do you fancy another ride of the property, or should I arrange for a bit of shooting? Fishing perhaps?" His throat tightened. Lizzy would scold him for his tone.

"You do not need to trouble yourself for my amusement, sir." Collins crossed his legs and cupped his hands over one knee. "I can tell, you are a quiet man and would much prefer solitude to my company."

Bennet flushed. Had Lizzy mentioned something? "Do not misunderstand. Your presence is most agreeable—"

"You are just not, in the general case, a lover of society." Collins tipped his head. "I do comprehend your condition. My father was much the same, if you will forgive the comparison."

Bennet grumbled.

"You are far more considerate in your discomfort than he was ever able to be. I appreciate your efforts on my behalf. You have made me feel more welcome here than I felt in my own father's home."

"I am glad you are pleased." Bennet chewed his cheek. There was something to be said for a man who recognized he was an inconvenience.

"I do not wish to prolong your disquiet, so, by

your leave, let us discuss the significant matters before us." Collins dragged his hand through his hair and sighed. "I cannot tell you how distressed I am to know…well, you have thought through this enough on your own, there is no need to detail scenarios of your demise and its consequent unfortunate effects on your family."

Bennet sniffed and pulled a handkerchief from his waistcoat. "Since you mention it, an avenue for the clearing of your conscience is available, should you choose to permit me to mortgage the property."

"Ah, yes." Collins ran a finger along the edge of his cravat. "I am in a bit of a dilemma over that. My patroness, Lady Catherine De Bourgh, believes a mortgage could be of distinct disadvantage in the future and should only be embarked upon under the most careful of consideration."

Bennet grumbled low in his throat. "I have shown you the reasons for the need and exactly what would be done with the money."

"Indeed, and I can see you have considered the whole matter carefully and do not embark upon it lightly."

"I do not understand your problem."

"I am caught in a most difficult position, between two individuals I would most like to please. I owe so much to my patroness, I feel it my duty to bow to her wishes. At the same time, I owe a familial obligation to you." He dragged his fingers through his hair. "Lady Catherine insists, once the mortgage money is made available, no mechanism exists to ensure you use it the way you have discussed."

Bennet slammed the arms of his chair, and he rose halfway. "Are you calling me a liar and a cheat?"

Collins paled. He lifted open hands. "Not at all, sir! Please forgive me. I meant no offense. Those are her words, not my own. I tried to convince her of your character and sincerity, but she does not believe me. Though I would never accuse you of duplicity, Lady Catherine insists that I should be more wary. She tells me I trust too easily."

"You rely upon her opinions?" Bennet scowled and folded his arms over his chest.

"I owe her a great deal. Fealty is not inappropriate. However, the happy news is I believe I have found a way for all parties to be satisfied." Collins rubbed his thumb into his palm.

"I cannot imagine what you are thinking. Enlighten me."

Collins bowed his head and stroked his lips against his knuckles. "If you had a more direct stake in the estate after it passes to me, I could be certain of how you would employ the funds from the mortgage."

"I do not follow."

"If you knew your family would be provided for out of the estate after your passing…you would certainly invest the mortgage money as we discussed." Collins slowly raised his head, still not meeting Bennet's eyes. "Lady Catherine believes I should marry. I am well able to do so from my generous living. If I were to take a wife from among your fair daughters, then I could, in good conscience, approve the mortgage. You would be assured of provision for your wife and daughters, whatever the future might bring, since they would never find themselves displaced from Longbourn." Collins bit his lip and glanced up at Bennet.

"You wish to barter—"

"Oh, certainly not! What must you think of me?" He squeezed his eyes shut. "That is not at all what I meant to convey. I do not wish you to force any of your daughters to marry against their will."

"Forgive me. I should not jump to conclusions. As you know, Mary is engaged. It is a match not short on affection. I wish the same for all my girls."

"You are a most devoted father. I would not dream of going against your wishes." Collins smiled. "I, too, wish for a marriage based on mutual affection. Miss Elizabeth and I share many of the same tastes and mightily enjoy a good laugh. I hope we might be well suited to one another. If I win her regard, would you approve?" He tipped his head and lifted his eyebrow.

He was correct. Lizzy seemed to enjoy his company very much. If she was pleased with the arrangement, it would resolve so many of his worries. "I will not force her, nor even encourage her to make such an alliance. If it is her desire, with no pressure or inducement, I will not forbid it."

"Then I have your blessings?"

Lizzy would make a fine mistress of Longbourn and ensure her mother and sisters were cared for. Perhaps this was the hand of Providence. Collins could secure her future in a way no other man could offer. "You have my permission to try and win her esteem."

Collins rose and extended his hand. "Thank you, sir."

Bennet pinched the bridge of his nose. "I have only just gotten used to giving one daughter away. I need time to become accustomed to this idea. You will excuse me."

"Of course, sir, you are a most sympathetic father." Collins withdrew his hand and bowed.

Bennet's mind danced with far too many ideas. He needed time for repose, to order his thoughts. There was no one at Longbourn to entertain Collins. "Perhaps you would find it agreeable to pay a call upon Mr. Pierce. Like you, he is a clergyman. I have no doubt you share much in common. If you win my Lizzy, he will be your brother."

"What a delightful idea!" Collins rose.

"Let us be off then. His cottage is just a brief stroll from here." Pierce would certainly not begrudge his future father a small service.

Chapter 5

DARCY SAT IN THE Green Swan's parlor, near a sunny window, feet propped on an ottoman. Dust motes danced in the sunbeams, disappearing against his newspaper. He turned the page and snapped the paper into its crease. Bingley had chosen their accommodations well. Though quaint, the inn offered Darcy the thing he most required—privacy. The innkeeper attended his needs, but without fawning and had instructed his staff to do the same.

He drew a deep, relaxed breath. This rare venture into indolence made a welcome respite after all he had been through with Wickham and Georgiana.

"I say, you are the spit and image of your father."

Darcy jumped and tossed the paper aside. "Fitzwilliam! I did not expect you yet. Why did you not send word of your plans?"

"With the message you sent, you could hardly expected me to dally about." Fitzwilliam laughed and clapped Darcy's shoulder.

Darcy settled into his chair. "Sit, sit. Tell me of London."

Fitzwilliam dropped into a nearby seat. "Our sisters and Miss Lackley keep Mother quite occupied. Though she might say otherwise, Mother delights in a bevy of quality young ladies to guide into society!" He kicked his foot up onto the footstool and chuckled. "It was no place for a man."

"How fares Georgiana?"

Fitzwilliam leaned in on his elbow, all traces of mirth gone. "She has blossomed under my mother's guidance. You did right in sending her and her friend to Matlock House. What is more, Mother dotes upon Miss Lackley. The girl is a rare combination of enthusiasm and good sense."

Darcy dragged his hand down his face.

"You are not still flagellating yourself over Wickham, are you?" Fitzwilliam crossed his arms. His brows knit into rugged creases.

Darcy rolled his eyes. His cousin's commanding expressions and intimidating postures no longer impressed.

"For heaven's sake, man, let it go! Your sister is well. The scoundrel floats somewhere in the middle of the ocean, assuming he did not already succumb to the scourges of naval life. She and her reputation are safe." He cuffed Darcy's knee. "Why must you still brood? I say, you are just like your father."

Darcy raked his hair. "If only I had protected her, taught her better—"

Fitzwilliam smacked the arm of the chair. Others turned to stare. His dark scowl drove them back. "No more of this. If you wish to dwell on your inadequacies and the sad fact you are but a man, do so without my company."

Darcy squirmed in the confines of his chair. Once again, Fitzwilliam cut him off, not listening. Bradley listened so much better. Then again, Fitzwilliam rarely challenged him the way his vicar did.

"You are fortunate to be first-born. You would never have survived the life of an officer." He snickered. "And I cannot imagine you as a clergyman, or worse, at the law."

Darcy flushed. Did Fitzwilliam resent his lot in life? "Are you now retired from the army, or do I still address one of His Majesty's finest?"

"I finished the last of the formalities the day before I received your letter and am officially sold out. My life is once more my own." He laced his fingers behind his head. "Though the realities of a sedentary existence—"

Darcy chortled. "Enjoy a few inactive months. After you purchase your estate, you will wish for idleness again!"

"True enough. It is easy to forget the frenzy of planting and harvesting."

"Do not forget managing the livestock, maintaining the fences and houses, handling tenant issues and the parish duties—"

"Enough! You sound like the general I just left behind." Fitzwilliam raised open hands. "May I count on your assistance to find a proper estate for an earl's second son?"

"Once I am done here, I am at your disposal. I seem to be making a habit of this service." He balanced his right ankle onto his left knee. "I drew the line at crawling through Netherfield's attics with Bingley."

Fitzwilliam slapped his thigh, chuckling. "Oh, that is rich! What a picture, the proper master of Pemberley picking cobwebs off his lapels!"

How had Fitzwilliam survived his tours of duty with his sense of humor intact? Only the occasional shadow that veiled his eyes gave testimony of the horrors he had endured.

"Tell me, how did you meet this rare paragon of feminine virtue you wrote of?" Fitzwilliam's voice dropped to a whisper.

Darcy blushed as he recounted his tale of losing himself in Longbourn's woods.

Fitzwilliam's grin widened, and his eyes twinkled. "You, lost? Chasing raspberries? That is rich!"

Darcy shot him a sour glare.

Fitzwilliam only laughed harder. "Surely you have met her since, under more civilized conditions?"

"She and her sisters have called upon Miss Bingley at the inn. They are anxious to make her feel welcome in Meryton."

"Let me guess—you, and probably Bingley as well, happened to be here when the young ladies' called?"

"It was unplanned, but a pleasing occurrence nonetheless."

"You say there are five sisters?"

"Yes, though the youngest is not older than Georgiana."

"Well, as I do not need a silly young wife, I may rule her out easily. Clearly, you selected a sister for yourself, so which of the remaining do you choose for me?" Fitzwilliam winked and twitched his eyebrows.

"We are speaking of gently bred ladies, not common…"

"Relax, cousin! I jest." Fitzwilliam propped his other foot on the stool and crossed his ankles. "How unlike you! Tell me more of this mythical creature who moves you to dramatic letters and overt displays of emotion."

"Fitzwilliam…"

"I am serious. You know Mother insists I should settle down with an heiress of some sort."

"They have no fortune to speak of."

"I suppose a flaw was inevitable. That they provoked you to such a letter must be enough."

Darcy smiled in spite of himself. "Perhaps Bingley's proximity affects me."

"You need to find him an estate near Pemberley! You would do well to continue this reformation."

Darcy muttered under his breath. Fitzwilliam always took his teasing a step too far.

"So, tell me of these women we are to marry—did Bingley choose among them, too? He is a decent sort of fellow. I could accept him as a brother. What are we to do with the ones remaining? A maiden aunt to tend our children or perhaps—"

"Enough!" Darcy jumped to his feet and stalked out. He paused at the front door to give orders for his horse to be fetched.

Though he tried to wait patiently, he paced the steps until the hapless groom brought his animal. Darcy mounted and rode off toward Pierce's cottage in a cloud of dust. Enough of Fitzwilliam's disregard for propriety! If anyone had heard him prattling on, what gossip would ensue?

With her intelligence and wit, Miss Elizabeth resembled no woman he had encountered before, and he wanted to know her better. He could not be the source of further murmurings about her family and thus jeopardize his chance.

His horse nickered, and he slowed. Bother, where was he? He blinked dust from his eyes. Two familiar young women walked along the road just ahead of him, Miss Bennet and Miss Elizabeth. The tips of his ears burned.

They did not appear because he wished them there, but a touch of self-consciousness nipped at him all the same. Heartbeats later, they were close enough to notice his guilty conscience. At least he had met their father when Bennet visited Bingley at the inn and he might greet them without remorse.

He dismounted and bowed. "Good day, Miss Bennet, Miss Elizabeth."

"Good day, Mr. Darcy," they replied together. They adjusted the baskets in their arms and curtsied.

"Are you on your way to Netherfield, or do you seek more raspberries, sir?" Miss Elizabeth's eyes sparkled.

"Neither, madam." He tucked his hat under his arm. What fine eyes she had! "My horse and I have grown restless with too much time at the inn. We are not accustomed to a sedentary life." The horse nudged Darcy's shoulder and received an affectionate pat.

"He agrees with you, sir. May I?" Miss Elizabeth gestured towards the animal.

"Of course." Darcy held the horse's halter while she stroked its soft nose. "Do you ride?"

"A little and not on so fine a creature as this. He seems quite a delightful animal."

"Usually he is most high spirited." Darcy brushed

the horse's cheek. "I am sure he is gentled by the presence of—"

Rapid hoof beats bore down on them. Miss Bennet gasped and jumped to the side of the road.

Fitzwilliam trotted toward them on his bay. "Darcy!" He sprang from his saddle.

Fitzwilliam possessed the most astonishing timing. How had he survived the French when he lacked the sense to recognize his company was not wanted? Darcy huffed. "Ladies, may I present my cousin, Colonel Richard Fitzwilliam. This is Miss Bennet and Miss Elizabeth Bennet."

"A pleasure to meet you, sir." Miss Bennet curtsied, her eyes locked on Fitzwilliam.

Fitzwilliam bowed. "The pleasure is all mine, madam."

Where were Fitzwilliam's manners? Must he gawk? Aunt Matlock had taught him better. "My cousin has just arrived from London." Darcy forced himself not to glare at Fitzwilliam.

"Are you and your horse restless like your cousin, or have you a destination in mind?" Miss Elizabeth clearly noticed Fitzwilliam's rapt gaze at her sister.

Fitzwilliam chuckled and broke his stare. He turned to Darcy with raised brows.

"We are going to pay a visit to our friend, Mr. Bradley, at Mr. Pierce's cottage." Darcy gestured down the road.

"Our path takes us past Mr. Pierce's as well." Miss Bennet smiled.

"Perhaps we might walk together?" Fitzwilliam reached for Miss Bennet's basket.

"Thank you, sir." Miss Bennet relinquished her hamper and glanced at Miss Elizabeth, who nodded.

Miss Bennet walked ahead with Fitzwilliam, while Miss Elizabeth hung back a few steps to walk with Darcy. For several minutes, they strolled silently, listening to her sister and Fitzwilliam's lively conversation.

Not for the first time, Darcy wished for his cousin's ease in company.

"I met your friend Mr. Bradley. He joined my family for dinner a few nights ago." Miss Elizabeth peeked at him.

"What is your impression of him?" He held his breath.

"I did not much like him."

Darcy's feet turned to lead. His face cooled as the blood drained away. Miss Elizabeth was not the woman he had hoped. "Why might that be?"

"Because he intends to take our Mr. Pierce from us…and with him, my sister." She offered a watery-eyed smile.

Blood prickled back into his cheeks. He had judged her too quickly.

"Your Mr. Bradley shows a peculiar devotion to his parish. Few clergymen care so deeply for their people. Mr. Pierce is cut from the same cloth."

"I am surprised by how much you discern in so brief an acquaintance."

She shrugged. "My family has known Mr. Bradley since before I was born. My aunt grew up in Lambton, in his parish."

"Indeed?" What a ridiculous response! But better words eluded him.

"My aunt writes me often. Her letters are filled with stories and wise advice that originated with the curate who taught her as a girl. Though we only recently met face to face, he is an old friend."

He exhaled a heavy breath. "What do you truly think of him?"

They walked several more steps. Perhaps she did not hear?

"I like him very well."

Darcy's heart settled back into its right spot and his breathing eased. He could not fathom a wife who did not approve of Bradley. A wife? Where had that thought come from?

Bennet rapped on Pierce's door. With any luck, he would be able to introduce the two men and leave them to their own conversation while he slipped out for a bit of solitary reflection.

The door creaked open.

"Mr. Bennet! Come in, you are welcome—and your friend, too." Pierce ushered them into the front room.

A fleeting twinge of guilt pinched Bennet's conscience. Bradley sat near the sunny window, a book in his lap, feet propped on a soft stool. The poor man obviously wished for quiet, too. However, the old vicar would find it again much more easily than he.

Bradley looked up and set his book aside. He heaved himself to his feet and trundled toward them. "Good morning."

Bennet removed his hat. "Mr. Bradley, Mr. Pierce, may I present my cousin, Mr. Collins."

Bradley's eyebrows shot up.

"Mr. Collins is vicar—"

Collins bowed. "At Rosings Park, my patroness-"

"Lady Catherine De Bourgh," Bradley finished.

"You know of her?" Collins's eyes widened, then narrowed as he stared at the old vicar.

Bradley flashed the barest shadow of a smile. "We have met."

Pierce gestured for them all to sit. Collins settled on the sun-faded settee.

The visit was shaping into something most unexpected. Bennet selected the chair nearest the dusty bookcase. The far side made a wonderful place to observe, but not engage, in the conversation.

"Mr. Collins, did you know, Mr. Bradley is a vicar as well?" Pierce asked.

"Where is your parish, sir? Who is your patron?"

"Is not what we do more significant than where we do it or the patron who appoints us?" Bradley's voice sharpened to a fine point.

"Of course," Collins stammered, "I meant no offense. I thought it only a common pleasantry to exchange."

"Some men are exceedingly proud of their station." Bradley parked his elbows on his knees, his eyes drawn into a severe glare.

Pierce frowned and glanced at Bradley.

How astonishing! Bennet chewed the inside of his cheek. Even the saintly Bradley could have a cross day. Collins's reactions were proving quite interesting. Perhaps he would stay a bit longer.

Collins shook his head and blinked rapidly. "You said you have met Lady Catherine."

"At one time she offered me the living I expect you now hold." Bradley's lips wrinkled as though he drank sour milk.

Collins mouth hung agape. "You did not accept?"

"I preferred my curacy in Derbyshire." Bradley lifted his foot onto the stool with his hand. He grimaced and scooted back.

"Derbyshire?" Collins's brows knit, and he bounced his knuckles against his lips. "Lady Catherine's nephew's estate—Pemberley—is there. You are not—"

"I am indeed."

Collins's jaw worked soundlessly while Bennet stifled his laughter. Perhaps it was cruel, but Collins's discomposure seemed appropriate payment for the discomfiture Bennet suffered.

"Mr. Darcy is your patron?"

Bradley nodded.

"He is a man of consequence and connection, the Earl of Matlock's nephew, as well as Lady Catherine's. You are indeed blessed."

"I am, but not because of his wealth or connections. He is an excellent master to his estate and holds the highest of standards for himself and those with whom he associates. Those are true blessings." Bradley twined his fingers together. His knuckles popped loudly in the silent room.

Collins jumped. "Of course, I only meant—"

"I know too well what you meant and cannot agree. Neither wealth nor birth—"

"I said none of those things, sir. I am familiar with your opinions and would hardly contradict you." Collins glanced at Bennet and Pierce. "Such debates are not appropriate for refined company."

Pierce cleared his throat. "Too true, they are best saved for professional encounters."

Bradley grunted and folded his arms over his belly.

Full on guilt kicked his side, but Bennet could not

restrain himself. "I say there, Pierce, it was a most interesting sermon you preached Sunday."

Collins turned to face Pierce. "Indeed. What sermon writers do you favor? I am partial to the older ones myself."

Pierce hung his head and shuffled his feet. He exhaled heavily and looked at Bennet.

Bennet bit his lip. Perhaps he had gone too far. But Pierce would surely forgive, at least for Mary's sake.

"He writes his own," Bradley said.

"How…unusual."

Pierce shrugged.

"Come now, Mr. Collins, you have said a great deal more on that subject." Bradley sniffed and glanced at Pierce. "As I recall, you have voiced quite a strong opinion on the topic, on multiple occasions."

"How would you know that? You and I only just met."

"Like a pebble in a pond, a man's words cause much greater ripples than one might imagine."

Collins adjusted his cravat. "That was a good natured debate on the merits of—"

"— your own opinion?" Bradley's voice honed to a razor edge.

"I had no idea my remarks would be construed as such a personal affront. I beg your forgiveness for any offense I may have caused." Collins bowed his head.

Bennet tapped his fingers along the arm of his chair. Bradley's sharp tone and hostile demeanor meant only one thing: He did not approve of Collins. Whilst this saved Bennet the bother of asking his opinion, it was troublesome. Were there greater flaws in Collins's character than holding traditional opinions?

Pierce squirmed. Doubtless, he did not know what to make of Bradley's strident reactions either. Ah well, no man was perfect. Even Bradley should be allowed a prejudiced opinion now and then.

A loud knock cut off Bennet's thoughts and the clergymen's conversation.

Pierce answered and ushered in two well-dressed gentlemen.

Collins sprang to his feet. "Mr. Darcy, Colonel Fitzwilliam." He bowed deeply.

"Mr. Collins?" Darcy cocked his head at Bradley.

"You are acquainted with my cousin?" Bennet's eyes widened.

Bradley struggled out of his chair. "Mr. Darcy, Colonel Fitzwilliam, may I present Mr. Bennet of Longbourn, and my friend Mr. Pierce."

"A pleasure see you again, Mr. Bennet. Mr. Pierce." Darcy bowed smartly.

Colonel Fitzwilliam, who bore a strong resemblance to Darcy, scanned the room. "I fear we have intruded—"

"No, not at all. You are most welcome. Please make yourselves comfortable." Pierce gestured to a pair of worn chairs between Bradley and Collins.

How much more interesting would this call become? Bennet disciplined his twitching lips into a neutral expression. Though solitude had been his aim, all in all, this was far more entertaining.

"Thank you." Darcy sat and the rest followed.

"If I may be so bold as to ask, what brings you to Hertfordshire, Mr. Darcy?" Collins asked.

"My friend has plans to lease an estate here. I

came to assist him in the process." Darcy's thin smile did nothing to mask his short and clipped manner.

So, Bradley's patron held as low an opinion of Collins as his vicar, poisoned by Bradley's view, no doubt. Bennet pursed his lips and nodded. He should not take such pleasure in discovering another man's faults, but he did nonetheless.

"You are as generous as your aunt in your beneficence to those beneath yourself." Collins sat up a little straighter.

"Those below himself?" Colonel Fitzwilliam snorted.

"My friends, whoever they may be, are not below me." Darcy huffed and looked away.

Bradley's eyes twinkled. Did he just wink at the colonel?

"I…that is to say…Lady Catherine believes there to be few…" Collins stammered.

"I am quite familiar with what my aunt says and need not another repetition of her diatribes." Colonel Fitzwilliam crossed his ankle over his knee.

Collins opened and closed his mouth several times as though tasting his words before he spoke. "I am delighted to assure you of your aunt's and cousin's continued good health and prosperity."

Darcy smiled tightly. "How pleasing to know she has not begun a slide toward demise in just the few short months since I last visited her."

What diversion, to allow men to reveal their own foibles and flaws with so little effort on his own part. Bennet snickered under his breath.

"Do you plan to avail yourself of the local sport whilst you are here, Colonel?" Collins asked.

"Indeed, I do. Mr. Pierce, you must be the resident

expert, what can you tell me of it?" Fitzwilliam nudged Darcy with his boot.

Bennet glanced at his pocket watch. He had long overstayed Pierce's welcome. At the next break in the conversation, he cut in. "I thank you for your hospitality, Mr. Pierce, but it is time for us to return to Longbourn." He rose.

"Thank you for your visit, sir." Pierce showed them to the door.

The afternoon had warmed considerably since their arrival, and the sticky heat wrapped around him like a smothering woolen scarf. The heavy air hung uneasily between them. Bennet and Collins walked all the way back to the main road before Collins spoke.

"How long have you known Mr. Bradley?" Collins scuffed his boots though a pile of disintegrating leaves left from last autumn.

"Possibly longer than you have been alive." Bennet struggled not to scrutinize him openly. He settled for surreptitious glances from the corner of his eye.

"And Mr. Darcy?"

"I was recently introduced when I met his friend Bingley who is to take Netherfield."

Collins lifted his head, brow deeply lined.

"You do not seem pleased with either of them."

"We met in Kent."

"So I gathered."

"Do you know if they will be staying long in Hertfordshire?"

"I believe they only just arrived, though I am not privy to their plans."

"Then he has probably not come into the acquaintance of your daughters."

Bennet stopped short. "What do you mean by

that?"

"Nothing at all."

"Do not dissemble, Collins. If you are aware of some danger to my girls, I demand you speak frankly now." Bennet crossed his arms and glared.

"I do not mean to suggest he, or the colonel, poses any danger, not in the truest sense of the word. My patroness' nephews are not that sort of men. I just do not wish my cousins…ah…how does one put these things…to set their caps…upon either of them."

Bennet glowered. "My girls are not goosecaps, running after rich men."

Collins rubbed his face with his hands. "I am at a loss to express myself properly today. I mean no disrespect, to be sure. I hope to avoid any form of injury to my dear cousins. They are lovely girls and may attract Mr. Darcy's and Colonel Fitzwilliam's attentions. But men like them are known to bestow a young lady attention with the intention of harmless flirtation and nothing more. They will marry within their station and it would only wound my cousins to raise their hopes outside of their own sphere."

"I see." Bennet stroked his chin and resumed walking. Collins did make a good point. Any number of fine gentlemen had passed through Meryton and done just as he said. "I wonder though, if there might be an ulterior motive in your warnings."

Collins flushed and dipped his head. "I suppose that reflects meanly upon my character. Miss Elizabeth is such a gem in Hertfordshire. Is it wrong of me to fear she might garner the notice of a man with whom I could not compete? It is true though, what I said. Even if I did not like your daughter, I would still warn you against allowing them too much time in the company of gentlemen like them."

"I understand your motives, sir." Bennet stopped again and met Collins's eyes. "I will even confess that I like you well enough to allow you to pursue them."

"Thank—"

"But," Bennet cleared his throat, "I do not like underhandedness and concealed intentions. Those were your father's greatest faults. He sought to use others to his ends. I did not tolerate it from him, nor will I from you. Be straight with me and you will find our acquaintance mutually agreeable. Deceive me, manipulate me, take advantage of me in any way, and I will not hesitate to show you the door."

"Of course, of course, I would never imagine such a thing. Please, forgive me. My only excuse—"

"Yes, yes, no more apologies. It is all well enough if she likes you. But Lizzy and I are much the same, and if she senses any insincerity in you, your suit is lost."

"I will keep that in mind. I appreciate your patience with me."

Bennet grunted. He could not blame Collins. Men as wealthy as Darcy would make almost any gentleman feel insecure and a little foolish.

Darcy puffed a breath through his cheeks as Pierce closed the door behind Collins. He threw his head back, eyes squeezed shut. What a horrible man! Fine manners and handsome features covered mean opinions and limited information. He passed himself off with polish that admitted him into a level of society in which he would not otherwise be welcome. The sight of him made Darcy's stomach roil.

Pierce dropped into his chair. "None of you approves of my betrothed's cousin."

"It does not appear you do either." Fitzwilliam winked.

Pierce folded his hands over his belly and sighed. "I cannot choose her family. All families possess some troublesome distant relation. I expect we will have little to do with him."

"Too true, too true." Bradley settled into his seat. "A wise perspective to be sure. Each day has enough troubles; no need to search for more."

"We should go as well. I promised the afternoon to Bingley." Darcy stood and nodded to Fitzwilliam.

They left and took to their mounts. Darcy urged his horse into a fast clip.

Fitzwilliam matched his pace. "Though I have met only one of her sisters, I choose Miss Bennet. She is a lovely girl."

Darcy coughed.

"Do you find your Miss Elizabeth any less attractive having met her cousin?"

"Do be serious." Darcy pressed his mount for more speed.

"I am entirely serious. I could not care less about Collins. Miss Bennet was sweet, serene and sincere. She spoke with me out of an interest in me, rather than in the younger son of an earl. I cannot recall the last time that happened." Fitzwilliam drew his horse close and met Darcy's gaze.

Darcy started. All levity left Fitzwilliam's eyes. Shadows of pain deeper than any he had ever seen flashed across Fitzwilliam's face and disappeared as quickly. Darcy sat straighter, and his horse slowed.

Fitzwilliam had never been so transparent.

"I like her very much and want to further our acquaintance. Hopefully, Bingley will put me up at Netherfield for a while. The Green Swan is tolerable, but I would prefer less rustic environs, if possible."

"You do not find Collins objectionable?"

"Of course I do, and I always have. I did not approve from the moment Aunt Catherine gave him the living." Fitzwilliam nudged his horse back to a fast walk. "I fail to see what that has to do with the Miss Bennets."

"Would you wish to call him a relation?" The back of Darcy's neck prickled.

Fitzwilliam shrugged. "I cannot say I am pleased to claim any number of my relations, starting with my brother. As I have little to say on the matter, I try to think on it as little as possible. Why trouble myself with those things I cannot change? I advise you to do the same. Do not throw away your opportunity to know Miss Elizabeth better for the sake of her ridiculous cousin. If anything, you should be delighted in her connection to Bradley. You value his opinion more than any other."

"Bradley has many connections—"

"He is looking to raise Pierce up as his successor, and Pierce is to marry her sister. That should tell you everything." Fitzwilliam flicked the reins and pulled ahead.

Darcy remained behind. Fitzwilliam made it all look so easy. He did not have an estate depending upon him to make the right choice of mistress.

If Darcy erred, how many would suffer? How much easier to remain unmarried and allow Mrs. Reynolds to carry on the household tasks. Bradley's voice echoed in his ears. *By refusing to decide, you have still made a choice.*

Darcy squeezed his temples. Miss Elizabeth, with her fine eyes, witty intelligence and good humor, set him at ease. She was gently bred, and so many little things she said demonstrated she understood how to manage an estate and care for its people. Bradley approved of her family. What more could he hope to find? He encouraged his horse into motion. Fitzwilliam was right. He would pursue her acquaintance.

Chapter 6

THREE DAYS LATER, Bingley and Louisa waited near the Green Swan's parlor window. A wagon bearing their things from London would arrive soon. They would officially take possession of Netherfield Park and take the first step to fulfilling his father's dream. The Bingleys would join the gentry. He pulled his shoulders back a little straighter.

"Did Caroline's letter say when to expect the driver?" Louisa drew the curtain aside and peered through the window.

Bingley snickered. "As much as she resented making the arrangements, I feel fortunate she wrote to give me a date for the delivery."

"Do you think she enjoys London?" She tucked the drapes into place.

"Hardly, with whom will she find her amusement?" He picked up his newspaper. "Few tolerate her company."

She worried her hands together.

"Do not allow it to bother you. Remember, she refused to come. We only rejoiced in her decision."

She forced a smile.

"Look, the wagon comes." He tapped the windowpane.

They hurried to the front steps. The cart rolled to a stop before them, and Bingley trotted out to speak to the driver. The taciturn man pointed to a carriage stopped behind them.

Bingley's face prickled. No, it could not be. Impossible! He jogged to the coach.

"Charles!" a shrill voice cried. Caroline waved like a wounded bird until Bingley handed her down.

He edged away from her rustling skirts. "What are you doing here?"

"A fine greeting, indeed. Did you lose all your manners in the country?" She brushed dust from her sleeves.

His lips stretched tight over his teeth. "Forgive me, Caroline. How was your trip?"

"Ghastly." She peered around him and waved sharply. "Why does Louisa stand there so stupidly? She should be here helping me."

"I expect she does not know what to make of your arrival any more than I do."

Louisa shuffled toward them.

He shook his head, and she stopped. "What are you doing here?"

"Oh, do stop going on and on about that."

"You were at the town house."

Caroline smoothed her skirts and straightened her hat. "Yes, I was, and now I am here."

"Why?"

"Do I need a reason?"

He drew a deep breath, eyes to the sky. "You do not like to travel. Why would you make a journey with only your maid for company?"

"I found London dreadfully dull. I sat at home all day with no one to call upon and no one at home when I called. People flee the summer heat for the countryside, so I decided to follow suit."

More likely they had fled Caroline. He glanced over his shoulder. Louisa's crestfallen face begged comfort. How long would they be able to keep their newfound friends once they introduced Caroline?

He stared at her.

She flinched.

Blast it all! "You are following Darcy!"

She tossed her head. "Certainly not."

"Did not Mrs. Cooperton disabuse you of your desire to be mistress of a grand estate?"

"Disagreeable woman." She planted her hands on her hips and leaned in toward him. "Do not think I missed the little game you are all playing with me."

"What game?" He stepped back.

"Isolating me from your friends. How will I ever achieve an agreeable match if you will not allow—"

"Here in Meryton? You left London, in the height of the Season, to come to a quaint little market town and find a match? Have you taken leave of your senses?" He barked a strangled laugh.

"Do be quiet, before you make a spectacle."

He rolled his eyes. "You will not find it at all to your liking."

"I have already gone to the trouble and expense of getting here, and I will stay." She stamped. A little puff of dust swirled around her foot.

The wagon driver tapped Bingley's shoulder and whispered in his ear.

"Right, right, we must get this on to Netherfield so our things may be unloaded before dark. I suppose we can take this carriage, if the driver is agreeable." He signaled the coachman to make arrangements.

"I am not going any further. Three hours on the road—"

"You may stay here, by yourself. Louisa and I will attend to the house."

Caroline harrumphed and climbed into the coach.

Bingley trudged to Louisa. "I cannot believe she is here. I do not understand—"

"I do. She offended her last friend in London and with no one to receive her—"

"Gah!" He helped Louisa into the coach and followed her in.

"How far is this Netherfield Park from town?" Caroline picked at invisible specks on her skirt.

"A few miles." He kept his gaze to the side glass.

"That is tolerable enough, I suppose." Caroline sniffed. "What do you think of the house?"

"I am quite satisfied." Louisa studied at her hands. "The furnishings are somewhat older. I find them lovely and very homey."

"Well, I will determine just how suitable they are." Caroline tossed her head.

"Excuse me? What do you mean?" He flashed a wide-eyed look at Louisa.

She pressed her lips and shook her head.

"I am by far the best judge of the décor. You must allow me to conclude what is to be done."

"No redecorating. Our lease is a short term one. I

will not spend any money on the property at this point." He clenched his fists, his shoulders knotted.

"Mr. Darcy convinced you of that, no doubt." Caroline blotted her eyes with her handkerchief. "You are too cruel, Charles."

Bingley steeled himself for her tears. He would not be swayed by them today.

"Look, Longbourn!" Louisa pointed to the manor house on the horizon.

"What is that to me?"

"The home of the Bennets, our nearest neighbors," He muttered through clenched teeth.

Louisa twisted a fold of her skirts. "They are giving a dinner on our behalf on Friday to welcome us into the neighborhood."

"You must thank them for the offer when you decline. You cannot distinguish what sort of people these Bennets are, yet. We must take care to make the right impression—"

He glared. "We know what kind of people they are."

"And they are my friends," Louisa whispered.

"Besides, we already accepted their invitation!"

A florid stain crept up Caroline's neck. "Unaccept. It is easy to do and occurs often enough in the highest circles."

"I will not offend them by declining. They are gracious people, though. Perhaps they may deign to include you." He blew a long breath through his lips.

"You are far too naïve, Charles, You cannot possibly believe the invitation gracious in any way." Caroline rearranged the lace on her sleeve.

"The Bennets are my friends..." Louisa stammered.

"Friends? Friends? In a little more than a fortnight and a half, you think you have friends here when you have none elsewhere? They are nothing more than leeches, desperate for the influence of someone fashionable from London to bring interest to their drab little lives."

Bingley inched closer. "How dare you! They are the daughters of a gentleman—an advantage you cannot claim for yourself, I might remind you. They are ladies in the truest sense of the word…"

She waved him off. "These 'ladies,' as you call them, are in want of husbands, I am sure. What of their dowries? I expect they have none while you, my brother, are in possession of a fortune. Quite an eligible catch in their eyes, I imagine. Guard yourself lest they trap you with their arts and allurements. Our family should not be polluted by common chits!"

"Not another word! You will not insult our current neighbors the way you did our neighbors in town." He braced his feet along the floorboard and pressed against the squabs.

"Of what do you accuse me?" Caroline half rose in her seat.

"You insulted Mrs. Harrison and her daughters when they came to call," Louisa softly replied.

"I affronted them? No, Louisa, they offended me with their appalling manners. Have you forgotten? I did them a favor by making them aware. "

"No, your insults led them to cut you at the concert, in full view of all your acquaintances. No one desired to keep company with you afterwards. That is why you left London." Louisa wrapped her arms over her chest.

Caroline laughed thinly. "You were not even in

town when I attended the recital. How would you know?"

"Miss Wortham wrote me and told me exactly what happened. Stay home on Friday. The Netherfield staff is well trained. They will care for you."

"Who are you to tell me what to do? Perhaps I will go and show these Bennets what a fashionable lady-"

"No! I do not want you insulting my friends or embarrassing Charles and me."

The carriage lurched and stopped. Bingley pushed the door open and jumped down. He handed Louisa out and walked away. The driver could assist Caroline. He did not trust himself to do it.

He stared into the sky and massaged his neck. Storm clouds churned in his stomach and his knees turned to rubber. Standing up to Caroline would be a full time occupation, but a necessary one. If he did not start now, she would run their lives forever. He stretched his face with his hands and groaned. No better time to begin.

Though Caroline protested, Bingley directed the servants to move their belongings inside. He would be master of Netherfield and head of his family, whether Caroline liked it or not.

Darcy bit his tongue and tucked his feet to make room for the ladies' skirts. The coach would accommodate six men easily enough, but one never knew how much space women's gowns would require. He scooted a little further into the squabs. Why had he given in to Bingley's insistence that they all ride together to Longbourn? In the pleasure of his horse's company, he would have been on time, instead of fidgeting in the carriage, waiting for Miss Caroline to appear. Fashionably late, indeed—an oxymoronic concept at best! He cleared his throat and crossed his arms.

"Take a deep breath, Darce." Fitzwilliam pressed into his shoulder.

"To be intentionally late to make a statement of one's importance is the quintessence of bad taste and self-centeredness." Darcy craned his neck and peered through the side glass. "Finally."

"You would leave her behind to walk." Fitzwilliam stretched his legs and snickered.

"Indeed, I would. Arriving with her petticoats six inches deep in mud, just once, would cure her of this habit."

Fitzwilliam laughed into his fist.

Miss Bingley peeked in.

Fitzwilliam's laugh became a violent cough.

She stepped in, sat down and arranged her skirts "Are you well, Colonel?"

"Yes, yes." Fitzwilliam glanced at Darcy and composed his face into somber planes.

"My sister is on her way. Charles is…encouraging her." Miss Bingley smiled, though it was unconvincing at best.

"Of course, Darcy and I were discussing the comforts of coach travel over that of travelling on foot." Fitzwilliam elbowed him in the ribs.

The front door slammed, and tense voices filtered into the carriage. Miss Caroline entered and settled into the seat opposite Fitzwilliam. She straightened her skirts.

Bingley jumped in and pulled the door shut behind

him. He grunted and scooted past Miss Caroline to sit between his sisters. He glowered at Caroline. "We are off—at last."

"Do stop going on. It is only a few minutes." Caroline plucked the pleats in her sleeve.

"More than a quarter hour, closer to a half. Do not suppose we will brook your habit, either." Bingley sat back.

Miss Caroline squirmed to accommodate his shoulders. "Really, Charles."

"I think the Bennets most generous to host us for dinner. We must return the invitation as quickly as possible," Miss Bingley said. "It is the polite and accepted thing—"

"What do you know of entertaining? I will attend to the matter myself. Once we are properly settled in I shall plan a grand affair—"

"No, a small dinner party—"

"Do not be ridiculous." Caroline folded her hands in her lap. "I told you I will handle—"

Darcy squeezed his temples. Thank Providence, Georgiana was his only sister.

"There." Fitzwilliam pointed through the side glass. "We are at Longbourn."

Miss Caroline sniffed. "It appears no better now than it did when we drove past yesterday. I am certain the parlor is dreadful, and the food will be—"

"Served with warmth and grace in genteel company," Bingley cut her off.

Fitzwilliam cleared his throat. "I have attended enough high society events—"

"Oh, do tell us about them." Caroline batted her eyes.

Darcy pressed into the corner to increase the space

between them.

"No." Fitzwilliam shook his head. "They were dreadful, dull affairs with more posturing than a lawn full of peacocks. I prefer the kind of event I anticipate tonight."

The coach stopped, and Fitzwilliam shot out before Caroline could draw breath, Darcy close on his heels.

Mr. and Mrs. Bennet greeted them at the door. Darcy's ears burned as the buzz in the parlor quieted on their entrance. This was precisely why he preferred to arrive early. He scanned the room. Miss Elizabeth looked his direction and approached. His heart squeezed, then dropped into his stomach. She turned aside to Miss Bingley and Miss Caroline. Worse still, her cousin shadowed her like a puppy.

Darcy's sleeves suddenly became too short. He jerked them into place.

"You made it after all. I am proud of you." Bradley smiled and nodded as he approached.

Darcy drew a breath then closed his mouth when no appropriate response presented itself.

Bradley clapped his back. "The Bennets are excellent people—" He peered into Darcy's eyes and followed his gaze. "You have already discovered."

Darcy glowered, though his cheeks burned.

"Do not be so sensitive. She is a fine young woman. I encourage you to know her better."

"She is occupied—"

"Of course, she is acting as a hostess ought. You must not wait for her to come to you. Go to her; talk to her." Bradley nudged him. "She will appreciate your attentions."

Darcy glanced at her and sighed.

"Go, now." Bradley shoved him none too gently.

Darcy squared his shoulders, straightened his coat and walked through the crowd. An acquaintance with Miss Elizabeth was worth his discomfiture.

Elizabeth introduced Mr. Collins to the Bingleys and the Lucases. Charlotte and Maria both fell under his spell almost immediately. He had the happy gift of putting people at ease with his engaging conversation and personable manner. Yet his focus always returned to Elizabeth. She subdued her broad smile into something more demure. With all Mama's recent irritation towards her, his favor soothed her prickled soul.

Mama was in her element as the model hostess. She approached with a flock of older women in her wake. Elizabeth backed up to make room for them.

What was Lydia doing there in the corner? She stopped and focused on her sister. Lydia stood in the center of a small group of young ladies. In the midst of many giggles, she turned up her nose, threw her shoulders back and sauntered several steps in a most accurate affectation of Mr. Collins. Maria Lucas and Amy Long covered their mouths to contain their titters.

Darcy approached from the front hall. She acknowledged him with a tip of her head, but Lydia's behavior was a far more pressing matter. Hopefully, he would not deem her rude. She glanced from him to her sister, bit her lip and hurried away.

Why did everyone want their share of conversation with her now that she had somewhere she needed to be? Polite smiles and nods eased her way across the room to where Lydia aped the proud bearing of one Colonel Fitzwilliam.

Elizabeth blanched and searched the crowd. She exhaled heavily. Colonel Fitzwilliam stood at Jane's side, engaged in some delightful conversation, one which Elizabeth would much rather partake in than this.

"Lydia," she hissed.

Lydia stopped midstride. "What?"

"What are you doing?"

"La! A little harmless fun, that is all." Lydia looked from Maria to Amy.

"Mocking our guests where everyone can watch is your idea of harmless fun?"

"Do not be such a bore, Lizzy. No one pays any mind, and even if they did, how would they know—"

"I knew."

Lydia rolled her eyes and stuck her lip out in her characteristic pout.

"No more of this, or I shall tell Papa and ask him to send you upstairs," Elizabeth pressed in close, "for the rest of the summer."

"You would not—nor would he."

"You may want to reconsider that notion…in light of your other transgressions." Elizabeth glared.

At least Lydia blushed.

From the other side of the room, Mama quietly gathered the ladies to go to the dining room. Maria and Amy headed toward Mama. Lydia moved to follow, but Elizabeth caught her arm. Mr. Collins was too gracious to take offense at her juvenile behavior, but that was no reason to allow it to continue.

"After your disrespectful display you can stay with me and enter last," Elizabeth whispered. "Disliking our cousin excuses nothing."

Their eyes met and exchanged silent, barbed remarks.

Lydia dropped her gaze. "I will not do it again."

Elizabeth released her elbow, and they hurried to the dining room.

"I wish Mama would do what Lady Lucas does and allow the gentlemen to escort the ladies in," Lydia whispered, lower lip extended.

"Do stop complaining. Be glad Mama did not scold us for ignoring precedence." Elizabeth guided Lydia to sit near Mary and edged past her to take a seat close to Jane and Charlotte.

They both looked at her with the same longsuffering expression. Elizabeth frowned and shook her head.

The men filed into the dining room, and she bit her lip. Hopefully, Mr. Collins would sit close enough for conversation.

Darcy straightened his collar as he walked into the dining room. He felt the eyes on him, watching and waiting as he selected his place. How he hated being on display! Bingley, as guest of honor, sat beside Mrs. Bennet. The seat adjacent to him would be his safest choice, although it meant a seat next to Miss Caroline. Still, he would be near enough Miss Elizabeth to share some conversation with her. His spirits and his appetite both returned. Fitzwilliam's place beside Miss Bennet further buoyed him, though Collins's beside Miss Elizabeth did not. All in all, the arrangements might easily have been worse.

Bradley blessed the meal, and soup was served. Mrs. Bennet's cook had produced a fine carrot soup, not quite the flavor he was accustomed to, but that only added to his pleasure. From the way Miss Caroline wrinkled her nose, she lacked the same appreciation. Doubtless, the ride back to Netherfield would be full of disparagements of Longbourn's victuals.

"This is a delicious soup, my dear cousin." Collins dabbed his lips with his napkin and winked at Miss Elizabeth. "Though it is nothing to those served at Lady Catherine's dinner parties at Rosings Park."

Miss Elizabeth shielded her mouth with one hand and said softly, "Of course, we are to understand that Rosings Park is very fine indeed."

Collins and Miss Elizabeth giggled. Miss Bennet tittered while Fitzwilliam indulged in a hearty laugh.

Darcy closed his eyes. As much as he disliked Collins, he envied the easy humor and conversation Collins shared with Miss Elizabeth. If only his tongue could be so nimble.

"I mean no offense to your aunt," Collins said, his gaze directly on Darcy.

"Naturally," Darcy mumbled. His face burned. Must everyone stare at him so?

"Her palate is most…refined, is it not?" Fitzwilliam grinned. "Cauliflower, Miss Bennet? Miss Elizabeth?" He plated the vegetable for the two ladies.

A servant placed a platter of carved meat near Darcy. He served Miss Caroline, Mrs. Goulding and then himself a fine slab of roast mutton, one of his favorites.

Conversation buzzed around him. His head ached

as he tried to follow—too many voices, too many divergent trails and trains of thought. No sooner did he pick up one, but another distracted him. How did one even break into the give and take without interrupting or appearing rude?

"—Mr. Darcy."

He jumped and blinked at Miss Elizabeth. "Excuse me? I am afraid I did not hear you." He fingered the edge of the tablecloth.

She smiled so kindly, the outer layer of his anxiety melted away. "I merely asked if you found sufficient dishes to your liking. There are many at the other end of the table which may be brought for you to sample, should you wish."

"I…thank you…I am quite—" Why did she leave him so tongue-tied?

"I am certain it is a new experience for Mr. Darcy to be able to see the opposite side of the table." Collins chuckled, with yet another wink at Miss Elizabeth. "Though I have not observed the dining room at Pemberley, it can hardly be smaller than the one at Rosings Park, which takes a full day to circumnavigate."

Miss Elizabeth giggled into her hand, her cheeks a dainty pink.

Darcy's mouth went dry. "I do not find Longbourn's hospitality wanting in any way." His voice was raspy and low, coarse and unrefined next to Collins's droll banter. "Everything is most pleasing."

"Mama will be pleased to hear it." Miss Elizabeth's smile smoothed a fragrant balm over the prickly parts of his soul.

"He is right." Miss Caroline whispered in his ear.

Darcy's stomach roiled. He sipped his wine, now

bitter in his glass.

"Try as she might, our fine country hostess cannot hope to match what we are accustomed to." Miss Caroline took a tiny bite of mutton.

His brow furrowed, magnifying his headache. "Do not pretend to speak for me, Miss Caroline."

She clutched her chest. "By no means, I merely noted—"

"—most inappropriately given the current company. I would thank you to keep your opinions to yourself."

Her cheeks colored, and she turned aside.

Darcy tried to catch Miss Elizabeth's eyes. Had she heard Miss Caroline's biting remarks? If she thought—oh, that dratted woman, what damage had she wrought? He could not gain Miss Elizabeth's attention. She was engaged in a lively discussion with Fitzwilliam, Pierce, and Collins, trading quips and clever remarks so easily, the entire exchange might have been scripted by a master playwright. Darcy sighed and sagged into the seatback.

From the end of the table, Bradley cleared his throat loudly.

"Our old friend would like to offer a toast," Bennet announced, rising slightly from his seat.

Bradley lifted his wine glass. "To Mr. Pierce and his lovely betrothed, Miss Mary Bennet. Every blessing and felicity upon your upcoming union. May it be a long and fruitful one."

Everyone raised their glasses and joined the toast.

Miss Caroline inclined toward Collins and softly asked, "What is your opinion of your cousin's betrothal?"

Darcy blanched and nearly spat the last drops of

wine still lingering on his tongue.

"I am very happy for her." Collins dabbed his lips with his napkin. "I believe she has made a most felicitous union. A clergyman makes an excellent husband."

Miss Caroline and Miss Elizabeth giggled. Pierce snickered while Fitzwilliam rolled his eyes.

"You see," Collins focused directly on Miss Elizabeth, "he is neither too low nor too high in the world. Any lower, and he would not be genteel enough for a lady of my dear cousin's distinction."

"What if he were higher born?" Miss Caroline asked.

Collins folded his hands on the edge of the table. "Why then, he would be too genteel for her." He lifted his eyebrows and laughed.

Fitzwilliam leaned his forearms on the table. "If she is a gentleman's daughter and he a gentleman, how could one be too genteel for the other?"

"She might object to a dining table whose two ends require different post directions."

Miss Elizabeth and Miss Bennet chortled until tears ran down their cheeks.

Fitzwilliam guffawed. "Stuff and nonsense."

"How can you say that?" Miss Caroline asked. "You are connected to the finest of families. Your father, the earl—"

Miss Bennet started, and she blinked hard. Fitzwilliam did not look at her.

Darcy ran his tongue along the inside of his cheek. So, he had not told his angel of his connections.

"If I wanted to further those associations, I would be dining with the earl and viscount tonight." Fitzwilliam sought Miss Bennet's gaze and waited until he had it to continue. "I am not because I prefer much pleasanter company."

Darcy held his breath. Miss Bennet swallowed hard. Though her countenance remained serene, her eyes betrayed clear symptoms of particular regard. Oh, for a certain pair of fine eyes to train such an expression upon him.

Mrs. Bennet rose from the head of the table.

"Pray excuse us, sirs," Miss Bennet said softly as she stood.

The ladies followed their hostesses from the room. Darcy traded glances with Fitzwilliam. Without the ladies, this would be a long hour indeed.

In the drawing room, the older women gathered around Mary to discuss all things wedding. The youngest flocked to Kitty to discuss all things fashion. Lydia flounced and preened in the center of the group, clearly enjoying the attention that came with wearing Kitty's latest creation.

Jane stood with the Bingley ladies. Elizabeth moved to join them, but Charlotte caught her first.

"Your mother outdid herself tonight. It was a lovely dinner. Miss Bingley was most pleased to find her favorites on the table. I am always surprised at the little ways she finds to be so considerate." Charlotte glanced over her shoulder towards Mama.

"I am happy Miss Bingley approved. I fear her sister did not take the same satisfaction in our company." Elizabeth flashed a quick look at Miss Caroline.

"She does give the impression of being more

pleased in herself than she is in us." Charlotte's lips turned up at the corners. "Poor Miss Bingley has herself quite a sister, does she not?"

"I am reminded to be grateful for what I have. A lively disposition is far easier to live with than a bitter and taciturn one."

Charlotte smirked. "I must agree." She sat on the small settee near the fireplace and patted the cushion beside her. "Miss Bingley's brother is most agreeable."

"He is. Kitty has developed a good friendship with Miss Bingley, and he often joins her when she comes to call."

"Perhaps he has a preference for your sister." Charlotte's brow rose archly.

"She is full young for a beau and still very silly. What could Mr. Bingley want with a girl like Kitty?"

"I imagine he sees a pretty, agreeable girl, and with their family's connection to trade, a country gentleman's daughter would be deemed a good match for him."

Elizabeth chuckled. "Let us wait until Mary is married before we match any more of my sisters."

"Do not wait too long. It would not do for you to ignore the two most eligible and handsome gentlemen vying for your attention over dinner."

"No, not hardly."

"Yes, most particularly."

Elizabeth's face burned hotter than the flames on the hearth.

"The question, my friend, is what will you do about it?"

"What do you mean?"

"You must choose your gentleman and secure him

as soon as may be possible."

"Like a horse at auction?"

"There are similarities." Charlotte chuckled. "Choose and show him even greater affection than even you feel to make him decide upon you."

"Before I ascertain his character, his—"

"You will learn his faults soon enough. Why cloud the matter so early?"

"Charlotte!"

"I am entirely serious." She patted Elizabeth's knee. "I do not envy your choice. If you ask me, I suggest you fix on Mr. Darcy. He is better than twice the consequence of your cousin."

"There is more to the married state than—"

"Of course, however, you should not forget much strife is eased by sufficient funds." Charlotte folded her hands in her lap and leaned in on them. "While it is true enough that a woman may harm her reputation by setting her sights too high in a marriage partner, she must consider the future of her children. Mr. Darcy does not appear to be the sort of man to be seeking a country mistress to establish—"

"That is enough." Elizabeth rose. "I cannot bear to discuss this further."

"As you wish." Charlotte stood. "But do not hesitate for too long. Any number of young women in Meryton would be happy to distract either of your beaus from you." Charlotte glanced at Miss Caroline and joined Jane.

She slumped into the back of the settee. Mama hated it when she did not sit up straight. Charlotte usually spoke good sense. She sighed. Mr. Darcy could not possibly be interested in her. The shy, awkward, intriguing man must surely seek an heiress or the daughter of a peer, not someone like her. Mr. Collins's attentions were plentiful and pleasing. But, if it were possible, which man did she prefer?

Time crept through at least a century of discussions on politics and war and business. Darcy rejoiced when the port was finished, cigars smoked, and the gentlemen headed to the drawing room. If it were not for the promise of Miss Elizabeth's company, Darcy would have invented an excuse to leave.

"Mary! Mary!" Miss Lydia rushed past him. "The gentlemen are come, and you must play us a jig."

Miss Mary hesitated a moment and looked toward her mother. Mrs. Bennet nodded and Miss Mary walked to the pianoforte. Others scurried to move furniture for an impromptu dance floor.

Darcy searched for Miss Elizabeth, but Collins reached her first and led her off.

Miss Mary sounded a chord, and he scooted out of the way of the dancers. How patently unfair! Fitzwilliam had partnered with Miss Bennet and Bingley with Miss Kitty. Even Bradley danced with Mrs. Bennet. Darcy turned away. Miss Bingley stood slightly apart from the others. She sighed and glanced at the pearl ring on her left hand.

He straightened his coat and approached her. "Would you care to dance?"

"Thank you." She took his arm, her eyes bright.

Though he did not generally take pleasure in dancing, Darcy enjoyed the set. The easy informality of the drawing room reminded him of Pemberley and the company of his friends. The music ended too soon.

He joined the others to urge Miss Mary to play a second.

As the guests offered their musical suggestions, Darcy politely shouldered his way to Miss Elizabeth. "May I have the pleasure of this dance?"

The expression on Collins's face was worth the entire evening's discomfort. Darcy led her away, the warmth of her hand on his elbow sufficient payment for his troubles.

"Your sister plays nicely." He bowed.

"She does play the best of us all. I dare say it is because she practices more than the rest of us." Miss Elizabeth smiled broadly. "I hope you were not offended by my cousin's lighthearted remarks at dinner. Forgive my forwardness, but you appeared a bit uneasy with his levity."

"I was merely concerned you might have attributed to me criticism that in no way reflects my own opinions. I regret not finding a means to express this sooner." The words poured forth in a breathless, inelegant rush. At least it had been said. He panted slightly, heart thundering.

She studied him with penetrating eyes for far too many heartbeats. Her eyebrow arched. "If you had spoken for yourself, what would you have said?"

His mouth went dry. "The roast mutton was prepared in a way that is a particular favorite of mine. I do not know how your mother discovered my preference, but I am humbled by her gracious attentions." He dipped his head.

The music ended all too soon, and he led her to the side of the room. Her smile sparkled in the candlelight.

Blood rushed in his ears, and his vision wavered

briefly.

A young man carrying one side of a small table jostled her. "Excuse me."

She jumped, looked around and giggled. "Do you care for a rubber of whist?"

Whist? A dreadful bore at best, but in her presence—"Yes, thank you." He followed her to another table. Collins and Miss Lucas joined them moments later. He swallowed back a sigh. He could not expect to be allowed the pleasure of her company sans Collins for the rest of the evening.

Collins picked up the cards and shuffled with a flourish. He tapped them on the table top and dealt them with rapid precision. "Shall we place a few pence on the game for the sake of amusement?"

Miss Elizabeth and Miss Lucas traded glances and shrugged. "As you prefer. Mr. Darcy?"

He nodded, and Collins turned over the trump card.

Through several hands, Miss Elizabeth and Miss Lucas traded witty banter and conversation with Collins. How did Collins craft his every experience into an entertaining adventure? Darcy joined in as he could, though his responses came too late, or felt stiff and forced. Thankfully, Miss Elizabeth was gracious and made efforts to see him included. Never before had he worked so hard to participate in a conversation. But as long as Miss Elizabeth continued to bestow her smiles on him, he would continue.

"What say you we increase the stakes for the next rubber?" Collins asked over the rustle of shuffling cards.

Miss Elizabeth pushed back from the table. "No, sir. I never play for more than a few pence. Pray excuse me."

"Nor I." Miss Lucas stood.

Both ladies moved off into the crowded drawing room

"Mr. Darcy?" Collins's brows rose.

"Thank you, no."

As quickly as Darcy vacated his seat, others took his place. Collins called for bets and dealt a new hand with substantially higher stakes. Darcy smiled to himself. From the glint in his eye, Collins would be at cards for the rest of the evening and not in the company of Miss Elizabeth.

The last of their guests made their goodbyes, and the door shut behind them. Elizabeth propped herself against the wall in the foyer. What an agreeable evening! Excellent food and even better company, and Mama so easy throughout the whole of it, she could not ask for more.

Lydia dropped back against the wall beside her with a tired groan. "Did you note how much he bet on his last rubber?"

"Who?"

She elbowed Elizabeth in the ribs and nodded toward the drawing room where Mr. Collins was helping Kitty and Mary restore the room to order.

"Do not gossip, Lyddie."

"I am not gossiping. I saw him do it. He put fifty pounds on—"

"You certainly misheard. Surely he said fifty pence, not pounds."

"He did not." Lydia stopped herself mid-stomp.

"I am sure he did. He could not possibly repay half the sum you suggest, nor do I believe any of our neighbors able to accommodate so high a wager. Do not spread rumors about him, for it will only come back on you. Go to your room before he hears your speculations, and you both are embarrassed."

Lydia muttered something indecipherable as she stomped upstairs.

Elizabeth closed her eyes and pinched the bridge of her nose. Lyddie loved to be the center of attention and resented anyone who threatened to take it from her. It was one thing to be jealous of her sisters, but her resentment of Mr. Collins approached intolerable.

"Cousin Elizabeth."

She jumped. He stood at her elbow. How long had he been standing there?

"Forgive me, I did not mean to startle you."

"Do not worry." She giggled and caught her breath.

"You mother is an accomplished hostess. I scarcely remember the last time I so enjoyed an evening."

"I will be sure to convey the message to her."

He inched nearer and dropped his voice to nearly a whisper. "How did you find the company tonight?"

"Delightful."

"Including that of Mr. Darcy?"

A cold drop of discomfort splashed on her head and dripped down the back of her neck. Her shoulders twitched. "He is most gentlemanly. Why do you ask?"

"Your naivety does you credit. It is a trait as lovely as yourself. I find it entirely charming and most acceptable in a young woman." He edged a little closer.

His eyes were expressive, compelling. Her breath

hitched.

"I hate to discuss unattractive things in your presence, but I would not have you hurt."

Cold slid further down her back, fighting the flutterings in her stomach. How could one experience two competing sensations at once? "Please explain. I do not follow."

"I noticed the way Mr. Darcy looked at you tonight. I know his compliments flattered you, as well they should; however, you must remember his station."

"His station?"

"I mean no offense to your family, but Mr. Darcy's wealth and consequence far exceeds your own. He will marry prudently and to the credit of his family."

"Which, you imply, I would not be."

"You are not his equal in wealth or situation. His interest in you must be of a…baser nature. The only offer a man like him might make to you would be one most improper for a gentleman's daughter."

"You presume too much. You forget his friend—our friend—Mr. Bradley, speaks well of Mr. Darcy. Mr. Bradley would never—"

"I am aware of the old vicar's long history with your family. You must understand, Mr. Bradley's reputation—he is unconventional. I am not at all alone in finding many of his teachings questionable and do not forget, he enjoys the favor of his patron."

Elizabeth exhaled heavily and frowned.

"I do not wish to offend you, my dearest cousin—remember faithful are the wounds of a friend. I cannot bear the thought that your reputation or your spirits might be damaged by your association with a man like Mr. Darcy."

Her belly fluttered. "I still do not like your implication."

"Of course, you do not—your pure and faithful heart is one of your finest qualities. You are a most loyal friend." He took her hand and pressed it with his fingertips. "I dream that someday soon, I might win the smallest piece of your loyalty for myself. A selfish wish to be sure, but selfishness has no hope of cure." He lowered his head and touched his lips to the back of her hand. A heartbeat later, he was gone upstairs.

Elizabeth leaned against the wall, breathless and confused. Mr. Collins's words stung. Mr. Darcy did not seem like other rich men who came to Meryton just for sport, especially with Mr. Bradley vouching for him. Yet, was that reason enough to disregard Mr. Collins's warning? Charlotte believed both men liked her. Would she mistake baser interests for more refined ones?

Mr. Collins took her breath away and addled her thoughts. Mr. Darcy did not leave her tongue-tied and stammering, but he had tried so hard to talk to her when he was clearly uncomfortable in the crowd. His efforts were endearing and made her feel significant, as though all the things that Mama criticized in her might not matter so much. How could she choose as Charlotte pressed her to do?

Chapter 7

TWO DAYS LATER, Darcy rose before dawn and prepared for a trot along the bridle path. He made his way downstairs quietly, thinking no one else awake, but he found Fitzwilliam and Bingley already in the morning room. Bingley rarely awoke so early. It must be the country air—or sleeping in so late the day after the Bennets' dinner party. Whatever it was, they were amenable to a morning ride.

By the time their mounts were ready, the morning sun peeked above the horizon. Its first rays licked at the dew on the lush grass of Netherfield's meadows. Their horses walked together along one edge of the green. Soon, they increased their pace until their riders urged them on, exulting in the thrill of an impromptu race.

At the first turn, Fitzwilliam nosed ahead. Darcy made up ground in the straightaway. Bingley's horse disappeared from view by the time they reached the second corner. Fitzwilliam's mount matched Darcy's stride for stride down the long side of the field. The morning air buffeted his face. Darcy whooped a primal cry, echoed by Fitzwilliam, as they leaned into the final turn. Fitzwilliam's bay surged forward in a flurry of hooves and dust. He crossed their starting point leading Darcy's chestnut.

They slowed their horses to a walk, all panting as they began an easy lap around the pasture.

Bingley pulled his horse beside Fitzwilliam's. "What a fine animal!"

"I think it more the horseman than the horse!" Darcy brought his steed beside Bingley's. "All those years in the army certainly improved your seat, Fitzwilliam."

"Improved my seat? I was always the better horseman of the two of us."

"And how do you come to that conclusion?"

Fitzwilliam threw his head back and hooted. "How do I not? I seem to remember you thrown several times…"

"Thrown? Never. No, wait. I stand corrected, that demon beast of your father's!" Darcy turned to Bingley. "Twelve years ago, my uncle acquired an unrideable breeding stallion. So naturally, Fitzwilliam dared me to ride the creature."

"What happened?" Bingley glanced from one to the other and grinned.

"He managed to mount the stallion and was promptly thrown. Not to be easily bested, he tried several more times, to the same end. The expression on his face, lying on the ground, staring at the sky—" Fitzwilliam laughed heartily. "My father found him, and the only reason he did not thrash him proper—"

"Was I had already broken my arm. Do not leave off the rest of the tale." Darcy clucked his tongue.

Fitzwilliam raised his brows and shrugged.

"How easily you forget! After your father hauled me off, you had your share of excitement. The head groom carried you to the house, your leg broken."

"The horse did not do it."

"Yes, yes, you insisted that you fell from the fence. The groom told a different story." Darcy snickered.

"Come now, both of you!" Bingley patted his horse's neck. "Colonel, what say you of your first social affair since rejoining the civilian ranks?"

Fitzwilliam turned over his shoulder to Darcy. "Mother will be so disappointed. She intended to host a grand ball to reacquaint me with polite society."

Darcy snorted.

"Go on and say it, Darce, I was never introduced to *polite* company the first time."

Darcy raised his hands and shook his head.

"She may still throw her ball." Bingley glanced from one to the other.

"Oh, but to her, it is not the same. I am in your debt—or perhaps the Bennets'—having been spared me the pain of playing guest of honor at my second debut into society." Fitzwilliam chuckled.

"Why would you want to skip such an event?" Bingley asked.

"You have not endured the weeks of preparation with my mother at the helm. I would pit her against any general I served under." Fitzwilliam winked.

"I will tell her you said that." Darcy said.

"You do that—she will count it a compliment. As to your question, Bingley, I enjoyed dinner at Longbourn immensely. Dare I ask Miss Caroline's opinion?"

"No, you may not. I try to refrain from intemperate language in polite company—even yours." Bingley grunted and squinted into the horizon. "Excuse me. I must ensure my sister is awakened in sufficient time so as not to make us late for church this morning."

"You will understand if we take my carriage." Darcy nodded at Fitzwilliam.

Bingley's ears stained bright red. "Of course." He tipped his hat, flicked his reins and rode off.

"I will never complain about my sisters again." Fitzwilliam guided his horse into the field.

"I do not envy him."

"Miss Caroline aside, how do you find the company here?"

"Savage."

Fitzwilliam craned his neck and stared. A grin burst onto his face, and he chortled. "Tell me honestly now."

Darcy pressed his lips together to hide his smile. "I concede there are those whose company is most agreeable."

"We are of like mind."

"I noticed you much in the company of Miss Bennet."

"You would be a blind man not to."

"Are you not concerned you will raise her expectations?"

"Not in the least."

Darcy signaled his horse to stop. "You should be."

"Why? Perhaps I wish her expectations elevated."

"Did I hear you correctly?"

Fitzwilliam flicked the reins, and his horse moved

into a fast walk.

His cousin did not like to be challenged; he never had. Darcy urged his mount to catch up. "I do not approve of this game you play. The Bennets are a respectable family—"

"I am not playing games." Fitzwilliam's horse increased its pace.

"What do you mean?"

"I am not playing games."

"You have known her a fortnight." Sweat trickled down the side of Darcy's face.

"What of it?"

"I know you to be rash, but this appears extreme, even for you."

"That is your opinion of me? Rash and insensible?"

"Not at all. I am concerned for you and for the Bennets. I would not see anyone hurt in this affair."

Fitzwilliam wheeled his horse about to face Darcy. "I am entirely serious. I have managed my affairs carefully and just came into some inheritance from a distant relation. My fortune is sufficient—I no longer need marry one. I will be able to live simply and comfortably, and that is all I desire anymore."

"Indeed?"

"I have been nearly engaged twice, to beautiful heiresses of the first circles." Fitzwilliam waved his hand with a flourish.

"What happened?"

Fitzwilliam's shoulders fell. "The night I planned to ask the first lady, I arrived late for a dinner at her home. I told the butler not to announce my arrival and set off in search of her. I found her in conversation with several other young ladies and decided to surprise her. Ungentlemanly, you will say. I have learned my lesson since." He flashed a quick, thin smile.

Darcy's innards clenched into a tight little ball. Fitzwilliam had been deeply hurt. What more details did he need? He drew breath to stop the conversation, but his cousin plunged ahead.

"As I came through another room to join her, I overheard her tell her friends she planned to seduce me into compromising her and thus secure me! As if I were some kind of animal to trap! Worse still, one of the girls asked if she found me an amiable companion."

"Dare I ask what she said?"

"Nothing complimentary. I had allowed myself to become quite smitten with her. Hearing her true thoughts towards me was a shocking blow. Her only fondness was for my connections." Fitzwilliam shook his head sharply. "Father taught me marriage is a business affair, and love should be of no consideration. I have not honestly worked out how I believe on that point, yet. Still, if I am to share the same house together with a woman till death parts us, I want someone who I respect and can call a friend. I seek an amiable companion, a woman of sound judgment and faithfulness, one whose company I might take pleasure in each day…"

"Are those not marks of love? I think it not unreasonable. Your father might not agree, but your mother would be sympathetic."

Fitzwilliam rubbed his forehead. "The second young lady proved worse than the first. She, I heard tell her maid, 'He is an abhorrent creature, but for the sake of being in an earl's family, though, I would marry the family dog if necessary. I will tolerate his attentions only as long as it takes to produce an heir and a spare. Then I will lock the door between us and enjoy my privacy. He may retire to the country whilst I enjoy the diversions of the *ton*.'" Bitterness dripped from his voice.

"You were quite taken with her as well?"

Fitzwilliam scowled at the rising sun. "Much to my mother's dismay, I have abandoned the *ton* with its heiresses and socialites. I long for a simple existence with a companion who prefers a man to be more than a decoration on her arm at balls. Perhaps this is a place to find it."

"Perhaps."

"You are skeptical? Miss Bennet is exactly the kind of company I desire for now. She is a balm to my soul."

They locked eyes. The air between them crackled.

Darcy's lips twitched into a small smile. "I wish you good fortune in obtaining her favor. I am still concerned that a fortnight—"

"My time in the king's service taught me not to wait when I find what I desire. Life is far too brief—and fragile—to waste on unnecessary hesitation."

"Then go to it, man."

"I have your approval?"

"Do you need it?"

"No, but since Father will not grant it, I should like someone in the family to offer it." Though Fitzwilliam's grin said he teased, his eyes were more serious than Darcy had ever seen.

"I approve."

Monday at midmorning, Lydia, Elizabeth and Kitty walked into Meryton armed with lists and baskets. Mama gave them strict directions on what must be ordered and purchased. With Mary's wedding two weeks away, there was no time to waste.

At least the wedding plans distracted Mama enough for her to set aside some of her nervous distress at Mr. Collins's presence. Though still uneasy, she tolerated his company with only a few anxious flutterings and pains in her chest. The change was so profound, Papa suggested Uncle Gardiner travel to London to fetch his family for the wedding. Though Mama protested initially, Uncle Gardiner planned to make the journey on the morrow. Aunt Gardiner could not arrive soon enough.

Lydia kicked a small stone aside. "Mary's dress still needs more lace—what does Mary know about—"

"Her gown should be just as she fancies. Leave her be," Kitty scolded, head held high. "Besides, I do not have time to change it."

"What have you to do? Mama ordered the rest of her wedding clothes from the modiste."

"Jane's dress, Lizzy's dress, my own dress—"

"You are all getting new gowns? That is not fair." Lydia stomped and wrapped her arms around her waist.

"Lydia, do not pout." Elizabeth kept her eyes carefully away from her sister's tantrum. Censure would only draw out Lydia's sulkiness.

"Why should you all get new ones and not me?"

Kitty stopped and turned to Lydia. "Because we did not—"

Elizabeth grabbed Kitty's wrist.

"Well, it is true. We did not get into mischief

while—"

"Enough." She squeezed Kitty's wrist hard and frowned at Lydia.

Kitty snatched her hand away. "Ouch!"

Elizabeth glared at Lydia. "Bring your complaint to Papa."

"He will not listen to me. After all you told him, he barely will even look at me. This is your fault, Lizzy. I will never have any fun again. You hate me." She sniffled and rubbed her sleeve across her eyes.

"I do not hate you. None of us do. I am sorry you do not like the consequences of your actions, but what do you expect—"

"You do not understand. No one understands. You even turned Mama against me."

Elizabeth cradled her forehead in her hand. "Lydia, this is neither the time nor the place for this discussion. Right now, we must take care of things for Mama to get ready for—"

"Mary's wedding. I know, I know. All I hear is Mary's wedding. I am sick to death of Mary's wedding. What a clever girl she is for catching Mr. Pierce. How pretty she is! How good she is!" Lydia's lips drew back, and she stuck out the tip of her tongue.

Kitty leaned into Lydia's face. "You are jealous."

"I am not." Lydia tucked her arms around her waist. "But why must Mary get all the attention?"

"She is the one getting married." Kitty planted her hands on her hips.

"Stop, both of you. Kitty, go on and buy your thread and fabric." Elizabeth gave Kitty a small push in the right direction. "You come with me to place the orders."

"No, you do not need me. Do it yourself." Lydia

stomped off. Little wisps of dust trailed her footsteps.

If Mama's list were any shorter, she would have chased after Lydia, but if she did not accomplish everything, they would all pay the price for Lydia's tantrum. Elizabeth checked her list and headed toward the nearest shop.

Lydia scuffed her toes along the dusty street. No one cared about her, not anymore. Papa had not spoken to her since he scolded her the day he came home. Not that he ever talked to her much anyway. Little enough loss, except he cruelly took away her pocket money until harvest time. He never treated her sisters thus. He was so unfair!

Charlotte and Maria approached on the other side of the street. Maria would feel sorry for her, but Charlotte—she lectured as stridently as Lizzy. Lydia ducked into the nearest shop.

Lydia turned around and groaned. Of all places, how did she come to be at the bookseller? A familiar voice rumbled at the far side of the shop. Mr. Collins? How might things get any worse? Bad enough to keep company with him in the house every day, to be civil at mealtimes, and to entertain him in the time after dinner, she should at least find respite here in town.

He must not discover her, lest she be forced to accompany him afterwards. If only she had stayed with Lizzy. Why did everything always go wrong?

She slipped behind a shelf and crept along the wall. Her nose tickled. The shopkeep needed to dust more often. Mama would scold her for getting cobwebs and grime on her frock. How would she explain? Oh, bother!

"No sir, that is by no means a fair price." Mr. Collins shut the book on the counter loudly.

Lydia parted two books and peered through.

"This volume is hardly new. Here the spine is creased. Any number of pages are dog-eared and even written upon." The bookseller flipped the book open and rifled the leaves.

"Examine the title, though—a most uncommon volume." Mr. Collins pulled the tome from the shopkeeper's hands and held it in front of his face.

Lydia gasped and stuffed her fist in her mouth. That book—it was Papa's, a gift from Uncle Gardiner for Christmas. The blue and red cover with gold letters was so pretty, even if it was full of words she did not understand. She bit her lip. Why did Mr. Collins have Papa's book? Why was he trying to sell it? He had played for high stakes at the dinner party. Surely he needed funds to pay his debts. Her eyes bulged.

She must tell Lizzy, then Lizzy would dislike him as much she did. Lizzy would deem her as clever as Kitty or Mary. Perhaps this would be a good thing after all.

First though, she must escape without being seen. Inch by inch, she edged along the shelves while the men dickered. Another customer walked in, and she darted out behind him. Where would Lizzy have gone?

Elizabeth scanned her list, pencil in hand, and ticked off the last few items. The process went faster without towing a protesting Lydia along.

"Miss Elizabeth."

She lifted her face. Miss Bingley and her sister stood before her, arms laden with packages.

"Good afternoon." Elizabeth pushed her list into her basket. "Have your errands been successful?" Given the stacks they carried, hardly anything would be left in the shops.

"Well enough, I suppose." Miss Caroline sniffed and curled her lip.

"Thank you for showing me the best shops." Miss Bingley smiled broadly.

"I am glad to be of assistance."

"Did you come into town with Mr. Collins? We passed him in the road a moment ago." Miss Bingley asked.

"No, I had no idea he came to town as well." Elizabeth looked over her shoulder.

Lydia, dusty and disheveled, ran towards them.

"My gracious," Miss Caroline hissed. "What is that horrid creature?"

"Miss Lydia?" Miss Bingley gasped.

"You best get her away from town quickly. Your Mr. Collins will not wish to be associated with such a shabby little thing." Miss Caroline tipped up her nose and turned aside.

"My Mr. Collins?"

"Yes, of course. We all noted the way he stared at you last night. Is it too early to wish you joy?"

Miss Bingley grabbed her sister's elbow. "Caroline!"

"What?" Miss Caroline's nostrils flared. "You demonstrate excellent taste to choose a man of her own sphere and standing. It is so vulgar to set one's sights beyond one's equals."

"Lizzy! Lizzy!" Lydia panted hard and clutched Elizabeth's arm.

Never had she been so grateful for Lydia's flamboyant displays. She clutched her sister's hand. "Pray excuse us."

Elizabeth dragged Lydia half a block along the busy street.

"Stop, Lizzy! You are hurting me. Let go!" She snatched her hand away.

"What happened to you? You look as though you crawled through attics." She brushed dust from Lydia's spencer.

"I have something important to tell you."

She pulled out her handkerchief and wiped smudges from Lydia's face. "Miss Caroline was correct—you are a fright."

Lydia pushed her away. "Stop it. You must listen. This is important."

"Tell me."

"I went into the bookseller's—"

"You? At the bookseller? Whatever for?"

"To hide from Charlotte Lucas."

Elizabeth rolled her eyes.

"Lizzy!"

"Go on."

"Mr. Collins was there."

"How is that shocking?"

"He was not buying books—he was selling one—one of Papa's."

Elizabeth clutched her temples. "Surely you were mistaken."

"No, no, the pretty blue and red one. Mr. Collins cannot have one like it."

"Why would he sell one of Papa's books?"

"I told you last night, the debt he incurred at cards—"

"— a creation of your imagination. No prudent man gambles more than he can repay."

"Then he is imprudent. You must listen to me, Lizzy." Lydia stomped and shook her fists. "He stole Papa's book and sold it."

"You are biased against Mr. Collins and are searching for reasons to vilify him with your fantastical stories."

Lydia folded her arms and pouted. "If you know so much, how do you explain what I saw?"

"They are the jealous rantings of a selfish little girl who is angry that she is not the center of attention."

"How can you say that?" Lydia turned her back.

"You have been set against Mr. Collins from the day he arrived and did not dote upon you."

"You do not believe me."

"No, I do not, and I would counsel Papa not to either. I am ashamed of you."

Lydia looked over her shoulder and stared into Elizabeth's eyes. "Mr. Collins is no better than horrid Major Sloane who traveled with Colonel Forester."

Elizabeth shuddered. "You compare our cousin to him?"

"Do you not grasp the similarities?"

"Certainly not."

"Well, I do. Mr. Collins is just like Major Sloane."

"No more, Lydia. I am going home. I suggest you come in through the kitchen so Mama does not see you." Elizabeth strode down the street and did not look back. Lydia had finally gone too far.

Elizabeth closed the front door quietly. A quick trip to the study would vindicate Mr. Collins and she could put Lydia's bluster to rest. Perhaps she could avoid—

"Lizzy, is that you?"

"Yes, Mama." She leaned against the wall and sighed.

"Well, come here, child. Tell me of your trip."

She trudged into the parlor. Her purposes would have to wait. The table lay strewn with lace and trimmings. A half adorned bonnet sat askew on the far edge, opposite a pile of drawings and several fashion magazines. Mama held out her hand. "Did you mark the list as I told you?"

Kitty and Jane scooted over on the settee. Elizabeth handed the list to Mama and dropped down beside Jane.

"I believe I took care of everything. Mr. Nash will make the deliveries as you requested—and yes, I saw him write it all down and did not trust it to his memory."

"Hill must be informed—"

"I will tell her." Jane said.

Mama fanned her face with her handkerchief. "Jane, write me a list. I need you and Lizzy to share a room when the Gardiners arrive. Sister Philips has offered to keep the children at her house, but we will need to prepare your room for my brother and sister."

Mary laid her hand on Mama's arm. "You are worrying for nothing, please stop."

"Your wedding must be perfect. Now tell me again…will you and Mr. Pierce—"

"Yes, Mama, he promised. We will stay for breakfast. We are only going to London." Mary closed her eyes and shook her head. "Mr. Darcy offered us the use of his townhouse for several days before we travel on to Derbyshire."

"He has shown you great favor. You must be sure to thank him properly, though I do not know who to credit for it all—Mr. Bradley, or you Miss Lizzy."

"Me?" Elizabeth touched her chest, eyebrows high on her forehead.

Mama cocked her head and sniffed. "You cannot tell me you missed those looks he gave you."

Mary pinched the bridge of her nose. "Mama, we should not assume—"

"Well, I am sure you are correct, Mary. He is not the sort of man to find an impertinent humor appealing in spite of a pair of fine eyes." Mama patted Elizabeth's arm.

Mary pressed her hands over her face.

"Do not despair, Lizzy dear, Mr. Collins is quite good enough for you. He shows you great attentions, and I expect he will continue. I would not be surprised to be planning another wedding soon. Who would have thought you might be the saving of us?"

A rush of cold splashed Elizabeth's cheeks, and she fell against the settee. The saving of her family—her? A painful knot settled into her stomach. She and Jane had promised one another they would marry for love, not deliverance from poverty. If she married Mr. Collins as Mama suggested, Longbourn might remain their home—always and so many of Mama's fears would be relieved.

She did like Mr. Collins. He was amiable and intelligent, with a lively sense of humor, an excellent situation, and most pleasant to look at. The prospect would have been most appealing were it not for the other visitor in their midst. The tall, handsome and shy man from Derbyshire intrigued her. Moreover, he sought her out, and none of his advances seemed as untoward as Mr. Collins had warned. She sagged back into the settee and sighed. What would she do if called on to decide between them?

"Lizzy?" Mama's voice cut through. "Woolgathering again? I need you to pay attention."

"Yes, Mama." She really should not be dwelling on her own flights of fancy when Mary needed her so. Elizabeth's deliberations would wait, at least for a little while.

Chapter 8

THURSDAY AFTERNOON SUNBEAMS poured through Pierce's front window, the perfect brightness and temperature for a pleasant catnap. Bradley settled into what had become his favorite chair in Pierce's parlor. Threadbare on the arms and lumpy in the seat, the cushions were soft on his aching bones, and not so fine he feared sullying the upholstery if he got comfortable. He settled back and closed his eyes. Slumber washed over him in downy waves.

Heavy footfalls approached. Bradley cracked his eyes open. Why did Pierce stomp everywhere he went? Doubtless Miss Mary would cure him of that habit.

Pierce burst in and paced along the fireplace, hands shoved in his pockets. "You must think me a terrible host. I did not anticipate any of this when I invited you."

"Stop worrying. You were not facing an imminent wedding when you suggested I come." Bradley chuckled and pulled himself straighter in his seat. "Mr. Bingley asked me to stay with him at Netherfield. I will be well situated. Darcy will come for me this afternoon, and you shall be free of my troublesome company."

"You do not think—"

"Of course not, be at ease. You must host your brother after he has traveled so far to stand up with you."

Pierce stopped and turned to face him. "I still cannot fathom…I asked…she accepted…and we will be married."

"The Good Book says our Lord is no respecter of persons. I believe He is no respecter of plans either. How often my best intentions have been thwarted because our Lord failed to inform me He had other plans in mind."

Pierce stared, agape. He took a few steps and fell onto a footstool, laughing. "How do you speak of the Almighty with such informality and reverence all in the same breath?"

Bradley shrugged. "I suppose many feel as you do. I quite scandalized poor Mr. Collins at Longbourn last week."

Pierce snorted. "Well, I hope one day to scandalize people so effectively as you."

"I will take that as a compliment of the highest order." Bradley leaned forward, elbows on knees. "What think you and Miss Mary of my offer?"

Pierce's eyes glazed over, an expression Bradley had often observed. How delightful to be in the company of a young man besotted with such a worthy young lady.

"She wishes to visit the parish and meet the people. If all goes well, we will accept." Pierce laced his hands together and rubbed his chin along his knuckles. "I will need to give Mr. Bell notice and allow him to find a replacement. I know several men seeking a curacy and he is not nearly as particular as you. I do not foresee difficulty on that count."

Bradley beamed. "Excellent. You may use the cottage I used in my curacy. Darcy will give it to you on most generous terms. In time, after the parish becomes accustomed to you, you may have the use of the parsonage whilst I return to the cottage myself."

"Mary thinks your plan a good one." Pierce ran his hands through his hair and sighed. "I cannot conceive, in a week's time, I will be married."

"A good wife is a blessing like none other. I still miss my own dear wife after all these years." Bradley pushed himself up from the chair. "Well, the time has come. Darcy's carriage approaches."

A few minutes later, his trunk loaded on the coach, Bradley bid Pierce goodbye and allowed Darcy to help him in.

"You could have sent your driver alone. You did not have to come." Bradley eased into the rich, padded leather. He preferred Pierce's worn chair. Perhaps he might find a comfortably shabby one somewhere in Netherfield. "I appreciate you securing Bingley's hospitality for me."

"He enjoys the opportunity for largesse. I must warn you though, Miss Caroline—"

Bradley lifted his hand. "I understand."

"If you prefer, I will pay for a room at the inn."

"I am certain my presence will bother her more

than hers does me. Do not trouble yourself further on the matter."

"As you wish." Darcy shrugged and turned to the side glass.

No doubt, the issue would not be so easily set aside. The moment Miss Caroline uttered a cross word to him, Darcy's protectiveness would appear again. It was one of his most admirable traits—sometimes a bit overdone—but touching nonetheless. Today, though, something beyond protectiveness fueled the brooding in his eyes.

Bradley chewed the inside of his cheek. "How do you find Hertfordshire?"

"It is a lovely county." Darcy did not turn away from the window.

Short answers, no eye contact, tight jaw and squared shoulders—what weighed so heavily upon him?

"Pierce appreciates the offer of your townhome for his wedding trip."

"I am pleased to oblige."

"What do you think of Miss Mary?"

"Nothing at all."

"Excuse me?" Bradley sharpened his voice just enough to make Darcy jump.

"I am sorry." Darcy squeezed his temples. "I have spent little time considering her. My brief interactions with her have been most agreeable. She will be an excellent addition to the parish and a comfort to you as well."

"And her sister?"

Darcy grunted and looked away.

As he expected, the source of Darcy's preoccupation. Bradley slid across the seat until he sat knee to knee with Darcy. "You are considering a Miss Bennet for yourself as well."

Darcy heaved a deep breath and raked his hair. "I seem not to know myself anymore. My thoughts are no longer my own. I read—has she read and enjoyed the same book? I walk—did she travel the same path? She creeps into my idle moments. I smell honeysuckle on the breeze and find myself searching for her."

Bradley nodded.

"I receive letters from my steward and wonder how she would judge my management, how her perspectives might be different, and how I need someone to help me make all these decisions. How she might handle the tenant dispute my steward wrote of and would she approve of my judgments? I want her approval as I have wanted none other." He scoured his face with his hands.

Bradley tapped his thumbs together. "Miss Elizabeth is an excellent lady."

"But? What are you not saying?"

"I admire her, but I am not without reservations."

Darcy straightened in his seat, his brow tightened. "Enlighten me. Tell me of her flaws."

"Oh, my reservations are not with her. They are with you."

Darcy's eyes bulged, and he sucked in a sharp breath. "You do not find me sufficient for her?"

"I said nothing of the sort."

"What are you saying?"

"You are aware of the disparity in your fortunes." Bradley flexed his hands. His knuckles popped.

"Yes."

"Will you begrudge her lack of fortune? When your sister marries, a sizeable portion of your capital will go with her. Miss Elizabeth cannot begin to replace what you will lose."

Darcy scowled. "I am surprised your concerns would center on our fortunes."

"I am not blind to the power of wealth." Bradley shrugged. "Though you like her, it would not be fair to her for you to pursue her if, in the end, you would come to resent her. In such a case, you would be better not to begin at all."

"You honestly think I would consider her fortune as significant as her character? You put years into teaching me otherwise."

"Knowledge does not predict how you will feel when you face the financial realities of a dowerless wife. What could that loss mean for your younger sons? You have worried for years over Fitzwilliam's future. You will want to provide your children—all of them—with the means to live the life they are accustomed to. How might you accomplish it? Even your wealth has boundaries."

Darcy crossed his arms and harrumphed.

"Noble ideas notwithstanding, the heart of a man is a dark place, not easily known, even by its owner. Better to confess your limits now than wait and cause deep hurt to both of you later."

The rasp of Darcy's grinding teeth sent prickles up the back of Bradley's neck.

Darcy pressed his palms into his face. At this point, he usually walked off in a huff to return later, contrite. He would surely call for the carriage to stop soon. Instead he sighed and opened his eyes. "It will still take some time to fully fund the bank account I set aside, but the plans are in place to restore the capital committed to Georgiana's dowry."

"Indeed?"

"As much as I did not wish to be pursued by fortune hunters I did not wish to be forced to become one myself. Even my Uncle Matlock would agree, I am free to marry as I choose."

Bradley swallowed a lump of pride. "I am impressed."

The corners of Darcy's mouth twitched upwards.

"What do you wish to do?"

"What should I do?"

"You know too well I cannot—nay, will not answer that question."

"Why do I bother to ask anything of you?"

"I have long wondered." Bradley snickered under his breath. "What do you wish to do?"

"I should think it obvious. Pursue her."

"What stops you?"

"Collins." He snarled the name.

Bradley gasped and choked on a laugh. "Collins? The man you dubbed 'Lady Catherine's ridiculous finger post'—pointing the way for all to go but never going there himself?"

Darcy faced the window again. "I am pleased you find this amusing."

"How is he an impediment?"

"He is constantly at her elbow—a guest in her house. He shares spirited conversations with her. She enjoys his company."

"You are unaccustomed to vying for a woman's interest. Are you jealous?"

"No…yes…I do not know." Darcy dropped his face to his hands and knotted his fingers in his hair.

Bradley peered at him. "No, not jealous. You are afraid."

"I do not fear him."

"Not of Collins, but of losing to him."

Darcy shook his head still cradled in his hands.

"This is the most uncertain venture you have ever attempted. What would it say about you if you lost to Collins?"

"I could not live with it," he whispered.

"Thus, your solution is not to try?"

Darcy's head snapped up. "How does one court a woman?"

"It is not a thing you learn from a book."

"What am I to do?"

"What would you tell Bingley or Fitzwilliam?"

Darcy looked up, wild eyed. "They never asked, nor do I expect they will seek my noteworthy expertise in the matter."

"What would they tell you?"

"Enough word games. Will you not give me an answer?"

"You do not need one."

"Then why would I ask?"

"You want someone to blame if your efforts do not go your way."

Darcy grumbled and growled like an unhappy tomcat. He stared out the side glass.

Would he fling himself from the moving coach? Angry as he was, he just might.

"I understand how difficult this is for you." Bradley stretched to grasp Darcy's shoulder. "Just because you do not like the answer does not mean you do not know."

Darcy fell against the seat cushion. "How am I to determine what to say or how to say it well?"

"Few things worth doing are simple or easy."

Bradley's lips screwed into a thoughtful pucker. "I believe she is a woman worth the effort."

"You do?"

"Yes. All my reservations are satisfied."

Darcy breathed a hearty sigh.

"I am honored my opinion means so much to you."

"As though you were not already aware." Darcy smoothed his hair away from his face. "Fitzwilliam hopes to offer for her elder sister."

Bradley's brows rose. "Lady Matlock will be disappointed." The corners of his lips lifted. "I am not. I believe them well suited. Miss Elizabeth will be quite pleased, too. She and her sister are close. Marrying your cousin ensures they will be able to remain so."

Darcy squeezed his eyes shut and sniggered. "To think I always feared a woman would want me for my money. I never considered she might want me for my cousin."

Bradley laughed from his belly. Darcy's humor was quite as clever as Miss Elizabeth's when he chose to show it. If he did that a little more often, she should like him very well indeed.

Two days later, after breakfast, Darcy, Bingley, and Fitzwilliam sat in Netherfield's oddly arranged parlor. Miss Caroline had already rearranged the furniture twice. Darcy suspected she was only trying to persuade Bingley to redecorate. Good man, though, he held firm on his refusal. Perhaps there was hope for him yet.

Darcy sorted through a stack of letters forwarded

from Pemberley while Bingley and Fitzwilliam faced each other at chess over a most inconveniently placed table.

Bingley rolled a black knight in his palms.

"You know he draws out his move to torment you."

"I do not." Fitzwilliam placed a bishop with a thump.

"You can hardly expect him to confess, can you?" Darcy snapped the creases out of his letter.

"Quit distracting the man and let him play." Fitzwilliam drummed his fingers along the edge of the table.

"My concentration is not compromised." Bingley raised his bishop and knocked over another black pawn. "Although you may wish it were. Check."

Fitzwilliam peered at the board. "How?"

"I told you he was a fair player." Darcy chuckled and returned to his letter.

Miss Bingley ducked into the room and braced herself against the wall.

"Louisa?" Bingley rose halfway.

She pressed a finger to her lips and shut the door ever so gently. As the latch clicked shut, she fell against the door and sagged.

"Whatever are you doing?" Bingley whispered and padded toward her.

She rolled her head along the door.

"You look like you are evading the French." Fitzwilliam folded his arms, brows drawn tightly together.

"I may as well be."

Bingley laid his hand on her arm.

"I desire to call upon the Bennets this morning."

"Without Caroline?" Bingley propped his shoulder

against the wall and tapped his foot.

Miss Bingley took several steps into the room and stopped short. "Of course, without Caroline. Who amongst us did she not embarrass at Longbourn?"

"You are trying to sneak out of the house?" Fitzwilliam choked on a laugh. He shaped his face into a mask of sobriety, though his eyes still twinkled.

"Yes, yes, exactly." Miss Bingley nodded. "Will you help me?"

Darcy counted silently…three…four.

Fitzwilliam snickered then hooted into his fist.

Miss Bingley's countenance crumpled.

Darcy squirmed in his seat. He never knew what to do when Georgiana cried. Certainly it would not be easier with Bingley's sister.

"Forgive me, madam. May I assist you in making your escape?" Fitzwilliam stood and walked toward her. "In fact, I will accompany you on your call if you will have me."

"Yes, thank you." She sniffled.

"I only laughed because you reminded me of my younger self, evading my elder brother." He bowed his head.

Darcy grinned. "He speaks the truth, Miss Bingley. I assisted him in the endeavor often enough." He folded his letter and tucked it into his pocket.

"You were rather good at it as I recall."

"That sounds like an invitation." He stood and glanced at Bingley. "I shall support you as well."

Bingley rubbed his hands together. "It does seem rather adventurous to try and evade her notice."

Darcy joined Bingley in the doorway and cracked the door open. How long had it been since he and Fitzwilliam stole through the halls of Matlock House, eluding detection? He ventured a look. No signs of Miss Caroline.

Over his shoulder, Bingley nodded.

Darcy slipped out and stopped a passing servant. "Where might Miss Caroline be found?"

"I am right here, Mr. Darcy."

Miss Caroline's voice burned like fresh vinegar. He shivered.

"What may I do for you?"

He stared at her, mouth agape, all power of speech lost.

Bingley appeared at his side. "So…ah…are you well this morning, Caroline?" He tugged at his collar.

"I am quite well, as you see."

"Excellent, then we may leave upon our errands directly." Bingley stepped away.

"Oh, where are you going?"

"Nowhere of interest."

"I am most interested. In fact, I may wish to join you. Where are you going?" Miss Caroline folded her arms and drummed her fingers on her sleeve.

Miss Bingley slipped into the hall. "Good morning, Caroline."

Her eyes squeezed into slits. "You are a part of these errands as well?"

Miss Bingley hung her head.

How did Miss Caroline reduce her sister to a recalcitrant school girl and her brother to a cowering whelp?

"We are off on a walk." Bingley shuffled his feet.

"Are you going anywhere in particular?" Miss Caroline's brows rose.

Fitzwilliam burst out. "In the direction of Longbourn."

"Just as I thought!" Miss Caroline whirled on her sister. "I told you yesterday, I do not want to call upon Longbourn or visit the Bennets again."

"Precisely why we did not ask you to come along." Bingley threw his head back and stared at the ceiling.

"You intended to leave me here, all alone?" Miss Caroline's voice approached a shriek.

Fitzwilliam leaned into Darcy's ear. "Perhaps she needs a governess if she cannot stay alone."

Darcy clamped his jaw shut. Snickering now would not improve the situation.

"Why subject yourself to company you do not like?" Bingley shrugged. "And why should we deny ourselves the pleasure of company we do. What better solution—"

"You should stay here. The grounds of Netherfield offer plenty of entertainment."

"We will enjoy our house party later," Miss Bingley said softly. "This morning, I will go to Longbourn."

Fitzwilliam extended his arm to Miss Bingley and strode toward the front door.

"The carriage is not ready." Miss Caroline ran after them.

"We are walking." Darcy did not look at her as he passed.

"You know I do not like to walk. I hate mud." Miss Caroline blocked the door.

"Stay home and away from the dirt." Bingley shouldered her aside. "We like a brisk walk." He swung the door open and gestured his guests through.

"Far be it from me to suspend any pleasure of yours." Miss Caroline huffed and stomped after them.

Fitzwilliam elbowed Darcy. "Remind me never to allow you to lead an operation again."

"I dare you to do better."

"I got us to the door."

Miss Bingley giggled. "At least we escaped, even if we must endure her company."

Despite her complaints, Miss Caroline proved herself a good walker, and they arrived at Longbourn with only traces of mud on their boots, faces brightened from the exercise. The housekeeper showed them to the parlor where three of the Miss Bennets sat.

"Do come in." Miss Bennet smiled broadly, her eyes on Fitzwilliam.

"Pray excuse my mother and sister Mary. They are in town at present," Miss Elizabeth said, looking directly at Darcy.

His cheeks heated.

"We are glad to find you at home." Bingley sat near Miss Kitty and Miss Bingley. Darcy and Fitzwilliam settled between Miss Bennet and Miss Elizabeth.

"How go the wedding preparations?" Miss Bingley asked.

Miss Kitty launched into a detailed discussion of dresses and breakfast plans that quickly numbed Darcy's mind.

Fitzwilliam edged closer to Miss Bennet for a softer and more private conversation. Darcy envied his situation.

"Mr. Darcy, upon reflection, how did you find our country dinner?" Miss Elizabeth cocked her head and smiled the funny little half-smile that accompanied her gentle teases.

Prickling heat surged from his face to his feet.

Miss Caroline batted her eyes. "It was, I am sure, the best that might be expected under the circumstances and should be appreciated for the efforts made if not the overall effect."

The warmth left Miss Elizabeth's expression.

How dare she attempt to speak for him, again! "Your attempt at gratitude is pleasing, I am sure, Miss Caroline." He glowered and bit his tongue against so much more he wished to say.

She started, eyes wide.

A cool nugget of satisfaction slid into his heart. "I, on the other hand, found the evening quite enjoyable. I prefer small, intimate gatherings, in honor of one's friends, to the crush of a large ball."

Miss Elizabeth beamed. "Indeed, sir?"

"Yes, I regularly conduct similar dinners at Pemberley for my friends."

Miss Caroline blinked at Darcy. "You cannot compare the dinner you held for…for…now what was the occasion?"

"Mr. Bradley's appointment as vicar."

"Yes, that is what it was. You do not perceive any similarities—"

Enough of her impertinence! "As a matter of fact, I do. Moreover, I would ask you, Miss Elizabeth, to petition your cook for her receipt for the lovely carrot soup you served. I am certain my housekeeper, Mrs. Reynolds, will find it a most suitable addition to Pemberley's table."

Miss Caroline sputtered and coughed into her hand.

"I will fetch some water." Miss Elizabeth dashed out, fist pressed to her mouth.

Perhaps now Miss Caroline would keep her troublesome opinions to herself. Darcy rose and walked to the window.

Footsteps pounded down the stairs.

Miss Elizabeth appeared in the doorway, the doltish Collins trailing after her. Blast and bother! He was the only person who could ruin this call more effectively than Miss Caroline. How many more trials would he be called upon to endure? Still, Bradley's admonishments rang in his ears and Miss Elizabeth's smiles warmed his heart. He would continue his efforts to be sociable.

Miss Elizabeth handed Miss Caroline a glass of water and returned to her former seat. Her youngest sister dashed in and sat near Miss Bingley while Collins pulled a chair close to Darcy and Miss Caroline. Would nothing go his way this morning?

"Mr. Collins," Miss Caroline inclined her head toward him, "do you miss Kent and your intimacies at the exquisite Rosings Park?"

"My modest parsonage is nothing to the lovely Longbourn House." He gazed into Miss Elizabeth's eyes.

Darcy's stomach tightened into a hard little knot. Surely she saw through his nauseating insincerity.

"I confess, I do miss the regular invitations to that most magnificent of homes." Collins stroked his chin.

Darcy swallowed bile. Fitzwilliam's cheek twitched, but his focus on Miss Bennet remained firm. Her eyes were only for him. How did he manage to keep her attention so fully on him?

Collins turned to Darcy. "Do you not find Rosings Park to be the most sophisticated, most magnificent, most—"

"—extravagant of homes? Indeed I do. I am afraid my tastes run toward simplicity." He glanced at Miss

Elizabeth. "Perhaps you share my preference, madam?"

"I believe I do, sir." She smiled.

Ah, that smile made the whole morning call worthwhile.

"How can you call your tastes simple, Mr. Darcy?" Miss Caroline pressed her hand to her chest. "Pemberley is far from simple. It is one of the finest homes, appointed with elegance—"

"Not in the style of Rosings Park." Darcy glared. He needed to escape from Collins and Miss Caroline, preferably with Miss Elizabeth. Then, he might enjoy the kind of conversation Fitzwilliam shared with Miss Bennet. "The weather is quite pleasant this morning. Have you an agreeable walking path nearby?"

"We do." Miss Elizabeth stood.

"What a capital idea, Darcy!" Fitzwilliam sat straighter. "Miss Bennet?"

"You all go on without us." Miss Kitty waved toward the door. "Miss Bingley wants to see my sketches."

"If you do not mind, I will stay with you and your lovely sister." Bingley had that look on his face— the only question: with which one of the younger sisters did he fancy himself enamored? Hopefully, Miss Kitty, who appeared infinitely more sensible than Miss Lydia.

Darcy extended his arm to Miss Elizabeth. "We know you do not like to walk, Miss Caroline. Do not feel the need to accompany us."

They headed toward the door.

Miss Caroline and Collins stared after them with identical slack-jawed expressions. He struggled not to grin. At last, Miss Caroline had nothing to say.

Fitzwilliam and Miss Bennet followed her sister out the garden doors and down a gravel path. They emerged into a shady trail, lined with ancient trees.

He breathed in the loam-scented air and covered Miss Bennet's hand with his. The weight of her fingers in the crook of his arm satisfied a deep longing he rarely admitted and never acknowledged in company. The constant unease that hummed in the background of his every thought quieted in her presence. Her peace spread over him, and for brief moments, he recalled what his life had been like before Napoleon.

"You seem preoccupied, Colonel." Miss Bennet peeked at him.

He patted her hand. "Please forgive me. I suppose I was."

"Do you find civilian life dull to you now?"

He chuckled, though the dark tones still came through. "You far overestimate the glamor of military service."

"Perhaps. The militia left here only recently. Lydia found them quite fascinating."

"I suppose they might be, with their uniforms and drills." Fitzwilliam shrugged. "You will forgive me. They are little more than overgrown boys playing at being soldiers."

"You think little of them?"

"They call themselves soldiers, yet will likely never encounter the battlefield."

"And you have." She pressed his arm more tightly. "You do not need to speak of it. I will not ask."

He stopped mid-step and looked into her eyes. "Truly? You do not wish to know?"

She blinked rapidly then turned aside. "Death is difficult enough to witness. You can have no desire to relive those experiences."

He raised an eyebrow.

"Death does not limit itself to the battlefield, sir. A death in childbirth can be every bit as bloody, and the screams—"

"Are burned indelibly on one's soul," he whispered, fingers tightening over hers.

"Yes." Her eyes shimmered, and she swallowed hard.

Fitzwilliam took a small step, and they walked on.

"Few ladies share your perspective. Most desire recounts of valiant exploits—"

"Do not speak of it further." She pressed her shoulder to his.

"Thank you." Her peace settled a little deeper into his soul. "Hertfordshire is quite lovely. I have never spent time in this county."

"I confess a fondness for it. My aunt insists Derbyshire much finer, though I have never seen it myself."

"Perhaps you might experience it for yourself."

"You favor Derbyshire as well then?"

"It is hard not to when my father's seat is there. Many boyhood memories involve the peaks and my cousin, Darcy."

"Of course."

"I…I would like to show you one day." He held his breath. Could she feel his heart in its wild gallop? Her eyes met his. Had there ever been a blue so compelling?

"I should like that very much."

Darcy glanced over his shoulder. Fitzwilliam strolled with Miss Bennet, a moon-eyed expression on his face. When had Fitzwilliam worn such a Bingley-like countenance?

"Your cousin appears well pleased with himself," Miss Elizabeth said softly.

How he enjoyed her arched brow. "Yes. I do not recall him ever appearing so…at ease in the company of a lady."

"I believe my sister finds pleasure in his company as well."

While Darcy appreciated the assurance of Miss Bennet's feelings for Fitzwilliam, a more significant question remained unanswered. Did Miss Elizabeth find pleasure in his company?

"Would I be impolitic to observe you do not appear to enjoy the company of Miss Caroline?" Her eyes glimmered with a hint of mischief.

He discarded the first two, somber responses that flashed through his mind. "Yes, quite impolitic."

She smiled! What joy in making a beautiful woman smile.

"She is an old acquaintance of yours?"

"No, I attended school with Bingley. He only recently introduced me to his sisters."

The brilliancy faded from her countenance. What had stolen the light from her eyes?

"Please allow me again to offer my apologies for any offense Miss Caroline may have caused."

"It is her responsibility alone, not yours."

"You are most understanding."

"Perhaps not so understanding as self-serving." She laughed under her breath. "With younger sisters such as mine—"

"They are quite pleasant society."

"My youngest sister is full young to be in company, especially with her lively temperament and even more lively temper…" She offered a wry smile.

"Say no more. My sister is close in age to Miss Lydia. Hers is a rather trying age. I should like you to meet her. She has few young women in her circles, and I think she would benefit by your acquaintance."

"I am honored. I would be delighted to meet her should the opportunity arise."

"She is in London with my aunt. Perhaps I might arrange a visit yet this summer."

"She would enjoy the companionship of Miss Caroline?" She arched an eyebrow.

Darcy shook his head. "Ah, no, I only considered your friendship. I quite forgot there were any other ladies in Hertfordshire."

A pretty blush rose on her dimpled cheeks.

Elizabeth knew she should tear herself away from his gaze but could not. What lay behind his penetrating looks? At moments, she believed he could see into her thoughts themselves. How much of her inner self lay bare before him? A flush crept up her neck.

"While I profess to dwelling upon what is pleasant, perhaps you take it to excess, if the habit causes you to dismiss half the population of an entire county." She raised an eyebrow.

"I am sure you are correct." He smiled the smile that dimpled his cheeks and crinkled the corners of his eyes and set her insides aquiver. "You are far more pleasant than other company, though."

Her tongue tied itself around her teeth and refused to speak.

A flurry of red calico rushed toward them.

"Mr. Darcy! Mr. Darcy." Miss Caroline called, waving wildly, an unladylike display, even in Elizabeth's estimation.

"Miss Caroline, is something wrong?" Elizabeth asked.

"No, no, not at all, quite the opposite, in fact." She stopped near them, panting.

Mr. Collins hurried behind her.

"I could not contain myself another moment." She pressed her hand to her bosom.

"Why?" Mr. Darcy's eyes narrowed, and his jaw tightened.

"You received some significant intelligence?" Elizabeth asked.

"After a fashion." Miss Caroline glanced over her shoulder. "Mr. Collins shared the wonderful tidings, and I could not wait to congratulate you."

Mr. Collins came to an abrupt stop behind her.

"I do not know of what you speak." Mr. Darcy's voice cut the air with a razor's edge.

"You do not need to be coy." Miss Caroline laughed. "She is a brilliant match."

Elizabeth's face chilled.

"What are you talking about?" Mr. Darcy snapped.

"Mr. Collins acquainted us all with your engagement to your cousin, Miss Anne De Bourgh—heiress of Rosings Park."

Elizabeth turned to Mr. Darcy, her tongue barely loosed. "You are engaged, sir?"

Mr. Collins dipped his head. "Please forgive me. I thought your betrothal would be common knowledge."

Mr. Darcy's jaw dropped, and he stammered something unintelligible.

"I wish you joy. The sentiment is long overdue."

"I am not engaged."

"I should have remained silent on the matter." Mr. Collins covered his mouth with his hand. "However, you cannot deny—"

"I most certainly can," Mr. Darcy growled.

Mr. Collins shrugged. "Lady Catherine speaks quite freely of your coming nuptials."

"I am certain you will be the talk of the society pages." Miss Caroline clapped softly.

The world wavered. Elizabeth clutched a nearby tree. He was engaged? "Excuse me. I need to return to the house." She hurried away.

What a fool, to allow her ego to be flattered by the attentions of a man of such consequence! She deserved no less for lifting her hopes so far beyond her own rightful sphere.

"Cousin Elizabeth."

She increased her pace. No conversation, no company, not now.

"Cousin Elizabeth."

A hand on her arm forced her to slow. She wanted to tear from his grasp and run, but she was a lady, and ladies, even foolish ones, did not run through the countryside.

Mr. Collins peered into her face. Sweat trickled down the side of his cheek. "I am sorry you found out in such a brutal way."

"You knew this whole time?"

He nodded and placed her hand in the crook of his arm. "I tried to warn you. I am sure he did not intend to deceive you. His motives may not be unsavory, but he is interested only in friendship."

She blinked furiously. Foolish girl! She would not weep, not here and not in front of him.

"I fear you may have anticipated—"

"You presume too much." She pulled her hand away.

"Forgive me. I should not pry. You just dashed off so quickly…"

"I appreciate your concern."

"May I escort you to the house?"

She nodded.

They walked a dozen steps in silence.

"I expect you suffer some disappointment, but please, know my affections and hopes are unchanged. I am by no means the man Mr. Darcy is, though I might make an acceptable substitute."

She stared at him, mouth agape. How could she reply? Her hands and feet tingled. Numbing cold crept toward her heart.

"You must forgive me. I have no desire for company now." She wrapped her arms around her waist.

"Of course, I understand. If you have need of anything, you have but to ask." He bowed and walked away.

qDarcy had never struck a woman nor been so tempted to do so. Every fiber of his being tensed in herculean self-control. He would not strike Caroline Bingley.

"Did I misunderstand something?" She batted her eyes.

He glowered. The look usually frightened servants and the occasional small child. Apparently she lacked the wit of either.

"Did I say something wrong?"

"I do not want to speak with you." He strode away as fast as he possible without breaking into a run.

"Mr. Darcy? Mr. Darcy?"

Why did that blasted woman shriek?

Fitzwilliam stood close to Miss Bennet in quiet conversation. Darcy stalked past, near enough to growl, "I am returning to Netherfield."

He did not clear a hundred yards before Fitzwilliam jogged beside him. "Calm down, Darce! You will give yourself an apoplexy."

"I am in no mood."

"What happened?"

Darcy snarled and increased his pace.

"What happened?"

"Collins and Miss Caroline."

"I watched them approach. What was said?"

Darcy stopped and glared. "She, on intelligence from that insufferable prat, Collins, determined to wish me joy on the occasion of my engagement."

"Your what? You made an offer to Miss Elizabeth?"

"My engagement to Anne. Our cousin, Anne."

"Anne? You gave in to Aunt Catherine?"

"Certainly not." Darcy strode away.

"I cannot decide who is worse—"

"It does not matter. Both were calculated to distress Miss Elizabeth most acutely."

"What are you going to do?"

"What is there to do? She thinks me a cad. I do not expect she will listen to my defense. With Collins whispering in her ear and Miss Caroline parading her ignorance, I hardly expect—"

"You will just walk away—a woman like Miss Elizabeth interested in you, and you will surrender her to Collins?"

"No, by no means."

"That is a relief. You have not entirely taken leave of your senses."

"It is surely a comfort to know you can find humor in the midst of my misery." Darcy grated his teeth.

"Listen to yourself." Fitzwilliam guffawed. "You are besotted."

"As though you are not a moon-eyed—"

"Guilty as charged and most pleased for it." Fitzwilliam grabbed his shoulder. "You overlook the fact that your sudden misfortune is very much my own."

"How are you affected?"

"*My* Miss Bennet is the sister of *your* Miss Bennet, and they are close. Your offense is likely to be applied to me."

"Surely not."

Fitzwilliam shook his head. "I am not taking any chances."

"What do you mean to do?"

"I will plead your cause with Miss Bennet with the expectation she will take it to her sister. You, then, will find a way to talk with Miss Elizabeth—perhaps at the coming assembly. Yes, that will do nicely. Tell her the truth of the matter, and I will vouch for you."

"The assembly is weeks away, and Collins is in her house." Darcy raked his hair.

Fitzwilliam shook him. "Calm yourself, man. Did you not observe her stalk away from Collins? No, of course, you did not. You were too busy stomping off yourself."

"What?"

"She did not run to Collins. She dismissed him. I think it unlikely she will receive his attentions anytime soon. Besides, Miss Mary's wedding is between now and the assembly. The household will be far too distracted for her to pay Collins much mind."

"I still do not like it."

"Do not forget, I will go to Miss Bennet immediately and explain. Miss Elizabeth will immediately hear of your innocence. It will be to your benefit to give her some time to review and consider the situation."

Darcy screwed his eyes shut. "Very well, I have no better ideas. Try to win Miss Bennet to your side. I shall…I am not sure what I shall do, only that it will be far away from Miss Caroline."

Chapter 9

BRADLEY WAS NOT ACCUSTOMED to the energy of a house party and the late evenings had begun to catch up with him. Netherfield was quiet, its occupants away on morning calls, the perfect environs for a nap. He sat in the parlor, feet propped on a stool, near a window overlooking the front lawn.

He had tried every chair in the room, actually every chair on the first floor of the house, in search of one as comfortable as the one in Pierce's cottage. He finally found a suitable one, upholstered in weathered blue brocade.

Previous occupants had left it tucked into a dark corner of the parlor, hidden from view by a screen obviously made to display some forgotten young lady's handiwork. Doubtless, Miss Caroline would ignore the effort he expended to drag it into position near the window when she next rearranged the room.

At least he could be assured of finding it hidden behind the screen yet again. Still, Bingley had given him leave to make himself comfortable, and Bradley took him at his word.

He settled in and closed his eyes. This chair remained a mite stiff, and one misplaced bump directly under his left shoulder bothered him, but it would do well enough for a brief nap. The warmth of the sunbeams penetrated his knees that ached from Netherfield's many stairs. Ahh, just what he most needed.

The front door flew open, admitted several sets of angry footsteps, and slammed shut behind them.

Bradley pinched the bridge of his nose and rubbed his eyes. No more rest for this afternoon. Who would be first to discover his place of repose?

Miss Bingley dashed in and pressed the door shut behind her. The poor dear, her eyes red and cheeks tearstained, studied a wingback chair as though she might use it to block the door. She threw herself onto the settee and wept.

He kept his distance for several minutes. She needed to release some of her anguish. As her cries quieted, he rose and whispered, "Miss Bingley."

She started. "Oh, sir, I am so sorry." A sob strangled her words.

"No need to apologize." He moved nearer. "May I sit?"

She sniffled and nodded.

"What happened?"

Tears poured down her face.

Bradley produced a handkerchief and tucked it into her hand.

"The same thing that always happens."

"Your sister?"

She nodded again and stared into the linen square.

"I met your sister at Pemberley earlier this year."

"Oh, dear!" She pressed her hand to her mouth. "I cannot apologize enough for whatever she said to you."

"Why do you say that?"

She wrung the handkerchief. Good thing it was not a particularly fine one. It would probably never be the same after this.

"Because I know my sister. She says terrible, offensive things to everyone."

"Why are you sorry? Are you responsible for her behavior?" He lifted his brows and cocked his head.

She blinked at him, forehead furrowed as though unable to make sense of his words.

"Your sister's unkindness to me is in no way a reflection upon you and your brother."

"Please forgive…"

"My dear girl, it is done. Answer my question, though. Why do you apologize?" He extended an open hand.

"I must…"

"Her actions are hers alone. You are not responsible for her conduct. Allow her to be accountable for herself. Do not rescue her from the consequences she will reap from whatever she has done."

"You cannot image what she did this time." She twisted the handkerchief fiercely. "I fear the Bennets will never speak to us again and I enjoyed their company so much."

"I would like to believe the Bennets are better than that. What did your sister do?"

"While we called at Longbourn today, Mr. Collins

told Caroline that Mr. Darcy and his cousin, Miss De Bourgh—"

He slapped his forehead. "He promulgated the notion that the two of them were engaged?"

She nodded. "Caroline dashed from the house and accosted Mr. Darcy and Miss Elizabeth in the garden. She said she could not contain her joy and wished to congratulate him."

He rubbed his eyes. This was worse than he had expected. All his efforts to encourage Darcy out of his shell might be undone by her one, wretched, thoughtless act. He did not sigh, lest Miss Bingley think it directed to her, but his shoulders sagged.

"Now you understand. I am sure the Bennets will never speak to me again." She hid her face with the wrinkled handkerchief.

He tapped steepled fingers on his chin. "What do you think will happen now?"

"Caroline will get what she wants, as usual. She will pick and choose what little company I keep and command my attention for herself."

"You are satisfied with this outcome?"

"No! What can I do?"

"I suppose you can ignore what she has done as you have in the past." He ticked off points on his fingers. "You could instead confront her—"

She gasped and covered her mouth with her hand. "Oh no, I could never do that!"

"Why not?"

"It would be unkind."

"More unkind than her actions?"

Her forehead knotted, and she studied her hands. "No."

"What makes you think it cruel?"

"She would be upset."

"Her feelings are more important than those of the ones she injured?"

She shook her head and tied the handkerchief in a knot. "Caroline behaves so awfully if we try and tell her she is wrong."

"Perhaps she uses that to discourage you from telling her what she does not want to hear."

She blinked several times. "I never thought of that."

"In my experience, Miss Bingley, a person never changes until it is less painful than remaining the same."

Her lips shaped into a silent 'o.'

"I fear I have intruded too much. I should leave you now." He bowed and shambled towards the door.

An hour later, composed and momentarily calm, Louisa paced the length of her dressing room. By all rights, the carpet should be as threadbare as her own soul by now, but the makers had woven it of sturdier stuff that she.

Could she stand up to Caroline as Mr. Bradley suggested? The idea was fantastical, unheard of in her family, so close to fiction it tried her sensibilities. She whirled about for another trip past the dressing table.

What choice had she? Caroline had already announced her intentions to join Louisa on her wedding trip and live with her and Hurst afterwards. She loved Hurst too well to subject him to the life she and Charles endured. If she did not do something now, her marriage would be ruined before it began.

She drew a deep breath and smoothed her bodice. At least she would try. She sucked in as much air as her lungs could hold and marched to Caroline's door. Her knuckles stung as she rapped on the heavy oak. A muffled voice came through, and she turned the knob hard.

Caroline sat at her mirror, brushing her hair. "My hair—that awful walk utterly ruined it, just as I feared. This is your fault. Do find my maid and tell her I need her."

Heat rose in Louisa's belly. "No, I will not. Get her yourself."

Caroline turned to look over her shoulder slowly, her narrow-eyed, looking-down-her-nose expression the same one she used on the servants.

She was little better than a servant in her sister's eyes. The revelation scoured like sand across Louisa's cheeks. Her heart threatened to break free from its confinement in her chest.

"You forget yourself!" Caroline stood, hands on her hips. "How dare you use that tone with me!"

White hot strength coursed through Louisa and fueled her quivery voice. "You are a selfish, self-centered, mean-spirited excuse for a woman, who is never happy unless she has made someone else feel lower than herself."

"No more of this—get out!" Caroline walked toward the doorway.

Louisa followed her. "You will listen to every word I have to say." She pressed her back to the door.

"Leave! I do not want your company."

"No one wants yours either." Blood thrummed in Louisa's ears. Perhaps it was best she could not hear her own words. "You are unpleasant, unkind, and nigh on intolerable. You injured Mr. Darcy and Miss Elizabeth!"

"I only wished him joy. What is wrong with that?"

"Do not treat me like a simpleton. I see what you are about."

Caroline folded her arms and donned her most intimidating sneer. "Perhaps you will enlighten me. What exactly am I about?"

"Taking vengeance on Mr. Darcy by embarrassing him in front of Miss Elizabeth."

A blotchy flush broke out over Caroline's face and crept down her neck.

"Do you know he is not actually engaged? The colonel returned and explained—"

"How has that any bearing on me? Mr. Collins gave rise to the misunderstanding, not I."

"I thought London would have taught you not to repeat gossip."

Caroline pushed her aside and yanked the door open. "Take Mr. Collins to task if you will, not me. Get out!"

She poked Caroline's shoulder. "You are the one who should leave. No one here wants any more of your company."

"How dare you!"

"Easily, it is long overdue that I speak my mind as freely as you."

"I am your sister! You cannot—"

"It never stopped you." Louisa grabbed the door knob. "As soon as Charles returns, I will ask him to make arrangements to send you to Scarborough."

"You have gone too far! I do not want…"

"I did not ask you what you wanted."

"You cannot—"

"You never asked me if I wanted you to join me on my wedding trip, or if I wanted you to live with Hurst and me. I will tell you now, I do not. Are you not glad I have taken a lesson from you? Since this is how you have treated me, I will return the favor in kind." Louisa stomped out and slammed the door.

She took three steps down the corridor and collapsed against the wall. In her chambers, Caroline shrieked and pounded the wall, denouncing the way she had been treated.

What had she done? Lightheaded and breathless, Louisa covered her mouth with her hand and laughed until tears dripped off her cheeks.

Late in the afternoon, Miss Caroline paraded into the drawing room, dressed in taffeta, hair perfectly coiffed. She sat with a flourish and looked around the room "Are we to continue this little demonstration all day?"

Darcy glanced up from his letter. Her saccharine voice set his teeth on edge. At least she noticed no one had spoken to her the entire afternoon. He returned to his correspondence. Just a few more words, he would sand it, seal it and quit the room and her presence.

She rose and approached.

He wrote faster, but she reached his shoulder before he could sign the missive.

"I must say, I am surprised to find you so put out. You act as though I did you some kind of disservice."

"You portrayed me as a man who would pay attention to one woman while promised to another. I do not consider casting a shade upon my character a kindness."

"By all accounts I have done a favor both to you and to Miss Elizabeth."

Darcy sanded the paper, spilling a bit on the floor and Miss Caroline's gown.

She jumped back and brushed her skirt.

He stood and stared down at her. "What favor do you believe you granted me, madam?"

"Her expectations were far too high. Your intentions—"

He grumbled low in his throat all the words not fit to say to a lady. "Pray tell, how are you acquainted with my intentions?"

"Surely you recognize what kind of women the Bennets are. Knowing you as I do, I am certain they are not the sort with whom you would wish to affiliate yourself."

"You claim far more intimacy with me than exists."

She laughed, a thin little sound more annoying than the condescending sneer on her face. "My dear Mr. Darcy, their reputation precedes them. I learned of them in London, long before coming to this forsaken little town."

"Excuse me?"

She closed her eyes and shuddered. "Miss Lydia Bennet…such a hoyden."

"I know nothing of it." He leaned against the edge of the writing desk.

"You should consider that family's atrocious reputation before you, or your cousin, are tainted by their stain."

He flexed his hands into fists, glad for the sharp sting of his nails as they dug into his palms. "Those are serious accusations."

"As are their transgressions! Miss Lydia attempted an elopement whilst she visited with the wife of the militia colonel…in Meryton. Her father's indolent negligence left it to Miss Elizabeth to stop the entire disgraceful affair." She flashed a thin affectation of a smile. "What say you to that?"

Darcy worked his tongue along the roof of his mouth, but the vile taste remained. Miss Caroline would be scandalized to learn of Georgiana's similarities to Miss Lydia. "Who provided you with this intelligence?"

"The previous tenant of Netherfield, a Mr. Carver, whom I met whilst in London. His reasons for leaving Meryton are most interesting."

"I am sure I do not care."

"Perhaps you should. Mr. Carver is guardian for his two younger sisters. He found the Bennets an inappropriate influence on his sisters and returned to London to remove them from the Bennets' company."

"Mr. Carver shared such personal information with you?"

"No, no, whilst in town, I made the acquaintance of Miss Martha Carver, the younger of Mr. Carver's sisters. We shared tea several times, and she told me of the horrors of Meryton and, most especially, the Bennets."

"Did any of them actually witness the alleged elopement?"

"No."

Darcy harrumphed.

"However, Miss Carver received a letter from a Mrs. Carter, formerly a Miss Bond prior to her elopement with a militia lieutenant. The foolish girl confessed the whole thing and named Miss Lydia Bennet as the instigator of the entire shocking event."

"How would she be to blame?"

"She introduced Miss Bond to the officers and arranged for meetings with them in town, at Colonel Forster's house. Miss Martha said Miss Lydia shamelessly flirted with the officers and encouraged Miss Bond to follow suit." Miss Caroline rubbed her hands together. "The teas led to walks in the woods, where the colonel himself found Miss Lydia allowing an officer to place his hands on her person."

The blood drained away from his face. Had his friends not shielded Miss Caroline from the truth, she would be saying the same things of Georgiana. The back of his neck twitched.

"You have yet to explain Miss Lydia's responsibility."

"Miss Lydia suggested the elopement and planned the event. She even assisted Miss Bond in packing for her flight to Gretna Green. Can you deny that makes her responsible?"

Foolish and immature yes; responsible, no. Miss Caroline would be surprised if she perceived his thoughts, but he would not give her the privilege.

"These are not the kind of people with whom any of us should associate! I implore you—help me separate my family from them before the situation becomes worse."

He sprang to his feet and stalked toward the door.

"You cannot condone a family of hoydens and public women!"

"I cannot condone your judgmental attitude. Do you not realize the measure you use to judge them will be the one used to judge you? Can you stand under the scrutiny?" He turned on his heel and stomped back to her. "Are you completely unaware of your own reputation?"

"My reputation?" Her hands flew to her hips, her voice a glass-shattering screech. "My reputation is impeccable."

"Hardly." Darcy pulled himself to his full height and glowered, "Many have warned me to avoid *your* company."

Her face blossomed with crimson patches.

"Caroline!" Bingley stood in the doorway, his color high and eyes wild.

"Charles? I thought you—"

"Here and properly horrified." He stomped in, sputtering. "I am shocked, dismayed and astonished. After all the suffering you managed to inflict upon Louisa and me—"

"Do not inflate a trifling misunderstanding to the level of a real breach of propriety."

"Shall I share your humiliation with Mr. Darcy?" He stood toe to toe with her.

She inched away.

"Perhaps I should leave. This discussion does not require an audience." Darcy turned toward the door.

"No, please stay." Bingley beckoned him.

Darcy blinked. Bingley was capable of anger after all.

"Charles, no!" She stamped.

"You should taste the vitriol you so freely dispense." Bingley crossed the distance to them in three purposeful strides. "Do you recall that day in Hyde

Park?"

"Nothing happened," she hissed through clenched teeth.

"Lord and Lady Whitmore's daughter stumbled and fell into you. You accused her of being a street urchin and a pickpocket."

All color drained from her cheeks, and she turned away. "You may stop now."

Bingley grabbed her by the upper arm and spun her to face him. "You shook the child and threatened to take her to the magistrate to be hung! A six-year-old girl!"

She yanked her arm away. "Unhand me!"

"You did not unhand Lord Whitmore's daughter until his footmen disengaged you."

Darcy edged back. Whitmore had shared the incident with him, but not the name of the perpetrator. Miss Caroline was very fortunate he had not pressed charges against her.

"You may stop now, Charles." Her icy whisper trailed a chill down Darcy's back.

"Oh, no, not until the entire story is told. Remember, you arrived at their house, uninvited. The footman did not permit you entry, and you called apologies through the door for nearly an hour."

Her mouth opened and shut, but only odd squeaks came forth.

"You immediately left to visit your friend in Manchester. Louisa and I paid the price for your egregious behavior."

Darcy gritted his teeth to hold back words he might later regret. Bradley would appreciate the irony of her ignominy.

Bingley leaned into his sister's face. "I forbid you

to speak of the Bennets—"

"You forbid me? I hardly think—"

"Exactly, Caroline! You hardly think! What you did this afternoon proves—"

"I only intended—"

"No, we all know what you intended."

"Stop! You are humiliating me." She pumped her fists at her sides.

"Precisely what you did to him." Bingley glanced at Darcy.

Darcy felt her eyes raking him, the sharp claws of a trapped animal. A most effective tool of manipulation, but it would not move him.

"You are cruel. How can you treat me—"

"Enough!" Bingley stomped. The heel of his boot echoed off the hardwood. "You must leave. I will make arrangements with our aunt in Scarborough. Be careful not to offend her. I doubt Louisa or I will ever welcome you back into either of our homes." He pointed toward the door. The veins stood out, purple against the white skin of the back of his hand.

She gasped and fled the room. Pounding steps dashed upstairs. A door slammed. At least they would be free from her company for a little while.

Bingley mopped his face with his coat sleeve.

Darcy led the way for them to sit near the desk.

"My sister has been a selfish creature all her life, never held accountable for her actions. My mother coddled her. My father encouraged her to think far too much of herself. She expects to be the center of attention at all times. I do not believe she has ever admitted to being wrong." Bingley combed his hair back with his fingers. "What am I to do with her?"

"You cannot change her, but you can change yourself. Remove those things that encourage her selfishness and refuse to tolerate any more of it. If she changes, excellent. If not, at least you will be able to respect yourself."

"I suppose you are right." Bingley stared at the ceiling. "I spoke to Miss Kitty and Miss Lydia and explained to them the error of Caroline's declarations. They promised to talk to Miss Elizabeth on your behalf."

Darcy forced his lips upward. Bingley needed the encouragement, though it felt like a lie.

"I do not think Miss Lydia is partial to Collins. She appeared most pleased to hear he was mistaken." Bingley offered a weak smile. "I expect Miss Lydia will readily share my intelligence with all who will listen."

Darcy looked out the window. The lengthening shadows cut the last sunbeam from the room, leaving an empty chill in its wake. "I am sure she will."

"I am so sorry. I—"

"Leave it. What is done is done." Darcy shrugged.

"For what it is worth, Miss Kitty did not permit Louisa and me to leave until we promised to call again, without Caroline, of course." He sighed. "She insisted none of them blamed us for…what happened. I am certain Miss Elizabeth will feel the same way once she understands—"

Darcy lifted both hands and pushed back the heavy air between them. "Enough please."

"Will you be returning to the inn?"

"Were you serious?"

"I will send her to Scarborough."

"When?"

"I shall send an express to my aunt. I will go into

town tomorrow and make arrangements for her and her maid to travel, by post."

"Post?"

"I will pay to ensure she does not sit on the roof."

Darcy choked back thin laughter. "No, surely—"

"Yes, I am most decided." Bingley crossed his arms and furrowed his brows in what must have been an attempt to appear determined. It seemed sadly out of place on his easygoing countenance.

"Then I will stay for a while longer."

Two days later, Fitzwilliam accompanied Bingley and his sister on a call to Longbourn. Miss Kitty and Miss Bennet welcomed a break from wedding preparations. They were easily persuaded that a refreshing turn in the garden would be quite the thing to soothe their ragged nerves and tired hands.

Miss Kitty selected a path through Mrs. Bennet's roses—some of the handsomest Fitzwilliam had ever seen. No gardener at Matlock estate achieved such blooms or fragrances. Lady Matlock would envy this shrubbery. Heady perfume filled the air and petals rained upon their feet with every accidental brush against the canes.

"I never sewed so much in my entire life." Miss Kitty laughed and shook her hands before her.

"Better you than me." Miss Bingley shrugged. "I am an indifferent seamstress at best."

"Do not think so meanly of yourself." Miss Kitty frowned. "I have seen your embroidery and it is lovely."

Thank you. Bingley mouthed and nodded at Miss

Kitty.

Fitzwilliam patted Miss Bennet's hand, warm and snug in the crook of his arm. She glanced up at him, eyes half hooded by generous lashes. Bathed in a sunbeam, her face glowed. In her aura, he forgot anything had ever been amiss in his life.

He paused to smell a particularly colorful blossom dangling at his shoulder, and the others slipped out of sight. He glanced at her. Either she did not mind the illusion of privacy or desired it as much as he did. He hoped for the latter.

"Are you fond of roses?" she asked, her voice a soft caress.

Fitzwilliam winked. "I would not recognize a garden without them."

Her response took two breaths longer than it should. His gut pinched.

"Do you find these to your satisfaction?"

He pressed her hand and sighed. That prat Collins threatened to spoil his acquaintances as well as Darcy's. This nonsense would end now. Tension gripped his shoulders.

She stiffened beside him.

No, this would not do. She must not think his ire directed toward her. He must be gentle—something the army had ill-prepared him for. "Please forgive me if I still carry an officer's directness. I believe there are matters between us which I must address."

"What matters?" she whispered in a voice so thin it might tear on the next breeze.

His free hand flexed into a fist. What damage had already been done? "I am concerned you misunderstand my expectations."

She sucked in an abrupt breath and stopped mid-step. "Oh."

His stomach turned over and tried to edge his heart aside. "Please allow me to explain."

She tried to pull away, but he held her fast.

"Do not be concerned. There is no need to explain." She turned her face away.

"I must." He guided her to a short stone wall and urged her to sit. Blossoms crowded in to cloak her in petals, a fairyland princess holding court for her unworthy subject. The tableaux stole his breath away.

"Sir?"

He jumped. "Yes, yes. Ah…Mr. Collins and Miss Caroline made note of my connections—Lady De Bourgh and…my father—"

"The earl."

"Yes, the House of Matlock." He rubbed his chin against the back of his hand.

"They mention those connections readily."

"They seem to think more of them than I do."

Her eyes grew wide and forehead knotted.

A forgotten breath rushed from his lungs. "Many find their worth in their connections. At one time, I did too. But no longer." He stared into her eyes. What questions lay in those depths?

"Indeed?"

"Are you concerned I compare Longbourn to my family's estate? I do not. Nor do I compare you to any peer or heiress in my acquaintance for none of them can stand in your shadow." He lifted her hand and stroked her knuckles with his thumb. "Though your mother's roses are lovely, they do not compare to you."

Her blush deepened, matching the blossoms blanketing her shoulders.

"My expectations are different to most men in my station. I seek to make a quiet life for myself and my family—in the country, away from London and the *ton*, and all their complications."

She blinked and shook her head.

"It is true."

Her mouth curved into a smile that lit her eyes.

He should not kiss her now. He must not kiss her now. Still, he drew her hand to his lips and brushed them over her gloved fingers. It was not enough, but for now it would have to do. He offered his arm again, and they continued through the garden. Was it his imagination, or did she hold his elbow more tightly now?

A pair of birds startled and burst from the bushes nearby. She jumped and gasped. Her hand flew to her mouth, and she giggled.

What a beautiful sound, one he would never tire of. "I hope you will pay your cousin's remarks no further mind. Miss Caroline should not trouble you for very much longer either."

"How so?"

"Her behavior vexed Bingley deeply. He is making arrangements to send her to her aunt—in Scarborough."

"Oh, my, I never imagined—"

Fitzwilliam laughed. "I think her equally surprised."

"I would like to tell Lizzy, if you do not object."

"By all means. How is she?"

"Mr. Collins follows her around, attempting to explain himself, but she dismisses him. I repeated your intelligence regarding Mr. Darcy and Miss De Bourgh.

She listened but will not speak to me about the incident either. I believe she is angry and confused. "

"I suppose that is the best one may expect for the time being. Thank you for permitting me to call upon you, despite their current awkwardness."

"The pleasure is mine."

"Then I assume I have your permission to do so again." He turned aside. If she saw his smile right now, it would appear entirely too self-satisfied for his comfort.

Much to Elizabeth's satisfaction, Thursday evening, Uncle Gardiner's carriage pulled up to Longbourn in time for him and Aunt Gardiner to take dinner with the family. Elizabeth said little, both during the meal and after the ladies retreated to the drawing room. Mama and Lydia monopolized the conversation, which naturally focused upon Mary's wedding.

Somehow, the news of Mr. Darcy's alleged engagement left Mama unaffected. Whether she ignored it, or the presence of the still eligible and attractive Mr. Collins mitigated it, Elizabeth could not fathom. Whatever the case, no one objected to the continuance of Mama's good spirits.

Elizabeth pressed her temples to subdue her throbbing headache, the one that appeared with each thought of Mr. Darcy. Jane, Kitty and Lydia all protested his innocence, with the Bingleys' and Colonel Fitzwilliam's testimonials to support their pleas. With every consideration of the situation, she became more perplexed. She wanted to like both Mr. Darcy and Mr.

Collins, but, in all likelihood, one of them was reprehensible. The question remained—which one?

The gentlemen filed into the drawing room. Mr. Collins caught her eye and walked toward her. She ducked out the garden door. His attempts to apologize and make amends for his offence had graduated from courteous to ingratiating. She could not stomach another repetition.

The door behind her opened with a soft click. A woman's footsteps approached. At least he was not following her this time.

"Lizzy dear?"

Dear Aunt Gardiner! A warm hand on her shoulder made her turn. Her aunt stood close, her eyes full of concern.

"Oh, Aunt." Her throat pinched shut.

Aunt Gardiner led her to a bench just beyond the patch of light from the tall windows. Elizabeth wrapped her fingers around the cool stone's edge.

"Tell me what troubles you. You have not acted yourself all evening." Aunt Gardiner tucked a stray tendril of hair behind her ear. "I know you far too well to believe you jealous of Mary and all the attention she is receiving."

"Heavens, no!" She covered her mouth with her hand. "I delight in Mary's good fortune. Mr. Pierce is a wonderful man, and they are well suited. Mary has so often been ignored. I do not begrudge her a moment of mama's doting. I expect, though, she would prefer less of it, if the truth were told."

Aunt Gardiner's brows lifted. "Poor Mary's patience appeared sorely tried at dinner."

"Indeed. I do not know how she maintains her equanimity. I certainly would have opted for Gretna

Green by now."

"You would do no such thing!" Aunt Gardiner tapped Elizabeth's shoulder. "At least do not say so. You will send your mother into fits."

They both laughed, and some of her melancholy slipped away. She drew a deep breath. The tightness in her chest eased.

"Will you not tell me the source of your discomfiture?" Aunt Gardiner pressed her arm to hers.

"Where do I begin?" Elizabeth laid her head on her aunt's shoulder.

"The beginning is generally considered the standard place."

"When I was five years old—"

"Lizzy, please."

Elizabeth straightened and cupped her cheeks with her hands. She pulled in another breath to explain all she remembered of Mr. Darcy, Mr. Collins and the alleged engagement. The words tumbled out so quickly, Lydia would have been hard pressed to interrupt.

"My goodness," Aunt Gardiner chewed her knuckle, "that is quite a story."

"Take pity upon me and advise me as to what I should do."

"You credit me with the Wisdom of Solomon, and I do not deserve such praise."

"You must! To hear Mama, I should expect Mr. Collins to throw himself at my feet at any moment. Yet Charlotte Lucas insists I should throw myself upon Mr. Darcy's feet as he is easily ten times the consequence of my cousin." She threw her hands in the air. "And I cannot discern the character of either one."

"Have you a compelling reason why you must settle upon one of these gentlemen?"

"I only wish to resolve my confusion. They both carry the appearance of goodness, or at least I believed they did. Now, I do not know if either has the truth of it."

"I see."

Aunt Gardiner rose and led her on a turn about the space lit by the windows. "Since I know only what you have told me of either man, I cannot advise you as to the particulars of the matter. However, I may be able to offer you a few thoughts."

"Yes, anything at this point would be much appreciated."

"You will not be surprised to hear this is how Mr. Bradley once advised me."

Elizabeth chuckled. "How did our friend instruct you?"

"He told me a man's words may lie, but the fruits of a man's life will always speak the truth of him."

"I am not certain I understand."

"Many plants appear similar until they bloom and produce fruit. At that time, one may reliably sort out which is which."

"Unless they soon sport blossoms and berries like a woman's hat, how does one find the fruit a man bears?"

Aunt Gardiner's placid countenance dissolved into giggles. "Can you see your father and uncle parading about town, their hats festooned as the ladies of the *ton* decorate theirs?"

The picture sprang to her mind, so clear and absurd, Elizabeth bent double laughing. Breathless, she wiped tears from her eyes. "Papa with fruit on his head— that image will haunt me the rest of my life."

Aunt Gardiner smiled wryly. "I do like a touch of the ridiculous at times. Perhaps, it would be better if men might be judged by their hats. I do not expect that to come to pass anytime soon. So, we must be astute observers of the human condition, a talent which I know you to possess."

"What am I to observe?"

"What are his relationships like? Will any speak in his defense? Do those who know him respect him? Is he a man of his word? Is he prudent with his money? Generous to those in need? Does he call attention to his virtues, or is he clothed in humility? Does he demand his own way? Is he rude and self-seeking?"

"Some of those are things are not easily seen."

"No, they are not. Perhaps that is why many look at wealth and consequences and connections instead. They require far less time and effort to discern."

Elizabeth sighed. "I would rather they simply wear hats."

"As would I, my dear." She patted Elizabeth's hand.

Friday morning, the last day Mary would carry the name Bennet, the family rose early. Mama kept everyone except Mr. Collins, who escaped into town, busy checking tasks off her lists. Trunks were packed, checked and packed again. Everything that could be polished was shined until it glowed. By late afternoon, Mama's lists were completed, and everyone scurried away to prepare for dinner.

All Mary's favorites appeared on the dinner table. Mr. Collins squirmed at the sentimentality expressed by one and all. Elizabeth chewed her lip. She knew his father was a harsh man and such mawkishness must be foreign to him. Certainly that must explain his apparent discomfort.

After dinner, they adjourned to the drawing room, but the evening grew cold quickly, and they all were exhausted. The family retreated upstairs earlier than usual.

Elizabeth and Jane withdrew to Mary's room. They sat together on the bed heaped high with pillows. Elizabeth brushed Mary's hair in the crackling firelight. Her hair was beautiful and always well-behaved, submitting serenely to the plait and pins.

"Contemplative again, Lizzy?" Mary looked over her shoulder. "You are. I can see it in the melancholy turn of your lips." She clasped Elizabeth's hands.

The door behind them squeaked. Lydia and Kitty, clad in their dressing gowns, peeked through the doorway.

"Come in, come in." Jane beckoned them in and slid toward the head of the bed.

Elizabeth patted the counterpane beside her. Lydia and Kitty rushed in and piled on the feather bed, tucking their feet underneath them.

"Do you remember how we used to do this when we were small?" Kitty giggled. "Mama would get so cross when she heard us laughing. She called us her 'little titter mice.'"

Jane wrapped her arms around her knees. "I think maybe she and Aunt Philips used to do the same thing."

Mary pulled her shoulders into a funny hunch and looked up like an old woman craning her neck. Her voice thinned to a brittle cackle. "Remember how

Lizzy read us stories and did all the voices for the characters."

Elizabeth guffawed. She would miss those times.

"You must promise to do that for my children," Mary said.

"And mine," Jane added.

Kitty clapped her hands softly. "You shall have the most delightful children."

Elizabeth rolled her eyes. Not if any of Mama's predictions were correct. "Hardly, they will be all mischief and nonsense, to be sure. Mary's, though, shall be saints, like her."

Mary's cheeks glowed. "Not if they resemble their father." She turned aside.

"Indeed?" Kitty scooted closer and balanced her chin on Mary's shoulder. "You must tell us— genteel Mr. Pierce is not as he seems?"

Mary laughed. "No, no, nothing so outrageous. He was a most high-spirited lad, or so he tells me."

"Not like staid Mr. Darcy, I am sure." Kitty blinked with the same feigned innocence she used on Mama so often. "Nor like excessively…excessive Mr. Collins."

"I still do not like him." Lydia hunched and crossed her arms over her chest.

"I think you do, Lizzy." Kitty sidled close to Elizabeth and pressed their shoulders together.

Elizabeth gasped and traded looks with Jane. If her face burned any hotter, it would burst into flame.

"Kitty, please," Mary said.

"But everyone—" Kitty sat back on her heels and pouted.

"Kitty!" Jane's voice became sharp.

Lydia leaned forward. "I heard Mr. Collins tell Papa that he would agree—"

"No gossip, Lydia, please." Mary cocked her head.

Lydia pushed her lip into a pout.

Jane gathered Lydia's hair along her back and brushed it. "What pranks did your high-spirited Mr. Pierce favor?"

"His brother told me he liked climbing trees—"

Elizabeth covered her mouth, unable to contain her amusement. "Forgive me, Mary. I pictured him coaxing you to climb a venerable old oak on Mr. Darcy's estate, only for Mr. Bradley to catch you both."

Jane fell onto her knees in helpless peals of laughter. Mary and Kitty dropped on each other's shoulders in breathless giggles. Even Lydia tittered along. Mary wiped her eyes on her sleeve. Kitty pulled the sheet and dragged it over her cheeks.

"I shall dearly miss these times." Jane blotted her face with her handkerchief.

"I will, too." Elizabeth's mirth faded away. "I cannot imagine what Longbourn will be like without you."

"I never imagined being away from home and all of you." Mary blinked rapidly, her eyes bright. "I am quite certain I shall write so often you will tire of paying the post."

"You must, Mary—truly you must." Kitty bit her lip. "May we come to visit you?"

"Absolutely—"

Jane clutched her breast exactly as Mama did. "After all, she might put you in the path of other desirable men."

A fresh wave of laughter nearly choked them all. Jane's talent as mimic was a well-kept secret. Did

Colonel Fitzwilliam know yet? Doubtless, he would soon.

Elizabeth sighed. The way he looked at Jane, they might soon bid farewell to another Bennet sister. "Perhaps you might be able to come for Christmas."

"I hope so." Mary dabbed her cheeks with her sleeve.

"May we do this when you come to visit?" Kitty asked in a very small voice.

Elizabeth winked. "We cannot call it a proper visit without an assembly of Mama's titter-mice."

They all chuckled again, but it sounded a little hollow. Their lives would never be the same after tonight, and more change would surely follow.

"We need to let you sleep." Jane rose and helped Kitty and Lydia to their feet. One by one, they embraced Mary and padded toward the door.

Elizabeth stood.

"Lizzy, wait, please." Mary pulled the counterpane up a bit and patted the featherbed in front of her. "All the to-do with Mr. Darcy and Mr. Collins has upset you."

Elizabeth sat beside her, head bowed, eyes squeezed shut. "You wish to advise me toward Mr. Darcy's wealth as does Charlotte or Mr. Collins's charms as does Mama? Or have you another match in mind for me?" She pinched her temples. "Please, Mary, no more advice."

"I have no advice."

Elizabeth peeked up.

"There are some things I think you should know."

"Indeed. Tell me." Elizabeth drew her knees under her chin.

"Mr. Bradley said Mr. Darcy did not wish it made

public, but I…I…you need to understand. His generosity does not end with the use of his townhome for our wedding trip. If we take the curacy, Mr. Darcy will rent us a fine cottage for a pittance. What is more, Mr. Darcy is paying a full half of the generous wage offered us, perhaps more. He instructed Mr. Bradley not to allow money to be an issue in the choice of curate."

Elizabeth pressed her forehead to her knees. What kind of man shunned credit for generosity? She swallowed hard. "And what of Mr. Collins?"

"Lydia does not like him, and it is a rare man indeed that she does not like." Mary chuckled and sighed. "Oh, Lizzy, I wonder why Mr. Collins would choose to protect you by humiliating a man of so generous a nature—and with accusations entirely untrue. I suppose it might be a simple mistake—but what a way in which to make an error."

"I do not know what to think right now."

"Perhaps Mr. Collins erred in judgment because of a desire to impress you."

"Should I admire such a reason?"

Mary laid her hand on Elizabeth's. "Be careful, Lizzy. With your lively disposition, you could not live with a man you do not respect."

"That is the soundest advice yet." Elizabeth smiled wryly. "I should leave you to sleep now. A bride should not sport dark circles under her eyes." She opened her arms, hugged Mary and slipped out the door.

She slumped against the cool wall and rubbed her head against the paneling. The sharp little lumps and bumps felt oddly reassuring. Had Mary talked with Aunt Gardiner? What matter? Aunt Gardiner's advice was solid and Mary's observations accurate.

Perhaps it was possible Mr. Collins's charms were merely the appearance of goodness while Mr. Darcy had more the substance of it?

Chapter 10

MARY'S WEDDING DAY DAWNED, cool and clear. The breeze promised rain on the morrow, but today would be fresh and comfortable. Elizabeth leaned out the bedroom window and drew a deep breath. The house already bustled with activity. Mama's shrill voice punctuated the hum. She threw on a day dress and trotted downstairs. One of Cook's scones, maybe two, and jam—definitely Hill's raspberry jam—would be essential before she dressed to stand up with her sister.

Hill had laid the breakfast table with fragrant, freshly baked offerings, bowls of jam, cold meat and stewed fruit. The morning breeze wafted the fragrance throughout the first floor. Elizabeth's mouth watered.

"Good morning, Cousin Elizabeth." Mr. Collins gazed at her over the rim of his coffee cup.

She jumped. Why had she not noticed him in the corner behind a book? "Good morning."

She served herself and sat opposite him. Mary needed Mattie's assistance this morning, so she and Jane would help each other dress. They should make an early start since Mama—

"You seem quite preoccupied." He placed his cup on the table and folded his hands atop his book. "Is something amiss?"

She shook her head sharply. "Not at all. I was sorting out the morning's tasks."

"How much could remain after yesterday's monumental efforts?" He chuckled, his half-smile enigmatic.

"You said your sisters were much younger, did you not?"

"Yes."

"Then you do not understand what is required for a party of ladies to prepare for an event, much less a wedding. You should consider retreating with my father to his study as soon as may be possible." She scooped jam on her second scone.

"I will take that under consideration. You are by far the expert on the matter."

She dabbed the crumbs from her lips and sipped her coffee.

"I realize you are busy, but you usually take a morning stroll. Perhaps I might convince you to steal a moment for a brief turn about the garden."

He smiled his heart-stopping smile, the one that should not still affect her, but did anyway. How very thoughtful! A few minutes out of doors would be a welcome tonic to fortify her for the rest of the day.

"I believe I will." She rose.

He followed her outside.

"Does your patroness favor rose gardens?" She paused to press her face into a large white blossom.

"Indeed, she does. Rosings Park boasts three sizeable rose beds. The roses in my own modest garden are grown from cuttings from that estate."

"You grow roses as well?"

"I try…mine are nothing to hers. I only hope my small shrubbery pays homage to the original." He bowed his head.

"Of course, I am sure little compares to the splendors of Rosings Park." Though she avoided rolling her eyes, the sharpness in her tone remained. Any more talk of his patroness, and she just might scream.

"You think my admiration of Lady Catherine excessive." He glanced at her.

She gazed at the blossoms on the other side of the path. His question was far too pointed for her to meet his eyes. "At times, you seem to talk of little else."

"Forgive me." He clasped his hands behind his back and moved several steps ahead of her. "I suppose someone not in my position would have difficulty appreciating my devotion to her."

She winced. He was right. "I am willing to learn if you will explain."

"I hoped not to burden you with my trials, but perhaps it would be best to make it plain to you. Be patient with me. These are difficult things to say." He lifted his face to the brightening sky. "Without inheritance from my father, at no time have my prospects ever been secure. In many ways, Longbourn's entailment made my future as uncertain as yours."

Her cheeks burned. How selfish! She never considered his perspective.

"I studied for a place in the church. Without a living in our family or connections with one to offer, a curacy was the best I might hope for. Few share your Mr. Pierce's blessing to find a position on such good terms. My own prospects were rather grim." He did not look back at her.

The possibility of genteel poverty loomed for him, too? How similar their lives were. She rubbed her hands along her shoulders. Mary and Mr. Pierce might suffer the same, except for the generosity of Mr. Darcy.

He cleared his throat. "With these concerns hanging over me, I had the prodigious good fortune to be introduced to Lady Catherine." He turned to face her. "I still do not comprehend the serendipity which brought me into her favor. You must understand. I owe her everything –my home, my income, my future are all the product of her benevolence in giving me the living."

"I see." Of course, he was grateful. He should be.

"I count it my duty, nay—my privilege to accommodate her preferences and desires whenever I am able." He caressed a large blossom and it shattered in his hand. Petals rained over his feet. He looked at her.

Something in his eyes changed. She swallowed and edged away, the hairs on the back of her neck prickling. "Your appreciation is admirable."

He inched still nearer, too close for propriety or comfort. "I have even more for which to be thankful. Do you realize it was she who sent me here?"

His warm breath tickled her ear. A thorny cane poked her side. "I understood you came to conduct business with Papa."

"A pleasing coincidence, but no, I am here at the

behest of my noble patroness."

She sidled along the flower bed until the way opened behind her. "Why would she send you to Longbourn?"

"To find you."

His smile fluttered her heart in all the wrong ways, his bared teeth no longer so friendly, but alarming. She inched back.

"She advised me, 'Mr. Collins, you must marry. Choose well, not one too high born, for she must make the most of your modest income. Let her be a prettyish girl for your sake—one of your cousins from the estate you are to inherit would suit very well. When you bring her here, I shall visit her. I will see she understands her proper place in our society.'"

Bile burned her throat. Insufferable, conceited, arrogant woman—and he, too, for submitting to such a command.

"You are far more than merely prettyish or useful. I am convinced—"

"Stop, Mr. Collins, I beg you! Stop—lest scenes arise most unpleasant to us both. This is Mary's wedding day. Your comments are most untoward—"

"I forget myself. Please forgive me. I shall honor your sister's day. I fear I offended you." He reached for her arm.

She flinched away.

He pulled his hand back. "My patroness damned you with faint praise. Please allow me to speak to you of my esteem."

"This is neither the time nor the place for speeches. We are beyond sight of the house. Our situation is most inappropriate."

"Of course, how thoughtless of me. I will not

mention your impropriety—"

Her impropriety indeed! Insupportable, judgmental—

"Like you maintained Mr. Darcy's secret?" The words were vinegar in her tight throat.

His eyebrows drew together. "You do not appreciate my warning?"

"One delivered in a most insensitive fashion. You publically embarrassed him with incorrect information. I wonder at your character."

"I am surprised you find it so objectionable."

Her eyes stretched wide. "Do my objections make your actions right or wrong?"

"Forgive me. I am a man whose judgment is clouded by so violent a love—"

"Enough, I must return." She ran to the house. Once inside, she peeked through the window. He did not follow.

She trudged up the stairs, feet heavy, chest too tight to breathe. In the relative quiet of her room, she dressed. Her numb fingers struggled to fasten the tiny buttons along her back.

Mr. Collins loved her? She had seen no signs of particular regard. Favor, interest, yes. Violent love? Surely not. And what of her feelings? Did she love him?

No.

She liked him, or at least she had, but not love.

Cold splashed against her cheeks. Sensation trickled into her fingertips. Soothing cool air rushed into her lungs and softened the knots riddling her insides. Her eyes burned with hot tears that refused to be blinked away.

She would not marry a man she did not love,

much less one she was not certain she even liked anymore. Mama might not approve, but she was accustomed to that.

The door creaked.

"Lizzy?" Jane slipped in. "I am glad you are nearly ready. Mama fears we will be late."

"If you help me with the last few buttons and my hair, I will be done. Do you—" She glanced at Jane. "No, you do not need any help. You look radiant."

"You should see Mary. She is stunning."

"Help me pin my hair, and I shall." She handed Jane her brush.

"Quit fidgeting." Bradley slapped Darcy's knee. "One would think you were the groom this morning."

Darcy braced his feet against the floorboards as the coach lurched over a deep rut. He grabbed Bradley's elbow to steady him.

"I am not part of the family. I do not belong at the wedding."

"You were invited. You belong."

"An invitation of obligation is not the same as belonging."

Bradley straightened his cravat. "No, I suppose not."

"How do you do it?"

"Do what?"

"Walk into a room full of unfamiliar people and act as though they are all long lost friends?" Darcy balanced his chin on laced fingers. "You make it look so easy."

"Perhaps I missed my calling. When I was young, I

considered the stage."

"You are acting?"

"Not an act, a choice."

Darcy groaned. "One you are about to tell me I must practice, no doubt."

"No doubt." Bradley patted Darcy's shoulder. "You will be fine. Pierce and Miss Mary regard you quite highly."

"Not after—"

"Yes, even after that. Fitzwilliam and Bingley championed you. Miss Mary is an astute judge of character. She and Pierce are firmly on your side."

Darcy shifted in his seat, aware of every lump in the cushions.

"Do not wait any longer. You must talk to her."

"The look in her eye when she ran off said she wanted nothing more to do with me."

Bradley nodded. "Perhaps in the moment, but she has heard the truth since. Give her the chance to prove herself. You desire no less for yourself."

Darcy licked his lips and swallowed the dry frustration clogging in the back of his throat. "How does one begin such a conversation?"

"Surely you can devise a more original excuse. Do what you know to do. It grows easier with practice."

The coach slowed and stopped near the picturesque stone church. Pierce paced outside the doorway.

Darcy pushed the door open and leapt out to help Bradley. The old vicar's knees buckled a little, but he quickly regained his balance.

Pierce rushed to them. A flurry of words poured forth so fast Darcy could not keep up. Bradley leaned on Pierce's arm and ambled into the church. Unless he missed his guess, Bradley deliberately slowed down to give Pierce time to talk. He was not the first anxious groom Bradley had soothed.

The pair slipped inside while Darcy lingered near the coach. Would he ever be the nervous bridegroom Bradley calmed? Not so long as the only woman he had ever considered would not even speak to him. He had to convince her he was not the scoundrel Collins intimated he was. To do that required he speak to her. Somehow, he would.

Another coach approached. He dismissed his driver and ducked into the building. His conversation would wait until afterwards.

Through the windows, he watched Miss Mary, her parents and Miss Elizabeth emerge from the coach. He supposed the bride lovely—they all were according to Miss Bingley. But Miss Elizabeth outshone her sister in every way.

He should have remembered more—the bride's gown, the expression the groom wore as he took his place beside her. Yet only two things remained in his mind after the ceremony ended and he left the church. The first he would never forget: Miss Elizabeth walking down the aisle ahead of her sister, her eyes, her far too distracting lips, the cut of her gown. The pale sarsenet showcased her assets, yet it concealed as much as it revealed—a perfect balance of demure and daring. He could not abide another man looking on her—and yet he had no choice, for Collins was the other image seared into his memory. The face of a hungry, rabid dog as Collins's gaze followed Miss Elizabeth. Anywhere else, Darcy would have called him out for ogling at a gentlewoman—at his Elizabeth—that way.

His Elizabeth?

He exhaled hard. Yes, his Elizabeth. No point in further denials.

She had captured him heart and soul. Would she have him though? Regardless, he would protect her from her wretched cousin, somehow.

Elizabeth stood in the drawing room, greeting guests with her parents. Her smile grew with each compliment to Mary's beauty and good fortune. Today of all days, Mary should be recognized for all her excellent qualities. It had been too long in coming, but at least it finally had.

Though the house bustled with guests, she was keenly aware of Mr. Collins's presence. With a little luck, he would not recognize the minute contrivances she devised to keep him at bay.

Mr. Bradley trundled past.

"Why do you not sit, sir?" She slipped in beside him. "Please forgive my forwardness. I saw you limp as you walked in. Might you be more comfortable if you put your feet up?"

"You are a dear girl," Mr. Bradley said. "You have far more important people to tend to. Do not trouble yourself—"

"Yes, he would be far easier off his feet." Mr. Darcy appeared at Mr. Bradley's shoulder.

Mr. Bradley chuckled and shrugged. "My most esteemed patron has spoken. I suppose there is little for me to do but genuflect and obey."

Mr. Darcy hooted into his fist.

"No, sir." She slipped her hand into the crook of

Mr. Bradley's elbow and urged him toward a chair. "Those affectations I might believe of another, but never of you."

He patted her fingers. "Too true, I am afraid, for I am apt to make trouble wherever I go."

"That is far closer to the truth." Mr. Darcy pulled a footstool close and helped him settle in.

She crouched beside the chair. "Mama will not call us to dine for at least a quarter of an hour. May I bring anything for your comfort whilst we wait?"

"I would dearly love Miss Maddie's—your aunt's—company, if she is not otherwise engaged."

"I shall send her to you directly." She rose and went in search of her aunt.

She wove through the crowd and delivered her message to a much pleased Mrs. Gardiner. On her way back to the drawing room, she almost ran into Mr. Darcy. "Excuse me—"

"Thank you for your concern after Mr. Bradley. He is not apt to seek his own comfort."

"My pleasure. He is dear to us. I confess I am a bit jealous of my sister's good fortune to move into his parish and enjoy his company quite regularly."

"You will visit her often?" His eyes brightened, and he smiled in such an unexpected way.

She blinked and dropped her gaze. Heat rose on her cheeks. "I doubt it will be so often."

"The trip is but three days by coach and only a few hours on the third day."

"Only three days." She laughed and shook her head. "I think the distance quite formidable. Unlike you, I cannot simply call for the carriage and be off wherever my whim may direct me."

"I stand corrected, madam. I trust you will forgive

my enthusiasm." He stared at her, dark eyes filled with something she could not name.

That something, whatever it was, set her heart fluttering and skin prickling. "Of course, I know it was most kindly intended."

Mrs. Bennet hurried by.

Elizabeth watched after her. "She will call us to the dining room in a moment."

Mr. Darcy licked his lips and ran his finger along his collar. "Perhaps after breakfast you might be available for a walk?"

She hesitated, her morning outing a bit too fresh in her mind.

The corners of his mouth drooped. "Forgive me. I am sure you will be occupied. I should not impose—"

"I expect Kitty and Lydia will be most keen to discuss the morning with Maria Lucas. We might join them on the excursion, if that is to your liking." The words tumbled out of their own accord.

"I will look forward to it." He bowed.

Mrs. Bennet gathered the ladies to the dining room. The men followed Mr. Bennet a few minutes later.

Bradley introduced Darcy to the Gardiners at the breakfast table. Their fine manners, refined tastes, and fondness for the old vicar made them easy to talk with. Their conversation delivered him from Collins's nauseating prattle, a debt he could not soon repay.

How did Miss Elizabeth tolerate his ingratiating attentions and still respond so graciously? The white soup soured in his stomach.

Did she actually favor his company? No, no. He nearly muttered the words aloud. A woman so intelligent and perceptive must recognize his loathsome character.

The requisite social niceties seemed to drag on for at least a week by the time he excused himself to return Bradley to Netherfield.

Miss Elizabeth awaited his return! He urged his horse into a trot. The wind in his face renewed his spirits. Tension fell from his shoulders, and he enjoyed the scenery. Longbourn House came into view. Soon he would be in the company he most desired.

He handed his mount off to a waiting groom. The youngest Bennet sisters almost bowled him over as they dashed through the front door.

Miss Elizabeth appeared behind them, cloaked with poise and grace. "Please excuse my sisters. They are impatient to recount the wedding to their friend."

"Not at all. My younger sister occasionally demonstrates similar exuberance." He offered his arm.

"I hardly imagine your one sister could muster so much energy as two young ladies together."

He chuckled. "I suppose you are correct. Though, I maintain there are similarities."

A shadow passed across her eyes. A tiny crease appeared between her brows, disappearing a moment later. "Of course, I give you leave to be the brother of a very lively younger sister."

"Thank you. I would not wish to do so without your permission." Habit tried to force his smile into something more dignified. The smile prevailed.

"I hope you do not think me untoward, but … thank you for what you have done and promised to do for my sister and Mr. Pierce." She peeked up at him.

His cheeks and ears burned. "I did not realize you were aware—"

"I know you did not want her to speak of it, but she felt I needed…Mary regards you so highly, and she—"

"Cousin Elizabeth!"

The pleasant sensations drained away, forced out by acrid bile and revulsion. Of all times for him to appear!

"At last!" Collins panted, hands on thighs.

"Is something wrong?" she asked.

"No, no, not at all. I just would rather not walk to town alone." He tried to edge between Darcy and Miss Elizabeth.

Darcy sidled closer to her. He squared his shoulders and pulled himself up a few inches taller into his most imposing master-of-the-manor bearing.

Collins stepped back, cleared his throat and did the same.

Pompous addle-pate.

She glanced from Darcy to Collins and back again.

Why did she not dismiss him and be done with it? Darcy would be happy to do the service for her should she but look askance at the interloper.

She resumed their trek. "What is your errand in town, Mr. Collins?"

"Ah, my errand is not precisely…in town." Collins looked everywhere except at her.

Prevarication was ugly indeed.

She peered at Collins.

Darcy forced back his scowl. What good fortune that Collins would prove himself a fool without being provoked into the display.

Collins sighed.

A touch of melodrama now? How repulsive.

"I should not dissemble. I beg your forgiveness."

She stopped, arms folded across her chest. "Why would you go out of your way to offer false information I did not request in the first place?"

The corner of Darcy's lips twitched. He willed that expression under control as well.

Collins closed his eyes, frowned and shook his head, a countenance surely crafted for effect.

"It was not my intention to distress you—I purposed quite the opposite, I assure you."

"And from what manner of provocation did you intend to protect me?"

"Your youngest sister."

"Lydia? Whatever for?" She glanced over her shoulder. Miss Kitty and Miss Lydia disappeared around a bend in the road.

"I feared she might be upset because of the wedding this morning. I hoped to offer comfort—or assistance should her behavior—"

She gasped. The color drained from her face. "What are you suggesting?"

"After her unfortunate…ah…episode, shall we call it…with the militia…the wedding may have reminded her of her own unhappy state—"

"Unhappy state? What are you talking about?" She balled her fists and rose on tiptoes.

"After Cousin Mary's most felicitous marriage, it must remind her she will never be so advantageously aligned, and that she materially injured your—"

"You have said quite enough," Darcy snapped.

"Sullied as she is, you can hardly expect—"

She quivered, cheeks flushed. "What I expect, is that you would honor our family's privacy and not bring up difficult matters in a public context!"

"Badly done, sir." The words escaped Darcy before he could stop them.

"I am acting in service to you both."

Darcy fought back the urge to retch. "Under what delusion are you operating?"

"You would ally yourself with a family whose daughter came within a hair's breadth of eloping with a militia officer, particularly when you owe your duty to Miss De Bourgh?"

"You have no place—" Darcy stepped closer to him, fists held tight to his side.

"Indeed, you are mistaken. I wish to protect my cousin from the inevitable rejection she would suffer at your hands when you discovered the truth."

"Do not presume to know my mind," Darcy snarled.

Collins turned to her. "Can you not see the danger you are in, trying to ally yourself with a man so far outside your sphere? He must cast you off at the slightest hint of impropriety in your family. Consider the behavior of your younger sisters, your mother and even your—"

"You may hold your tongue," she snapped and held her open hand up toward his face.

"I speak in your best interest—"

"What do you know of my—or anyone else's—best interest?"

"I am a clergyman. It is my business—"

"You know nothing of that business either." Her words ended in a sob.

"Indeed, you do not." Darcy slipped closer to her.

"You think your doddering old fool Bradley—"

"Enough finger-posting!" Darcy's voice boomed through the branches overhead. Several birds fled in its wake.

"Pray excuse me." She dashed away.

Darcy and Collins stared at each other. Collins pulled back his shoulders and lifted his chin. "Regardless to what either of you believe—my motives were to protect you both. Cousin Lydia's transgressions are the talk of Meryton. You could hardly remain ignorant of her deed."

"And you can accurately anticipate my reaction?"

"What doubt can there be?"

"How dare you assume—"

"You would allow your home, your sister to be associated—"

"You will keep your counsel. I do not give you leave to make assumptions about me or my family ever again."

"As you wish, sir." Collins bowed and turned on his heel.

Darcy stood, feet rooted while the despicable toad hurried off toward Longbourn House.

He slowly uncurled his fists, exhaling as each finger relaxed. Once again, Miss Elizabeth was not speaking to him due to Collins's ill-timed intrusion. Coincidence could not explain that.

He must talk to her. But how? From the look on her face, she would not relish his company anytime soon—not after Collins embarrassed her so profoundly. Perhaps Fitzwilliam and Miss Bennet might be prevailed upon. He would find a way. Whether or not Miss Elizabeth liked him, she must not believe he thought ill of her.

Large, heavy feet pounded the ground behind her. Mr. Darcy was too dignified to run after her. Would Mr. Collins not leave her alone?

"Cousin Elizabeth," he panted. "Wait, please."

"I do not desire company." She increased her pace.

He matched her step easily and remained stubbornly at her side.

"Please, sir, leave me now."

"You must hear me."

"Some other time perhaps. Not now."

He dropped his large hand on her shoulder.

She stopped and whirled on him. "Unhand me!"

He pulled away as though burned. "Forgive me. I am not—"

"I do not care. Leave me alone!" Her thudding heart nearly drowned out her voice.

He raised his hands, but she had no confidence in his surrender.

"Just listen to me, please."

"Will you leave me then?"

"I promise."

She crossed her arms over her chest. Perhaps if she held her ribs tightly enough, her heart might slow and breathing ease.

"Everyone in Meryton is aware of Cousin Lydia's disgrace. Out of respect for you, they do not speak of it in your presence, but behind your back it is spoken of quite freely. Young ladies' indiscretions are not tolerated by society."

She glared. The whole of Meryton talking of it?

Surely not! But if not, how did he find out?

"I see now, I should not—"

"Indeed."

"I feared he would reject you once he found out. If he heard it from me, I thought I might be able to protect you."

She poked his chest with her index finger. "I do not desire, nor do I need, your protection."

"I beg to differ. A woman is always in need of a gentleman's protection."

"That is my father's role."

"Or your husband's."

Her cheeks prickled, and her lungs refused to draw breath. "You go too far."

"You said you would listen. Do me that service at least." He pressed his hand to his heart. "I am captivated, heart and soul. I cannot sleep but to dream of you—"

"Stop, I do not wish to hear another word. I insist you—"

"You gave your word."

"I did not agree to receive these attentions. Leave me at once, Mr. Collins." She pointed, arm quivering.

"Just consider—"

She turned and dashed away, listening for his steps.

He did not follow.

She ran to the top of Oakham Mount and dropped onto her favorite fallen log. It creaked beneath her. The fragrance of loam and faded honeysuckle filled her senses, familiar and soothing.

Twice now, Mr. Collins had revealed humiliating information under the guise of protecting her from Mr. Darcy. He declared himself violently in love with her. But love of this sort? Perhaps this was the fruit Aunt Gardiner spoke of. She worked her tongue along the roof of her mouth to rid herself of the bitter taste. At least she knew her mind toward Mr. Collins—and Mr. Darcy.

Her chest clenched. The look in Mr. Darcy's eyes assured her he had no interest in continuing their acquaintance. She swallowed the painful lump in her throat. Why had she not realized how much she valued his good opinion until it was utterly and irretrievably lost?

Two days later, Colonel Fitzwilliam persuaded the Bingleys of the material advantages to be found in a call upon Longbourn. Between Miss Caroline's pouting and Darcy's dour temperament, Netherfield was no place for good spirits.

Now he had his angel's arm in his. Her peace restored his heart as they walked through the wilderness near the manor. All might not be right in the world, but Miss Bennet's presence improved everything.

"I heard your sister's wedding called a great success."

She did not smile at his compliment. Her features fell, and her shoulders slumped. "Mama will be most gratified."

"I understand an assembly is planned for the end of the week."

"Yes."

"Would you do me the honor of reserving the first and last dance for me?" He tried to catch her gaze, but she refused.

"It is very kind of you to ask me—"

"You already promised them to another?"

"No."

"I can see your reluctance. Will you not tell me what is wrong?"

"I am not sure we will attend the assembly at all."

"Not going? What happened?" He stopped and stepped in front of her. "May I help?"

Her eyes glistened. "Perhaps it is best I return—" She turned away.

"No." He touched her shoulder. "I cannot let you go so easily. I insist you at least tell me—"

"What is there to tell?" Her voice pinched off in a shrill note. She dabbed a tear away with the back of her hand. "Surely you already know from Mr. Darcy. You must think us…" jumbled words dissolved into a sob. She pressed her fist to her mouth.

He guided her to a nearby stone fence, helped her to sit, and hunkered down beside her. "We both have been aware for quite some time. I fear ripe gossip does not stay quiet."

Miss Bennet covered her face with her hands, shuddering.

"Stop." His tone was sharp and commanding, a relic from the army he never thought to use with a lady.

She peeked up, eyes red, cheeks tear-stained.

Those eyes tore at his composure. If only he might gather her into his arms and kiss away her sorrow. How could she believe—he shook his head sharply. He must remedy that immediately. "I asked you to dance because you are a most desirable partner."

"But my sister—"

"Is not who I asked. I asked you."

A soft breeze dislodged a lock of hair from under her bonnet.

Propriety be hanged! He ran it through his fingers and tucked it back under her cap He trailed his fingertips behind her ear and along her jaw.

"You are not the only one with a silly younger sister."

She blinked rapidly, forehead knotted.

"Darcy and I both have younger sisters. His ran into a spot of trouble not many months ago. It is not my story to tell, but it is not unlike your family's tale."

"I am surprised."

"I hope you do not deem me or my cousin hypocrite enough to condemn you for the very thing we so recently endured."

She swallowed hard and nodded.

"Please, tell your sister. Darcy stomps about in high dudgeon over the whole situation." He offered his arm. They should not get too far separated from the rest of their party.

"She has been quite unsettled as well. She…we were unaware of the gossip circulating about town. It is most uncomfortable to think you are the topic of conversation amongst your friends and neighbors."

"Darcy and I face it every season with the *ton* and its marriage mart."

"I never considered that." Her step hesitated, and she glanced up at him.

"An unfortunate artifact of our position in society." He shrugged.

"I wonder if these things are not easier for a man than a woman."

He guffawed. "I suppose I would not know."

She leaned into him.

The knot in his belly released so fast his knees nearly buckled. He kicked aside a pile of leaves. "I meant what I said. It does not matter—not to me and not to Darcy. Say you will attend the assembly, and you will dance with me."

"You are a difficult man to refuse." Her lips curved into a tiny smile, her cheeks brightening.

"Though my men would have readily agreed with you, I have never heard a lady say so. I find it enchanting."

"Do not become too accustomed to it, sir."

Her eyes glimmered in a teasing expression most like her sister.

"Do you mean to tell me you are secretly a contentious harridan?"

"Possibly."

"No, you are the image of the goddess Irene. I shall not be contradicted."

"I suppose there is little else to say, since you will not permit it." She batted her eyes.

She was flirting! Had the sun ever been so bright? Now all was indeed right with the world.

Chapter 11

TWO DAYS LATER, Darcy climbed into Bingley's carriage. Miss Caroline, her maid, and Bingley waited within. He wedged himself into the farthest corner lest an inadvertent brush of Miss Caroline's gown be taken for something else.

Bingley insisted he needed Darcy's presence to bolster his resolve and not to succumb to his sister's pleas and promises of good behavior. For the promise of freedom from her, Darcy would endure a few miles confined in a carriage with the only company he enjoyed less than Collins's.

"I apprised our aunt of your itinerary. She will have a man there to meet you when you arrive." Bingley handed her a sheet of scribbled notes. "These are the accommodations for you and your maid, every stop is—"

"Really Charles! Your penmanship! You cannot

expect me to read this mess." She flung the list against his chest and folded her arms. "Enough is enough. You made your point. I will behave as you desire."

"No, you will only try harder to keep me from seeing your misdeeds. Even that will only last a few weeks, at best." Bingley glanced at Darcy who nodded slowly. "I am decided. You must leave."

"Mr. Darcy," she leaned toward him, her smile the epitome of insincerity, "tell him. I apologized and gave you my solemn word. I am a reformed woman."

He snorted and turned away.

"Aunt Rush reluctantly agreed to your visit. If you alienate her, your only choice will be to hire a companion and live like a spinster off your dowry."

"Charles!"

Darcy shuddered. Her voice set his teeth on edge and his hair on end. The sound could probably shatter a goblet if the opportunity arose.

Bingley blinked and shrugged. "I speak the truth."

"You torment me for your own amusement." She stamped and huddled into the soft squabs.

Her maid looked away, cheeks pink. Poor girl, such a mistress would be a sore burden for any servant. If a better situation appeared in Scarborough, doubtless, the maid would take it and wipe Miss Caroline's dust from her feet.

"I find no amusement in any of this. You do not understand how difficult this is for me." Bingley clasped his hands and rubbed his palms together.

"You seem easy enough. You and Mr. Darcy obviously plan to make a day of it once you are rid of me." She tossed her head and sniffed.

Bingley drew a tentative breath. Darcy shot him

the glare he had been commissioned to administer, and Bingley shut his mouth.

The coach rolled to a stop. Darcy jumped out first. He handed the maid down, but stepped aside to allow Bingley to perform the service for his sister.

Bingley escorted her into the office while Darcy instructed their driver to remove the luggage. He looked around the building. The post coach waited in the alley, remarkably on time and ready for passengers. He tipped the post driver to ensure Miss Caroline's trunks a place on the waiting vehicle. Nothing as pedestrian as her luggage would delay her departure.

Half an hour later, Darcy and Bingley stood on the side of the street and watched the post coach trundle down the main thoroughfare.

Bingley straightened his cravat and dusted his lapels. "It is done."

Too long in coming, but it was done. Darcy clapped Bingley's shoulder.

"Care to join me for a pint?" Bingley asked.

"I think not. It is a bit early for the pub."

"Probably, but this is a special occasion."

"True enough. You go celebrate. I will go to the bookseller and find you after I finish."

Bingley ambled away, his steps light, head held high. Darcy turned down the alley toward the bookseller.

In truth a pint appealed, though a little bit of quiet and relative solitude appealed more. Perhaps, by some chance, Miss Elizabeth would be there. Happy thought indeed!

He pushed the door open. A small bell tied to the doorknob tinkled.

"Good day, sir." A stooped shopkeeper in a dusty apron and smudged glasses hurried to his side. "May I help you?"

"I hope so. Mr. Bennet directed me here."

"Is there something particular you desire?"

Darcy looked around the shop. Shelves lined the walls and every available space. He ran his tongue along his cheek. He craved time to peruse each title at leisure, but Bingley waited. In lieu of that, a handbook on talking to ladies would do quite well. "Nothing specific, perhaps you can suggest something. My tastes run similar to Mr. Bennet's."

"Ah! Come this way." The shopkeep held up one hand and shuffled to a bookcase along the far wall. "Mr. Bennet has the selfsame volume, though it took him years to acquire it. Here." He stood on tiptoe to retrieve the book.

The shopkeeper handed him the blue and red, leather-bound tome. "I paid the seller dearly for this gem."

Darcy flipped through the pages. An inscription on the first page of chapter eight stopped him:

Bennet, you will particularly enjoy this chapter. I recommend it with a good glass of port—Gardiner.

His cheeks prickled. This was Bennet's book. How?

"The seller hated to part with it, but needed blunt for his debts. Right good looking young man, too handsome to be in gaol for debt. Though between you and me, sir, I think his debts were more of the gaming variety and gaol is the least of his worries."

"Tall, light hair—" Darcy gestured above his head.

"Curly-like, yes! You know the bloke? You must

ask him if he has aught else to sell. I'm always happy to pick up wares like these." He brushed dusty hands on his apron.

"Perhaps I will. In the meantime, I will take this." He paid the shopkeeper and tucked the book in his coat pocket.

If the wagers Collins placed at Longbourn were any indication, he owed far more than might be repaid. How loathsome, to steal from his host to cover debts! Surely the Bennets were not aware.

Darcy said little on the return to Netherfield and hurried upstairs to the library with only a nod to Bingley. Mercifully empty, the room welcomed him with the scent of books and leather and a comfortable chair in a sunbeam. He collapsed into the upholstery and pulled the book from his pocket.

What to do with this now? How he would relish the opportunity to drag Collins before the entire Bennet family, book in hand and reveal all. As satisfying as it might be, he would not lower himself to theatrics designed to injure another, no matter what Collins had done. He whistled out a long breath and traced the embossed cover with his fingertips.

"Darcy!" Fitzwilliam stormed in. "I must speak to you." He dragged a chair near and fell into it.

"What is wrong?"

"This just came, express." Fitzwilliam pulled a wrinkled letter from his pocket and pressed it into Darcy's hands. "Rosings' steward wrote us."

He wrestled the missive open. "What has happened now? More storm damage? A fire? Lady Catherine can scarcely afford more repairs to the estate this season. Do not tell me, she insists on refitting another drawing room despite her promise to wait?"

"Nothing nearly so simple. Skip down to the middle, just above the large ink blot." Fitzwilliam tapped the back of the letter.

"Five thousand pounds? What does she need five thousand for?"

"Her vicar announced he will bring home a wife soon."

Darcy's jaw dropped.

"It gets better. His wife will be chosen from among his cousins—*as she ordered.*"

"What has that to do with five thousand pounds? Why would she insist upon his marrying? And why from among the Bennets?"

Fitzwilliam braced his elbows on his knees. "She discovered her vicar owes serious gaming debts in the amount of—"

"Five thousand pounds," they said in unison.

"She must be livid." Darcy rubbed his forehead.

Fitzwilliam nodded vigorously. "The steward says Lady Catherine insists Mr. Collins stops his gaming, and a wife is just the means by which it will be best accomplished. Moreover, a wife attached to the estate he will inherit will be the one most apt to bring his behavior under control so as to preserve her family home."

Darcy cringed. "Please do not tell me—"

"Lady Catherine does not wish his situation to become known. As she has denounced those with debts of honor, the news would cast a shade upon Rosings and herself, particularly since she selected Collins against the advice of any number of people, not the least of whom was my father. She promised to pay Collins's debts if he vowed to stop his gaming and brought home the wife she required within a specified time."

"Her logic astounds me." Darcy raked his hair. "One lot of foolishness does not cure another."

"Thus her steward begs us to intervene and prevent this pointless and dangerous excess expenditure."

"Once she sets her mind upon something—"

"Like you marrying Anne—"

"Now is not the time."

Fitzwilliam scratched his head. "Forgive my attempts at levity—"

"We must warn the Bennets."

"Indeed. The question is how. We cannot violate Aunt Catherine's privacy." Fitzwilliam stroked his chin.

Darcy drummed his fingers on the hard book cover. Of course! "I have an idea."

Friday afternoon, Bennet retreated into his study to escape the feminine flutterings in anticipation of the evening's assembly. Since this was the first event since Mary's wedding, Mrs. Bennet's impressions of the nuptials would be in high demand. With some luck, she would return home gratified with her status as a new bride's mother. Until such time, he hoped to partake in a hearty dose of solitude and fortify himself for the evening.

Of course, these privileges were too much to expect with a man of a sociable disposition in the house. Some American, or was it a Frenchman, who said, guests, like fish, begin to smell after three days?

Whichever it was, he was right. No matter how pleasant Collins might be, Bennet simply could not stand that much of anyone's company.

Except Lizzy's, of course. She possessed the happy skill of quiet companionship, able to sit and be with him without demanding anything but his presence. Now that she was put out with Collins, it fell to him to entertain his cousin. Another few days and he would surely run mad.

"Good afternoon." Collins sauntered into the study, dropped into a chair and parked his elbows on the far side of the desk.

Bennet nodded. "Are you arrived to escape the assembly preparations or with business on your mind?"

"A bit of both. I am beginning to understand what Miss Elizabeth told me about women preparing for an event."

"Indeed." Bennet rearranged a stack of papers. "Have you considered the mortgage?"

"Yes and my offer still stands."

Bennet grumbled under his breath and brushed his knuckles together.

"You should regard this as good news. I believe one of my cousins harbors a *tendre* for me as I do for her. She is merely in need of a bit of encouragement from her dear father to overcome her natural and most ladylike reticence."

"You expect one of my daughters will accept you? Obviously not Mary, and Jane is clearly otherwise attached. Lydia cannot abide your presence, and you barely speak to Kitty. I am left to assume you mean Lizzy."

"Indeed I do, sir. Her company is most pleasant. It would be an honor to call her my wife."

"I am not sure she would agree with you. You are aware that she is quite exasperated with you."

"I sought to apologize. She will not hear me, but she may be willing to listen to you. I hope you will intercede on my behalf."

No wonder Lizzy avoided him—the audacity! "You must be joking. You wish me to plead your case with her? Absolutely not." He slapped the stack of papers.

"But it would be in her best interest and to the benefit of the—"

"I am unmoved. If you are unable to manage a misunderstanding now, marriage is a poor option for you."

"You must help me." Collins grabbed the edge of the desk.

Bennet shook his head. "In time, she may be willing to grant you an audience and hear you out."

"How long will that take?"

"You do not know ladies well, do you?" Bennet chuckled. The poor, clueless fellow. "One cannot predict—perhaps days, weeks, even months."

"Months? Surely you jest."

"Not at all. A courtship should not be conducted in haste. Do not think the speed of Mary's wedding any indication of the duration of their relationship. Their friendship and courtship was the work of nearly a year, all told."

"I do not have months!" Collins huffed and stared at the ceiling.

"What is your rush?" Bennet leaned forward on his elbows. "Do you suggest my daughter is not worth the investment of your time?"

"Oh no, not at all." Collins raked his hair. "I must

go back to my parish soon, and I had hoped to return married."

"Why the rush, sir? You waited this long. What is a little while longer?"

"My patroness—she will be disappointed. She wants me married."

"She can brook the disappointment. Besides, what can she do to you? She has not the power to stop your pay or dismiss you from your position."

"Of course, you are correct. I simply do not like to disappoint her."

"You may wish to consider whose disappointment means more to you, a wife's or your patroness's. Perhaps your priorities—"

Collins rose, a tight smile stretched his lips. "I am certain your advice is kindly meant, sir. Excuse me. I must finish getting ready for the assembly. I would not desire to *disappoint* the ladies." He dipped his head and rushed out.

Bennet grumbled and pressed his forehead to his hand. All possibility of a mortgage just departed with Collins. He should have expected it. So ready a solution could not possibly come to fruition. Perhaps Philips or Gardiner might help him find another way.

"Girls! Girls! The coach is ready. We must be away." Mrs. Bennet's voice was not quite a shriek, but would become one soon if the girls did not appear directly. Thankfully, she would not be forced to wait on Collins. He had planned to ride one of the horses.

He shambled to the door. His wife required his presence.

Darcy paced the foyer until Fitzwilliam convinced Bingley and his sister to leave for the assembly though it was still a quarter hour before their intended departure. In the confines of the coach, Darcy drummed his fingers on the cushion and fidgeted.

"Why the hurry, Darcy?" Bingley nudged his foot.

Darcy pulled his foot back.

"Relax, with five women to prepare and transport, the Bennets will not arrive before we do." Fitzwilliam chuckled. "I have sent an entire company on maneuvers with less to do than my mother and sister preparing for a party."

"I am certain your men were occupied with far simpler goals than a woman at a ball." Miss Bingley smoothed her skirts.

Bingley snorted into his hand. "I doubt outmaneuvering the French is to be compared with the strategies of catching a husband."

"Perhaps you are correct, but a woman does more than hunt husbands at a ball." She cocked her head and lifted an eyebrow.

Bingley stretched his legs and stacked his ankles. "What else must she do? Enlighten us."

Fitzwilliam snickered and winked at her.

"Have you not noticed married and engaged women attend balls as oft as unmarried ones? A woman attends a ball to be observed by other ladies as much as to be seen by men."

"Think of a hen house, Bingley." Fitzwilliam slapped his knee. "They must establish their pecking order. Why else would they adorn themselves with so many feathers?"

Darcy guffawed. Even Miss Bingley laughed merrily. Would Miss Elizabeth enjoy such a joke? No doubt, for she dearly loved to laugh.

How much longer until he could speak to her? Darcy tapped his heel. Bingley's carriage approached the Meryton assembly rooms with no sign of the Bennet coach on the street. Excellent, excellent, he would be able to meet her before anyone else sought her for a dance.

Assuming, of course, she—no, she would not refuse him at least one set. Whether she would accept a second was another question entirely. One that would be answered soon, for the Bennet coach rolled up the road.

Collins, on horseback, turned onto the street. A bitter tang rose on Darcy's tongue. He gulped it back. Miss Elizabeth would note his annoyance, and he could not chance her thinking it directed toward her. Fitzwilliam broke into motion. Darcy jumped and followed him to the Bennets' carriage.

Though smiling all, the Bennet ladies, save Mrs. Bennet, seemed reserved—probably Collins's doing with all his talk of Meryton's gossip. What hypocrisy, given Collins's own situation!

"Good evening, Miss Bennet." Fitzwilliam bowed. "May I escort you in?"

"Good evening." She smiled for him alone, so brightly Darcy felt the warmth.

Miss Bennet's poise and grace, her elegant manners and education—though unconventional—rivaled any of the peeresses and heiresses Fitzwilliam had mingled with.

Miss Elizabeth stepped out. Though her finery might not match the gowns of Almack's, she was a diamond of the first water. He should speak, but how with his mind as empty as a fresh sheet of paper?

What would accurately convey the breadth of his admiration?

She tilted her head, a little of the light in her eyes faded.

No! He must exert himself further—

"Cousin Elizabeth."

They both jumped. Darcy's mind filled with all manner of things to say, none of them fit to speak before a lady.

Her face shifted into a mask of politeness. She smiled at him, yet this empty mien for Collins? Darcy's entire evening was vindicated in this single moment.

"I throw myself on your mercies, my fair cousin." Collins bowed. Low.

She inched back.

"I received a promise of a dance from all my dear cousins, save you. Would you do me the honor of dancing the first and last sets with me?"

Curse the slowness of his tongue! Darcy ground his teeth. If only he had spoken sooner.

"I…I…" She glanced at Darcy. "I am not engaged for the first, but—"

"She has promised the final set already." At last his tongue loosed.

She nodded, but looked shaken. A touch of relief and possibly appreciation filled in her eyes.

"Then may I ask you—"

"No, sir. I will not dance a second with you. Surely your concerns with gossip—"

Collins smiled a tight, shallow expression. "Of course, your sensibilities are to be commended. May I—" He reached for her.

"No, sir." She pulled away.

"I offered to escort her, and she accepted." Darcy straightened as her warm hand tucked into his elbow.

He should not gloat, but the desire nearly overwhelmed his self-control. Collins may have claimed the first dance, but she denied him a second. He forced his face into neutrality and led her past Collins into the assembly rooms.

"I pray you forgive my forwardness," Darcy whispered.

She clung to his arm. "Not at all. Your invitation was both appreciated and well timed."

"Though, you would agree, not the most conventional way to petition for a dance."

She peeked up at him, lips quirked in a teasing curve. "As long as you do not make it a habit, I shall be content."

No man could endure such temptation unmoved. He stopped and bowed. "Would you grant me the pleasure of dancing the second set with me?"

The corner of her lips rose just the barest bit. Her eyebrow lifted in an arch expression that veritably demanded to be kissed. Oh, the cruelty of tempting a man so.

She curtsied. "I would not object, sir."

"I shall count myself most fortunate."

"Perhaps you should secure a partner for the first set, though. The musicians are prepared to start." She peered over his shoulder. "It would not be proper for you to sit out with so many young ladies without a partner."

He stammered, eyes darting about the room. Miss Bingley was already engaged.

"Charlotte Lucas approaches." Miss Elizabeth tipped her head toward her friend.

Miss Lucas and Collins arrived at nearly the same moment. Sir William Lucas, the Master of Ceremonies, strode to the top of the room and announced the number of the lady to open the dance.

"Oh, that is mine," Miss Lucas said, "but—"

"May I have the pleasure of this dance?" Darcy bowed from his shoulders.

Miss Lucas nodded, and they proceeded to the head of the room.

Elizabeth looked at her partner and swallowed her sigh. How wonderful for Charlotte to lead the first dance of the assembly—and with a prestigious partner! Though she cared for Charlotte, she would have gladly traded places. Ah well, she was about to pay her penance for those uncharitable thoughts.

Mr. Collins led her to the dance floor, far down the set. Alas, she could not avoid some conversation. As long as he did not apologize or declare violent love, it would be tolerable.

"I feared you might refuse to dance with me." He smiled.

The expression no longer affected her. When had that changed?

"Your mind is on a more desirable partner?"

"Excuse me?" She knew it inappropriate to glare during a dance, but some expressions simply could not be quelled.

"Please forgive me. I only meant a bit of levity."

Elizabeth held the tip of her tongue between her teeth. Glaring was one thing, but she would not sink to outright rudeness. She looked down the line of dancers. Their turn would not come soon enough.

"In my best efforts to protect and impress you, I accomplished quite the opposite. I cannot say how deeply I regret causing you offense." His eyes fixed on her, prickling like a woolly caterpillar.

"Then why did you do it—twice?" Her voice dripped treacle. She hated treacle.

He smacked his lips. Obviously he did not dislike it as she did.

She shuffled back until she could go no further.

"I plead ignorance, my dear cousin. You inspired me to do good, but. I knew not how. My education lacks the finest parts of refinement only a lady of your delicacy might impart."

Certainly he distilled his words, smooth as fine brandy, to ignite fire within her bosom. But wet kindling would not light so easily. "Your patroness is not an accomplished lady?"

"She is all elegance and propriety."

"Perhaps she should instruct you."

He pressed his hand to his chest. "I would gladly sit as her student. She lacks the time to spend on a lowly clergyman."

"Perhaps if you apply to her for assistance—"

"No, the role would be better filled by someone one much closer—"

The couple beside them finished their steps. What a relief to take his hands and begin their turn. She skipped down the line with far greater energy than she felt. Perhaps if she exhausted him with her vivacity, he might lack the breath to continue his unappealing conversation when their turn ended.

They stopped at the head couple. Charlotte's cheeks glowed. She grasped Mr. Collins's hands to begin a graceful turn.

Elizabeth took Mr. Darcy's hands.

"Are you well?" he whispered.

How did he recognize her distress so easily whilst her partner so easily ignored it? How dear his concern. "The room is very warm." She forced her face into a smile.

"You are a bad liar. Forgive me. I abhor disguise. You do not need to lie to me. I am your friend." His voice wrapped around her, warm and comforting and safe.

"I…I…" she stole a peek at Mr. Collins.

"I thought as much." Fine lines creased his forehead and the edges of his eyes. "The set will be complete soon."

She nodded. His fingers tightened over hers—a promise. The tension across her shoulders eased, and her final steps with Mr. Darcy were light and pleasant.

Mr. Collins took her hands and she almost stumbled. Who knew slippers could weigh so much?

"Your figure is shown to your advantage when you dance." He stared.

A hot flush crept up her neck. Could she impose on the staff to prepare her a bath when she returned home?

"A man could go a long way without meeting another figure like yours." His eyes fixed on her décolletage and below.

She wished for a shawl, a blanket, a curtain or even a tablecloth might do. One last couple and the dance would be over. She would be free. "Whilst I appreciate your desire to be complimentary, those are hardly—"

"How might I compliment you? Do you want to

hear that I think you the handsomest woman of my acquaintance?"

"I beg of you, stop. Say no more, please."

"How can I stop when you excite every proper feeling of admiration with your perfections, your beauty, your wit and charms?"

"Stop! Enough!" She raised trembling hands.

The music stopped, and the dancers applauded. The gentlemen bowed, ladies curtsied, and the dance floor cleared.

He approached her rapidly. She edged backwards, but the crowd prevented her escape. She glanced over her shoulder. Would they not move out of the way?

"Cousin!"

She turned back. Mr. Collins plunged toward her, hands outstretched and grasping.

A dark blur rushed in.

Mr. Darcy caught him by the elbow and yanked him to his feet, bracing his shoulders until he steadied. "Have a care, sir, lest you injure someone."

"Excuse me." Mr. Collins wrenched himself away. "My shoe caught on the floorboard." He lifted his foot and examined the sole of his pump. "It is damaged."

"You must refrain from dancing for the remainder of the evening. You would not wish to risk harm to you or your partners." Mr. Darcy's eyes narrowed, and he shifted from gentleman to *Master.*

Their eyes met. The air crackled with the intensity of their contest.

She inched back. Mr. Collins flexed his right hand and his wrist quivered. Would this come to blows?

Mr. Darcy squared his shoulders, his eyebrows lifted infinitesimally. His hands rested at his sides, but his little finger twitched.

Her lungs cried for air. When had she stopped breathing?

Mr. Collins tipped his head and broke eye contact. A smile, thin as muslin, pulled his cheeks. "Of course, you are correct." He shifted his weight and grimaced. "I believe I strained my ankle. Cousin Elizabeth, would you keep company with me—" He reached for her.

Mr. Darcy stepped between them. "She promised me this set."

"She has a higher duty to me. I insist." Mr. Collins shouldered in front of Mr. Darcy.

She gasped and pulled away. "If you need of assistance, I shall be pleased to alert my father—"

"I require you to do your duty to me."

"What duty do you expect?"

"Every proper feeling insists you do not leave me in my hour of need."

She smiled and forced an anemic laugh. "I scarcely consider this an hour of need. A turned ankle is hardly a mortal wound."

"You would diminish my pain? You are not so unfeeling—"

Mr. Darcy sidled closer to her. "Enough of this rot! You are a grown man—"

"How am I to know the ankle is not broken?"

"You stood on it a moment ago when you pushed in front of me." Mr. Darcy gestured toward the offending limb.

"An instant of inflamed humors overcame my discomfort. I assure you, it is most excruciating." He shifted his weight to his left foot, face screwed into an expression painful to look at.

"Allow me to help you to a seat." Mr. Darcy grabbed his elbow and slipped one hand under his arm.

"No, it is not necessary."

"No, no, I insist. The next dance should not start for a few moments. Perhaps Miss Elizabeth will take this time to notify her father of your dilemma." He jerked his head toward the card room.

"Yes, of course." She dashed away.

Where was Papa? What was she to tell him? She could not hide her distress, but what to say in so public a place? She stopped and surveyed the room. Oh, where was he?

"Lizzy?"

She jumped. "Papa!"

"Are you well, child?" He grasped her elbow and guided her to a quiet corner. "What happened?"

She pulled in a deep breath. "Mr. Collins, he turned his ankle and does not feel well enough to continue to dance."

Papa shrugged. "He will not be able to dance with your sisters. I expect they will be relieved." He chuckled and thumbed his lapels.

"I am sure you are correct." She flashed a quick smile. Her eyes burned. "He insists it is my duty to attend him in his 'hour of need.' He was rather…forceful in his declarations." She swallowed hard.

Papa blanched and searched the ballroom.

"Mr. Darcy—I promised the next dance to him—he came…and assisted Mr. Collins to a seat. He suggested I find you—"

He pulled his shoulders back and squared his jaw. "Let us go to him and see how I may be of service."

She led him to Mr. Collins.

Mr. Darcy stood beside him, keeping watch as a knight over a prisoner.

"I hear you are injured, Collins." Papa stopped close to Mr. Darcy.

"The heel of my shoe became loose. I turned my ankle—"

"When he tripped and nearly fell into Miss Elizabeth." Mr. Darcy glowered.

Papa stared at her. "Are you—"

"Mr. Darcy intervened before I was injured."

"You have my gratitude, sir." Papa nodded at Mr. Darcy. "Clearly you cannot continue to dance. Accompany me to the card room."

"I do not—" Mr. Collins clutched his ankle.

"There is no swelling. Your injury is not serious. Perhaps the life of a parson does not expose you to the minor mishaps common to country experience. You may take my arm, and I shall assist you to the card room." Papa hauled him to his feet.

Mr. Collins's eyes raked her, penetrating and threatening. Her breath hitched.

"I shall claim my partner for this dance." Mr. Darcy led her to the set as the musicians sounded the first chords of a familiar cotillion.

She lost herself in the intricate steps, relieved to be away from Mr. Collins and the burden of conversation for a few moments.

Mr. Collins had seemed quite fleet of foot on the dance floor. How embarrassing his fall could have been—with damage to her gown and all the ensuing talk! Her cheeks burned. Mama might even suggest she should marry him after such a mishap—an excellent way to secure a husband. What a fate!

"Are you well?" Mr. Darcy whispered as they joined hands and turned round each other.

"Yes, yes, I am fine. I simply realized I did not thank you for your timely interventions a few moments ago."

"I am most gratified to be of service to you." He smiled with his whole face. How had she ever found Mr. Collins's smiles so appealing? Mr. Darcy's were unparalleled.

Chapter 12

THE MUSICIANS RETUNED THEIR instruments in preparation for the final set. Fitzwilliam scanned the room in search of Miss Bennet. Their first dance had been the most pleasant of his memory. Her grace and beauty made her a highly desirable partner, but her charm in dealing with the clumsy oaf who collided with her and tread upon her toes gilded the lily. The poor man looked ready to die of mortification, and she gently reassured him and restored his spirits.

How rare those genteel feelings were among the ranked and privileged. Darcy and his father would call him impulsive, even rash. Little matter, he knew what he wanted, and nothing could stop him.

Her partner still tried to converse with her. She was too polite to turn him away. He would gladly perform the service for her. He straightened his jacket and tidied his cravat.

He strode toward Miss Bennet and passed Darcy in the middle of the room. They traded nods. Given the glint in Darcy's eye, perhaps impetuousness was contagious.

"Miss Bennet?" Fitzwilliam bowed.

The young man with her stared and stammered. Oh, the expression on the poor bloke's face! He must have desired the last dance with her, and now his hopes were dashed.

"Excuse me." She nodded to the young man and joined Fitzwilliam.

They took their places in the set and looked to the top of the room. The musicians trilled the first notes of the Finishing Dance. They danced the first few steps then settled in to wait for their turn. Ah, what he most anticipated.

"What say you of your evening?"

"Exceedingly agreeable." She graced him with a smile not bestowed upon any of her other partners, a smile for him alone.

His heart beat a little faster. She returned his regard. All night he had searched for some sign and now he received his prize.

"What a shame it must end so soon."

"Yes." Her smile faded a bit. "Especially given that the journey home cannot be nearly as pleasant as the one here."

"I was under the impression the discussion following a ball was on par with the event itself. Will not your mother and sisters provide most diverting conversation?"

"Our cousin injured his ankle after the set he danced with Lizzy and has worked himself into high dudgeon since. I doubt he will be able to ride horseback. He must take Papa's place in the carriage. I expect little merry talk with him present."

"A harsh punishment, indeed. He is an ungracious guest to interfere with your enjoyment."

"Do not judge him so harshly. We must consider his discomfort."

Discomfort my arse.

Fitzwilliam caught the words just before they tumbled out. "The times I noticed him, he appeared hardly inconvenienced."

"Indeed? When I attended him, he gave the impression of severe distress. Perhaps he simply did not wish to reveal himself before you, sir." Her eyes twinkled. "You are most formidable." The smile returned.

"I should like to think a colonel more formidable than a clergyman." He winked. "Unless, of course, you speak of Mr. Bradley—he I would not dare challenge."

She laughed.

How dearly he loved that sound!

The couple beside them stepped into the center for a double figure-eight. They quickly joined; both blushed for having nearly missed their turn.

Far too soon, the last chords faded away. Unwilling to relinquish his partner a moment earlier than necessary, he escorted her to the corner where Darcy and Miss Elizabeth stood.

"Oh, Jane, I am glad you are come," Miss Elizabeth said. "Mama called for the carriage already. She is quite concerned for Mr. Collins and wants us directly." She peeked over her shoulder.

Mrs. Bennet stood near the doorway, wearing a most unsettled countenance.

"Mama is content to ride with Mr. Collins?" Miss

Bennet's brows rose.

Miss Elizabeth glanced from Darcy to her sister. "I do not believe so. She would rather Papa joined her in the coach. I would be happy to ride home horseback if I could, but neither the horse nor I is dressed for it."

They all chuckled.

"Perhaps we might be of service." Darcy nodded at Fitzwilliam. "Our coach will accommodate six, though we are but four. No doubt, Miss Bingley would relish female companionship on the way back."

"What a capital idea!" Fitzwilliam grinned. Anything to extend his time with Miss Bennet was a fine notion.

"No, I fear it too great an imposition." Miss Bennet shook her head, though her eyes smiled.

"No inconvenience at all. Miss Bingley will certainly enjoy your company. Longbourn House is on the road to Netherfield. Where is the imposition in that?" Fitzwilliam nudged Darcy with his elbow.

"You said yourself it would ease your mother's burden," Darcy said.

"Perhaps we should ask Papa his preferences." Miss Elizabeth's gaze never wavered from Darcy.

"I see him near the card room." Miss Bennet and Miss Elizabeth nodded at one another and wove their way across the crowded room.

Mr. Bennet quickly agreed to the scheme and left his daughters in the care of the Netherfield party whilst he hurried off to attend his wife and cousin.

Darcy assisted the ladies into the carriage, the

Bingleys only too pleased for the additional company.

"What a jolly event!" Bingley bumped shoulders with both Darcy and Fitzwilliam.

Three sets of broad shoulders taxed the capacity of even Darcy's fine vehicle, but it was a small price to pay for Miss Elizabeth's presence.

"I have never attended a country ball before." Miss Bingley traced her fingers along the side glass as the coach pulled away from the assembly hall. Theirs was amongst the last to leave. "Are they usually so merry?"

"The ones in spring and early autumn are. In the winter, with fewer visitors in town, I fear we all grow tired of the confined and unvarying company." Miss Elizabeth chuckled. "You must be accustomed to a much wider circle of friends than you will find in Meryton."

"I thought you said you dined with four and twenty families?" Fitzwilliam turned against the side wall and freed a little space for Darcy to breathe.

"In Derbyshire, we are spread farther from our neighbors than you are here. We dine with but a dozen families on a regular basis." Darcy kept his eyes on Miss Elizabeth. Would she find so little society undesirable?

"An appealing sum, if good friends are included," Miss Elizabeth said.

"Indeed, the value of company cannot be measured merely by their numbers," Miss Bennet added.

Fitzwilliam, besotted puppy that he was, leaned forward, ready to capture every word and smile she might deign to bestow upon him. Darcy stifled his smirk.

"I find the London crush delightful. A large crowd

and a variety of companions are most exhilarating," Bingley said, "though I remain unable to convince Darcy."

"You must allow for differences among persons." Miss Bingley sighed. "Not everyone meets strangers as confidently as you."

"It is nothing to fear." Bingley shrugged.

Miss Elizabeth flashed a quick look at Darcy. "Not all are as fleet of tongue as you. Some struggle with what to say when meeting someone new."

Or someone they knew well. Darcy's cheeks heated. Her skin glowed in the moonlight, an ethereal light rivaled by the gentle sparkle of her wit. Oh, to be alone with her. "I believe Mr. Bradley would tell you, the aptness of a word is more significant than the volume of words spoken."

Fitzwilliam tapped Bingley's foot with his. "And, as you are well aware, he is always right."

"You may laugh." Darcy crossed his legs. "But he is rarely wrong."

"My Aunt Gardiner quite agrees with you." Miss Elizabeth quirked an eyebrow. "She relies on his advice and faithfully writes to us of his wisdom."

"He is a diligent correspondent with our aunt, despite the fact she moved from his parish many years ago," Miss Bennet said.

Darcy smiled. "I often come upon him at his writing desk—"

A crunch echoed through the coach. It lurched, swayed, and the right front side dropped. The ladies cried out and tumbled into each other.

"Is anyone injured?" Fitzwilliam shouted, hand braced against the ceiling.

"We are well." Miss Bennet pushed up from the fallen corner.

"We broke a wheel." Darcy wrenched the door open. "I will speak to the driver." He walked to the disabled side.

The driver met him. "Sorry sir, hit a rut in the road, and the fool thing cracked."

They knelt beside the broken wheel. Darcy ran his hand along the damage.

"It's broke clean through. Shall I take one of the horses and ride on to Netherfield for the Bingley carriage, sir?"

"Longbourn is closer."

Darcy jumped and looked over his shoulder. Miss Elizabeth stood, silhouetted against the full moon, hair temptingly disheveled. He rose and brushed his palms on his breeches.

"We are nearly at the drive to Longbourn House. Would it not be more expedient to go there?"

"I do not wish to impose on your father."

"As we imposed upon you?" She laughed.

He tipped his head and raised hands in surrender.

"Papa will not sleep until we are returned. Your man will not wake him."

He bowed and addressed his driver. "Go to Longbourn and inform Mr. Bennet of our situation. I am certain he will send his carriage."

"Very good, sir." The driver bowed and went to the horses.

Darcy turned to her. "Please accept my heartiest apologies for this inconvenience."

"You mean to tell me it was not your plan all along to break a wheel at this precise spot, where the road is wide enough to allow another vehicle to pass, but too far from either house for us to walk home? I thought you inordinately well planned, sir, yet you would deny your complicity in this scheme?" Her eyes twinkled, and her lips pursed into a kissable little bow.

He stepped closer. She did not retreat as she had from Collins. His heart beat a dance rhythm in his chest. Could she hear it? Would she dance with him here in the moonlight? Someday, he would dance with her under the full moon, not caring who could see them together. But not tonight, tonight he might only join in her mirth.

He inclined his head. "You uncovered my plot with your superior powers of deduction. I stand in awe of your remarkable abilities. No man will ever be able to keep a secret from you."

Even in the moonbeams, her cheeks colored. The teasing glint drained from her eyes, replaced by something he could not name but liked far better.

"My powers are neither superior nor remarkable; I simply love to laugh and will always find a way to do so."

"It is a rare talent." Her eyes drew him, held him fast in their snare. He tugged his coat straighter. A sharp corner in his pocket poked his ribs. Thank heavens! It would not do to forget!

He pulled out the volume he purchased from the bookseller and handed it to her. "I believe this belongs to Longbourn's library."

Miss Elizabeth turned the book over in her hands. She opened directly to the first page of chapter eight, and traced her uncle's inscription with her fingertip. Eyes wide, she stared at him. "It is indeed Papa's, a favorite gift from my uncle. How?"

"A book seller in Meryton."

"I do not understand."

"I am not certain, but I may have an explanation. Perhaps if you examine the volume carefully, you might come to better comprehend my conclusions." He separated the pages to reveal a folded note and closed the book.

A little crease appeared between her eyes, and her lips parted.

Voices approached from the far side of the carriage.

She slipped the book into her reticule. "Very well, sir."

"Thank you," he whispered.

By the time Elizabeth and Jane returned home, the rest of the family, save Papa, was all abed, asleep. Exhausted, they fell under their counterpanes with barely a muttered "good night."

Elizabeth awoke well after dawn. The pinks of sunrise were fading into the blues of the morning sky. None yet stirred, an ideal time for a walk to delve into the mystery of Mr. Darcy's book. She threw on her day dress and half boots, tucked the volume in her pocket and snatched her spencer, gloves and bonnet on the way out.

She paused at the stairs. They squeaked if one did not walk carefully. Hand on the railing, she stepped lightly and held her breath lest an ill-timed inhalation cause a noise. She dared not risk rousing anyone, particularly Mr. Collins, who would doubtless put a halt to her clandestine plans. In the foyer, she fastened her outerwear and fled outside.

She gulped in the morning air, fresh and full of potential, unmarred by the trials of the day. Glistening dew, her favorite gem, still twinkled on the grass blades and shrubbery. As a child, she relished the opportunity to rub her face in the dewdrops and enjoy the cool on her cheeks. They called to her, but today she could not indulge.

She needed privacy. Oakham Mount offered the best possibility, so she hastened there. At the top, she sat and retrieved the book from her pocket.

The embossed cover and bright colors had always fascinated Lydia while the contents had fascinated her. Papa treasured the volume. He was so careful with his books. How had it ended up in Meryton—

A breeze raised prickles along the back of her neck. She slipped into a sunbeam, but it did not ease them. Lydia had said something regarding Mr. Collins, a bookseller, and one of Papa's books. Elizabeth had dismissed it and chastised Lydia. She meant to check on the book when they had returned from town, but Mama had distracted her.

Her stomach clenched and hands trembled as she leafed through pages until Mr. Darcy's missive fell onto her lap. She turned it over. His seal held the letter fast and dared her to break it open.

She pulled in a deep breath and sighed. Her courage rose, and she cracked the seal. The crisp paper rustled and balked as she tried to smooth it over her lap. She bit her lower lip and focused on the neat, regular hand, as polished and proper as the man who penned it.

I pray you will forgive the forwardness of this note, madam. The news which I must impart to you is such I thought it best to permit you the utmost privacy to re-

ceive it. I am loath to bring distress to you, but faithful are the wounds of a friend—

A shudder ran down her spine. Mr. Collins had used those same words not long ago.

I came upon this volume at the bookseller and found the inscription identifying it as your father's. The shopkeep's description of the seller matched Mr. Collins. The bookseller went on to say that the seller desired to raise money for the payment of his obligations.

Be assured, my purchase was made with the intention to return it to your family, not defame your cousin.

How dear a friend! Were these the fruits of which Aunt Gardiner spoke?

Shortly after my acquisition, news of an alarming nature came to my attention, news with direct bearing upon your family. I have no option but to inform you though I know it will distress you. My aunt, Lady Catherine, discovered her vicar, your cousin Mr. Collins, carries debts of honor totaling over five thousand pounds.

She gasped. She closed her eyes and squeezed her temples. At the dinner party, Mr. Collins had spent the better part of the evening at the card table. If she had only listened to Lydia! He probably had wagered fifty pounds and Lydia was not a liar. Her stomach churned.

Whilst some in her position turn a blind eye to the vice of excessive gambling, my aunt does not. She offered to pay his debts on the condition he gave up gaming entirely and married. In specific, she desired for him to marry a daughter from the estate entailed upon him. She intimated such a wife would most effectively regulate his habits of excess. Her offer, though, was of limited duration, and his time is almost elapsed.

I do not wish to cast aspersions on his character, but if he paid attentions to your sisters or yourself, his affections may be influenced by a promise of deliverance from his debts.

Mr. Collins's warmth toward her was a farce. He wanted her for material advantage as surely as if she had been an heiress with a fortune to offer. Worse still—she swallowed the vile tang that rose in the back of her throat—he needed a keeper, not a wife. To think she had once considered him so attractive and desirable. She dropped her face to her hands.

No doubt, you will desire to share this intelligence with your father. Please do, in whatever way you deem appropriate. If you must reveal this letter to him, then do so. I am willing to accept his displeasure at my impropriety if it protects your family from harm.

Yours faithfully,

FD

Her heart somersaulted between warmth and revulsion. Mr. Darcy demonstrated himself the truest of friends, despite the difference in their social standings whilst Mr. Collins proved little more than a cad. She must find Papa immediately.

She hurried back to Longbourn to discover both Papa and Mr. Collins gone. Hill informed her Papa had taken him into Meryton to consult with a surgeon. She suspected Papa hoped the surgeon would deem the return to Longbourn too taxing and suggest Mr. Collins remain in town whilst he healed.

What a pleasing thought indeed! Yet, how would she contain herself until Papa returned?

Later that morning, Fitzwilliam walked with Bingley and his sister in the direction of Longbourn. The Bingleys had jumped at the suggestion of calling upon Longbourn. Darcy refused to join them, concerned for Miss Elizabeth's feelings. Dash it all! If he did not show his face once in a while, he might never convince her of his feelings. His dignified reserve could cost him a woman well worth winning. Ah well, that was Darcy's problem. Today, he had his own fair maiden to win.

He sighed and stopped short. Miss Bennet stood near the house, basket in hand, cutting flowers.

Bingley nudged him.

"I will join you shortly."

Bingley grinned and turned to his sister. "I hardly think so. We will offer your regards nonetheless."

Fitzwilliam tossed him a quick salute and sauntered toward the flower garden. He paused at a large oak and leant his shoulder against the rough bark.

Sunlight glistened golden off a lock escaped from her bonnet. He caught strains of a soft folk tune hummed under her breath. Some of the men he had served with on the continent had sung that refrain. He swallowed hard and shut his eyes.

Explosions, screams and the stench of gunpowder and blood overwhelmed him. He struck his head on the tree trunk and groaned. All his days here in Hertfordshire had been free of these ghosts. Why did they come to taunt him now? Would he never be delivered?

He stood in the midst of an idyll, tortured by the cries of dying men and the sound of cannon fire. She—so beautiful, so serene, so happy, tranquil in the face of any circumstance—and he a tormented man—what right had he to ask her for an alliance? She deserved a hero, not a broken down old soldier with nary a home to call his own.

Hoof beats pounded nearby. A large horse charged past, Fitzwilliam close on its heels.

She screamed and dropped her basket. He rushed her out of the horse's path and turned to the agitated creature. With one hand he grabbed the dangling reins, and with the other he soothed the horse. His confident, soft voice and expert touch soon brought it under control.

A moment later, a young groom ran up. "Beggin' your pardon, sir! Is the young lady well? I'm so sorry. The horse ain't properly trained yet. A dog scared 'im and 'e run off." A look of terror haunted the boy's eyes.

He passed the reins to the boy. "That's a fine animal, though a bit high strung. Keep to your training, and you will produce an excellent mount soon enough."

"Thank ye, sir." The boy bobbed an awkward bow and led the horse away.

He turned to her. She huddled against a tall bush. Quiet sobs racked her quivering form.

His angel required comfort. He eased his arm over her shoulder. "The boy took it away."

She clutched his lapels and buried her face in his

coat. "You must think me quite the fool. I am terrified of horses."

He smoothed his hand over her back. Bless the creature for sending her straight into his embrace.

She tilted her head up and wiped tears from her cheeks with her fingers.

He passed her a handkerchief.

"Foolish girl that I am, I did not bring one."

He brushed away another tear. "You are many things, but a fool is not among them. Will you sit with me?"

She nodded, and they sat on a nearby stone bench

"Thank you. I feel much safer now." Her eyes glittered.

If only he might kiss away those tears. "I am pleased."

"I feel like a princess delivered by her knight in armor." She peeked at him.

He laid his hand over hers. "You deserve a prince, not a soldier, broken and scarred from battle."

"I do not want a prince."

"What do you want?" He held his breath.

She licked her lips and glanced away. "My parents tried to shelter us from the reality of my mother's experiences. My Aunt Philips shared more than she should with me. I have walked in fear every day since I was twelve." She turned glittering, soulful eyes on him. "More than for castles or treasure or princes, I wish to feel safe."

He swallowed hard. What had happened to Mrs. Bennet? His shoulders twitched. Far too much could happen to a lady. "I thought you a tower of serenity."

"My mother's nerves are fragile, and she is oft fearful. If she sees fear in any of us…" She shrugged.

"You learned to hide your fear from her and from everyone. No one knew, not even your dearest sister, so you comforted your mother at the price of your own solace."

"I do not regret it." She bit her lip.

"Few things are in my power to give you, dearest Miss Bennet—Jane." He cupped her cheek with his palm. "But I can promise to protect and comfort you always." Could she hear his heart drum a tattoo against his ribs? "Would you allow me that chance? Be my wife, despite all I lack?"

She sucked in a soft breath. "Yes…Richard, because of all that you are, I will be proud to be your wife." She laid her hand over his against her face.

He crushed her to his chest. "I promise you will not regret me, Jane."

"I know."

Her bonnet slipped back, and he kissed the top of her head. Perhaps the old soldier could be her knight after all.

After an unsatisfying morning call on the surgeon, Bennet sat in his carriage with Collins on the way to Longbourn. The coach hit every rut and rock in the road. His nerves frayed further and further with each jolt. Collins muttered and groaned under his breath.

Mr. Whittington insisted none of Collins's bones were broken. Moreover, the swelling did not even indicate a bad sprain. He had no physical evidence to substantiate Collins's complaints. A well-wrapped foot, a walking stick, a few herbs for a compress and a generous bill were the best Whittington had to offer.

Bennet glanced at Collins. He slumped in his seat and gazed through the side glass with a mildly sour expression. Even attractive young men might experience bad days. Still, what part of his recent behavior resulted from unfortunate timing and what from deeper character flaws? He shook his head and stifled a chuckle. To think he agreed with Lydia, of all people.

He stroked his chin. If he and his youngest were like-minded, darker forces were surely afoot. It was time for Collins's visit to end. Whittington had insisted Collins should be back to rights in two days, so he would insist Collins arrange travel to Kent and depart in four.

Bennet pressed into the squabs and sighed. His home would soon return to normal. He might lack the mortgage he hoped to obtain, but he had made do this long and could continue well enough.

A mile from Longbourn, Collins found his tongue. In the few minutes it took to reach the house, his ears ached, and he nearly complained of his poor nerves. Quoting Fanny now? Collins had to go.

Bennet pushed the door open and hopped down. "My man will assist you."

"You are most gracious, sir—"

He strode away and did not look back. A door and a few feet of hall stood between him and blessed solitude and silence.

"Mr. Bennet, sir," Hill curtsied, "Colonel Fitzwilliam is waiting for you in the parlor."

He groaned.

Hill peered into his face, her brow furrowed like a spring field. "Do you wish me to send him away, sir?"

A loud clatter echoed behind him.

"Ugh!"

Bennet whirled. Oh, rot! Was Collins trying to drive him to Bedlam? "Hill, call Franks."

She bobbed and dashed away.

Colonel Fitzwilliam took her place. "May I be of use?"

"Yes, yes." Bennet hurried to the front steps.

Fitzwilliam shadowed him.

Bennet stooped over Collins's sprawled form. "Why did you not wait?"

"I did not wish to trouble you."

Bennet huffed and grabbed Collins's upper arm.

Fitzwilliam slipped between them. "Allow me, sir." He wedged his hand under Collins's arm. "Can you stand?"

"No, my ankle, you see—"

"Not to worry." In two breaths, Fitzwilliam hoisted Collins up and across his shoulders.

Collins grunted. One arm and one leg dangled impotently over Fitzwilliam's chest while his head lolled behind the colonel's shoulder.

"You are not the first man I have carried in from the battlefield."

Bennet held his breath and bit his tongue lest he laugh in Collins's face. At last, Collins was being treated with appropriate deference to his injury. He followed the two men inside.

While Hill directed Fitzwilliam upstairs, Bennet slipped into his study and poured two glasses of port. Whatever he desired, Fitzwilliam certainly had earned an interview. Bennet eased into his favorite chair.

Fitzwilliam rapped on the doorframe. "May I come in, sir?" His disheveled hair and disarranged cravat gave testament to his recent service.

"Come in, come in, and close the door behind you."

Fitzwilliam shut the door quietly and sat.

Bennet handed him a glass. "You earned this."

"Thank you."

They sipped their port in companionable silence, another point in the colonel's favor.

Glass empty, Bennet propped his feet on Lizzy's favorite footstool. "I expect you have a reason for this interview? I cannot imagine you waiting in my parlor for the opportunity to hoist my cousin upon your shoulder like a sack of grain."

"I pray I did not cause offense, sir." Fitzwilliam's eyebrows flashed up, and the corner of his lips quirked.

"Well, you may rest easy on that point. I have rarely been so diverted."

"I am pleased to be of service." Fitzwilliam chuckled and leaned his elbows on his knees. "I come on a most serious errand."

Bennet looked deep into Fitzwilliam's eyes. His stomach knotted.

"The creases in your forehead suggest you know why I am here."

"Jane?"

Fitzwilliam nodded. His eyes lost their focus and an easy smile lifted his lips.

Calf-eyed puppy. No, this man was certainly no puppy, but his affection was appealing, nonetheless. "She has no fortune. One in your circumstances generally seeks at least twenty thousand, or so I hear."

"That is the going rate for second sons." Fitzwilliam tapped his fingertips together. "You might say I am a bargain, though not one of His Majesty's bad bargains."

Bennet chuckled. A sense of humor, particularly a wry one was another point to his credit. "Why would you select a bride so imprudently?"

"I might try and spin you a flowery sonnet after the fashion of your cousin. Alas, I lack the skill. Simply, I admire your daughter more than any woman I have ever known. While a fortune does increase one's comfort, it does not ensure an amiable life with one's partner. The army gave me enough battle for a lifetime. I wish for peace in my home above everything else. My fortune is sufficient to secure a comfortable home and lifestyle for her and her children, not unlike what she is accustomed to."

"A significant step down for you, though?"

Fitzwilliam folded his arms over his chest. "What you mean to ask is whether I will miss the lifestyle in which I grew up? Will I grow to resent my wife for leaving me impoverished? Will my eye and person stray in my dissatisfaction?"

"I am familiar with what is acceptable in the spheres in which you travel."

Fitzwilliam sighed and rolled his eyes. "I am well acquainted with my brother's lifestyle. His wife tolerates a great deal to be viscountess."

"You do not approve?"

"No."

Bennet cocked his head and lifted his eyebrow. How unusual—and pleasing.

"I will not violate my sister's confidences. Suffice to say, I would not cause such pain to any woman, much less one I admire as much as I do as your daughter."

"Will you resent relinquishing that society—"

Fitzwilliam barked a coarse laugh. "How little you understand the nature of high society."

"You could live without it?"

"I detest it."

Bennet leaned back. "Strong words, especially from one in your station."

"True, nonetheless. I did my time in the marriage mart, and I will be happy to leave it behind. Not all battles take place with rifles and bayonets." Fitzwilliam's shoulders twitched.

"Is my daughter aware of your battle scars?"

"Yes, and with total honesty. She is a balm to my soul—what I want more than anything in my home." He met Bennet with a steady gaze.

"Your acquaintance is one of short duration. Surely it would be better to prolong your courtship, so you may know each other better."

"I do not need more time to be certain. I know. I watched too many men die regretting a lady not wed. I vowed once I found my lady, I would not waste any of the precious time given us. I will honor you as her father, and give you all the deference I do to my own father. If you insist we will wait. I ask you, as a son, do not require it of us."

Jane deserved this sort of man, one who saw past her beauty and treasured her character. Bennet sighed. "Only this week, I expressed my disapproval of short courtships, but you have my consent. You are fortunate to have won her affection." He rose and extended his hand.

Fitzwilliam stood and clasped it. "Indeed, I am, and I will not forget it."

"Be sure you do not." Bennet pressed his lips and

swallowed hard. "One day you will realize, a daughter is difficult to lose, even to a good man."

"I hope you will advise me on how to do it so graciously."

Chapter 13

ON REFLECTION, BENNET REALIZED he should have extracted a promise for a few days' peace as part of his agreement with Fitzwilliam. The notion came too late for the damage to be undone. Jane recognized the pleasure it would give her mother so wasted no time sharing her good fortune.

Mrs. Bennet's raptures stretched well into the night, extended, no doubt, by Collins's not unwelcome absence from the dining table and drawing room. Kitty sketched at least three wedding gowns before he excused himself and left the ladies to their enjoyments.

In the quiet of his chambers, his mind wandered from the pages of his book. Giggles and happy voices kept intruding. Between Pierce and Fitzwilliam, the hedgerows no longer threatened his family. He could devote himself to worry about their happiness, rather than their support. For the first time in two and twenty years, the entail mattered not. He released a deep breath and dropped into his pillows.

Now, where was such a man for his Lizzy? Collins had proven entirely inappropriate. She needed a partner to cherish her lively mind, one to relish her teasing and not think less of her for her love of laughter. Perhaps that Darcy fellow would do.

How much like Fanny he sounded! He chuckled. No doubt he needed quiet and solitude to restore him to proper masculine lines of thought. He blew out his candle and closed his eyes.

The next morning he slipped, undetected, into his study. He propped his feet in front of the fireplace and opened his book to where he had left off the night before. Ahh, few pleasures in life compared to those offered by a good book, enjoyed in the comfort of one's own home.

Three pages later, at the start of his favorite passage—*knock…knock…knock.*

"Come." He slapped the volume shut and threw his head into the soft upholstery. What was it about his closed door that invited interruption?

The door creaked, feet shuffled and a walking stick clacked—Collins. Dare he rescind the invitation now?

Collins fell into the chair nearest Bennet. "I will speak to you, sir."

"Indeed?"

"I insist." He rapped the cane on the floor.

"Why do you take that tone with me? The early hour is no excuse for ill-manners."

"You lied to me." The stick crashed down.

Bennet jerked straight. "How dare you accuse me of—"

"You deny it?"

"I do not have the pleasure of understanding you."

"Given your tendency to prevaricate, I am wholly unsurprised."

"Explain yourself or leave. I will not be insulted in my own study." Bennet gripped the arms of his chair.

Collins pitched forward, deep furrows in his brow. "Did you not tell me you disapproved of brief courtships and thus dissuaded me from pursuing your daughter?"

"I recall the conversation."

"Yesterday, you approved an engagement between your eldest daughter and Colonel Fitzwilliam after an acquaintance of less than two months!"

"What is that to you?"

"I believed you a man of his word. I almost granted you permission to mortgage this property based on your promise to use the money in accordance to your plans. How can I possibly trust you?" Collins's eyes bulged in his florid face.

Bennet sprang to his feet. "Do you forget you denied my request? Why judge my character now?" He stalked to his desk. "Enough of this!"

"Enough indeed!" He threw the stick aside and followed Bennet.

"What do you want?" Bennet slammed his fist on the desk. The inkpot rattled.

Collins braced his arms on the opposite side of the desktop and pressed close. "Your daughter as my wife."

"I will not compel any of my daughters into marriage."

"Grant me the same privilege you afforded the colonel. Permit me to offer for her and promise to consent when she agrees."

"*When*? Do you not mean *if*?" Bennet's lip curled into a sneer.

"She will not refuse me."

"You think highly of yourself."

"I am not fine enough for your daughter?" He tossed his head. "I am your heir, your equal."

"Whilst you may be a gentleman, you are not my equal, either in wealth or in wisdom. My daughter will have no scruples in familiarizing you with that fact."

"Will you give her the opportunity?"

Bulldog determination was not always a pleasing trait in a man. "I will concede on one condition."

"What? You desire your mortgage?"

Bennet knocked a book off the desk. "Hang the bloody mortgage."

"Such language! Most unbecoming in a *gentleman*."

"You may petition my daughter for her hand. When she refuses you—"

"If she does—"

"When she does, you will leave my home and not come back during the course of my lifetime. I will not entertain you under my roof again."

"You intend to throw me out?"

What a pleasing image! If only Fitzwilliam were there to do the job. "Your patroness desires your return. You will leave."

"My injury, you cannot expect—"

"Is obviously inconsequential. You stand before me with no difficulty." Bennet pointed at the fallen walking stick.

Collins gasped and grabbed the back of the nearest

chair. "The heat of the moment overrode—"

"Now who prevaricates?"

"Have you no charity—"

"The surgeon found no injury. You are fit to travel, and I am done with you. Leave me now." He squeezed his temples with his hand and covered his eyes.

"But—" Collins staggered toward the desk.

"Enough." Bennet grumbled under his breath. He strode to the doorway. "Hill!"

She appeared at his shoulder a heartbeat later.

"Get my man and instruct him to escort Mr. Collins to his room. I am going out." He stormed through the foyer and out the front door.

Insufferable man! A waste of good looks and charm on a weak mind and questionable morals. Just a few more days. Lizzy would dispatch his arrogance and leave Collins to slink away like a rat back to its hole. It could not come soon enough.

Mr. Collins's secrets burned in Elizabeth's belly. Oh, to release her burden to the one who should rightfully carry it. But when?

She sat in Papa's study on the footstool near his favorite chair. Papa's book lay tucked inside her writing desk while she engaged in the most mind-numbing task she could find. Open journals surrounded her. She furiously transcribed receipts and instructions from Mama's ledgers into her own.

Marriage had seemed like such a faraway business until recently. Losing Mary was difficult enough, but now Jane as well? How cruel that their happiness portended her loneliness! Perhaps she and Kitty—no, it would not be the same.

Selfish, unfeeling girl to begrudge them so!

Best return to Mama's receipts.

To clean breeches, a particular ratio of ox-gall to fuller's earth was most efficacious.

Four more pages and her hand cramped. Mama often warned her not to clutch her pencil so tightly. She should have learned by now. Obstinate, headstrong girl!

She dropped the pencil and pressed her face into her hands. Where was Papa to reassure her, to remind her of her admirable traits, that she met his expectations and was good enough? Mama did not mean to make her feel small, or so Jane insisted. She was just different to other girls, and Mama simply did not understand. Then again, Mama did not understand Papa either. Would she ever please Mama?

She stretched. Thunder rumbled in the distance. A sharp breeze whisked the scent of rain through the half open window. She clambered to her feet to close it.

The door opened and slammed shut. She jumped and whirled about. Papa never slammed the door. Mr. Collins strode into the room.

"Sir! Common courtesy requires you wait to be admitted before entering a closed room." She rubbed her hands over her apron.

"Excuse me. I did not realize you were here." He smiled, but his eyes belied the expression.

"This is my father's study. I must ask you to remove yourself until Papa returns." She balanced against the front edge of the desk. Where was his cane?

"I think not, Cousin Elizabeth."

If not for her hairpins, her hair would have stood on end like a cat rubbed wrong.

He stepped closer. "Do you recall our earlier conversation?"

Her cheeks cooled to ice. "We spoke of many things."

"I know it is the way of delicate females to extend a man's suspense by such means, but I beseech you, do not continue in this game."

"Rest assured, I do not play games." She swallowed hard. "Leave this room! Your presence here is highly inappropriate."

"My dear, your modesty only adds to your other perfections." He stared at her bosom.

She rearranged her fichu. How quickly might Hill prepare a bath? Was there enough scented soap in the house to wash away this stench?

"Almost as soon as I entered this house, I singled you out as the companion of my future life. My violent feelings will not be repressed. I must tell you of my love."

Her throat strangled her voice into a squeak. "I do not wish to hear this."

His lip curled back, and he inched nearer. "That does not change what I must do. I mot ardently, passionately—"

She sidestepped around the desk, opening her way to the door. "Stop! I never desired your good opinion and never knowingly sought it. Accept my thanks for the compliment you pay me, though I must decline you. Go no further! I implore you! This must become unpleasant for both of us if you insist."

He pressed his hand to his heart. "Before I am run away with my feelings, I should state for you my reasons for choosing to marry. First, I am convinced it will add greatly to my happiness." His eyes raked her body.

A walk in the storm might be necessary to wash his stain away.

"Secondly, I think it a right thing for every clergyman to set the example of matrimony in his parish. Moreover," his voice dropped to a purr, "it is the particular recommendation of the very noble lady, my patroness. 'Mr. Collins,' she declared, 'you must marry.' The notice and kindness of Lady Catherine De Bourgh is not the least of the advantages in my power to offer."

She shuddered. "Upon my word, sir, your response is extraordinary. I am perfectly serious in my refusal. You must excuse me—"

He waved off her protests and grabbed her hand. "I am by no means discouraged and hope to lead you to the altar ere long. I know it is the established custom of your sex to reject a man on the first application. Perhaps you even said as much to encourage my suit, consistent with the true delicacy of the female character."

She snatched her hand away. "Are you touched in the head? How am I to convince you?"

"A woman like you is in no position to refuse."

"A woman always has the right of refusal."

"Your fortune is so small it negates all your other charms. Without your eldest sister's beauty, I cannot imagine you will receive another offer of marriage. So, I must conclude you are not serious in your rejection." He stepped through the short distance between them and backed her into the bookcase on the far wall.

A large volume thudded to the floor.

She jumped and balled her fists. "I cannot accept you."

He grabbed her chin and forced her to look in his eyes. "Your father is an old fool who failed to provide you sufficient dowry, failed to bring you out into London society to seek proper matches and failed to run Longbourn to its potential. I offer you a home in the shadow of Rosings Park and an assurance of shelter and sustenance for your mother and sisters on his passing!" His forehead turned blotchy red.

She quivered under his touch. "My future is none of your concern."

"I thought you a sensible woman."

The stench of his hot breath soured her stomach. She pulled away from his hand. "What sensible woman wants a man who would gamble away a fortune he does not possess? I know your dear patroness discovered your debts and bribed you to take a wife—one she thinks will rein you in like a governess does a child." She darted around him.

He blocked her path. "You should consider your words more carefully. You have all the makings of a confirmed shrew."

"You are a hypocrite in the worst possible form. It sickens me that you should be a clergyman. You fail in every regard to the task." She pushed his chest. "I will not marry you."

He forced her into the shelves. "Why, with so little endeavor at civility, am I thus rejected?" He glanced over his shoulder and knocked another book to the floor. “I offer you everything a woman desires, a home and good income—”

“To lose on cards in a single evening? I pity the parish forced to suffer under your weakness of character." She thrust him aside and dashed for the door.

He grabbed her arm. She stumbled and barely kept herself upright.

“You are the last man in the world—”

“I perfectly comprehend your feelings, though they do not matter to me in the slightest.” He shoved her.

She fell into the bookcase. “Leave me alone!”

He leaned close to her face. “You shall marry me.”

“Never!” She kicked his shin. Pain shot through her foot. Wellingtons would have been much better suited to the task than her slippers.

He clutched his leg with one hand and grabbed for her with the other. His fingertips caught the hem of her bodice. The fine muslin ripped.

She shrieked.

“Scream, cousin, scream! Bring in witnesses to this scene!” He pressed forward.

She ducked under his arm. The carpet bunched under her feet, but she regained her balance and sprinted away.

He turned to follow. His foot caught under the edge of the rug, and he fell. The thud blended with a thunderclap.

She flung the door open and pelted down the corridor. None of the family was home. She could not remain here with him.

She fled down the garden path into the cover of the trees and ran until her breath ran out. Clutching a tree trunk for support, she cast about. Thank heaven— no sign of him following.

Her dress gaped open. Nothing less than Kitty's sewing kit could hold it together. She fumbled with the knot in her fichu. A branch rattled behind her. She squealed.

Silly girl, only a bird, nonetheless, she set her feet into motion. Trembling hands vexed her; but after three attempts, she arranged her fichu to disguise the damage to her gown. Awkward, to be sure—

Flash. Crack!

She screamed and jumped. The wind whipped her dress. A sharp chilled edge sliced through the meager protection of her skirts. Cold raindrops splattered her cheeks. Thunder boomed. The drops turned to sheets driven by shrieking, frigid wind. A vast expanse of gloomy clouds promised the storm would not abate soon. She needed shelter.

Netherfield! Had she come so far? Yes, behind the murky sheets of rain, the outline of the house was visible. Her feet slipped in the mud. She crashed to her knees. The dread of Mr. Collins spurred her on.

Numbed by the cold, she felt nothing as she ran. At last, the front steps. She forced herself to slow and walk carefully. A fall on these would be far less forgiving than the mud. She rapped on the door. Please, let it open soon.

The housekeeper cracked the door open and hurried her inside, calling for the maids to bring towels and blankets.

"Miss Elizabeth?" Mr. Darcy stared at her over the housekeeper's shoulder.

Her teeth chattered too hard for a reply.

He stripped off his coat and wrapped it around her.

Oh, it was so very warm. She pulled it tight.

He guided her into the drawing room and helped her sit near the fire.

"What happened?" He looked deep into her eyes. "I can see, something happened—Collins?" He spoke the name like a curse.

She nodded, throat too tight for anything more than a whisper to slip through. "I…I…was waiting for Papa…to tell him. He came…"

His nostrils flared with heavy breaths. "Did he?"

"No." She swallowed the sob poised to escape.

"Thank God."

"Miss Elizabeth!" Mr. Bingley called from the doorway. He charged in with Miss Bingley, Jane, Kitty and two maids trailing behind.

Mr. Darcy backed away. Jane and Kitty took his place. One maid pressed a bowl of hot broth into her hands. She sipped it while the other maid plied her with warm, dry things. Her shivering faded into deep weariness.

Slim, sure hands guided her upstairs to a bath and finally, a delightfully heated bed piled high with pillows and two counterpanes. She was asleep before the door clicked shut.

Darcy slipped out to allow the ladies to tend Miss Elizabeth. Despite his best efforts, she had been harmed. He scrubbed his face with his palms, unable to scour away the image of her huddled in his coat.

Fitzwilliam came alongside and grabbed his elbow.

He guided Darcy into the study and closed the door. "What happened?"

They dropped into a pair of chairs near the fireplace. Darcy screwed his eyes shut and shook his head.

"This was more than getting caught in the rain."

Darcy groaned. "Collins."

"Collins?"

"She said little, only that it was him and that she escaped before he truly harmed her." He knotted his hands into fists. "Her dress was ripped, though whether it was by him or her dash through the storm only she knows. I fear the hell-hound may claim to have 'accidentally' compromised her to try and force her into marriage."

"I cannot imagine her father would approve, given my discussion with him." Fitzwilliam's lips turned up in a lopsided grin.

"I see no humor in this."

"I grant you, this is most serious, but remember, she was not materially harmed. More importantly, she is here now and safe. We may accompany the Miss Bennets home tomorrow and talk with Mr. Bennet ourselves."

"I should have told him myself." Darcy jumped up and paced in front of the fire.

"Do not find more reasons to wallow in guilt. You were right to allow Miss Elizabeth the privacy to manage the affairs of her family as she thought best. When your friends became involved with Georgiana's—"

"Collins appears little better than Wickham. I came here to escape—"

"You must come to grips with this thing, not escape it. The look in her eyes will haunt you until the day you die."

Darcy bounced his fist off the mantle "Precisely how is that useful to me?"

"As long as you try to find escape, you will spend your life in hiding and never achieve peace. Trust me, I know."

"What do you recommend?"

"At the risk of sounding like Bradley—"

"Anything but that!"

Fitzwilliam joined him at the fireplace. "I will tell him what you said."

"And I will tell him you tried to play sage."

"Not play his role, merely relay what he told me."

Fitzwilliam had sought Bradley's counsel?

"I see I have your attention. Good." Fitzwilliam nodded.

Lightning flashed very near the window. Thunder rattled the glass with a boom so loud their ears rang. They both jumped.

"Bloody hell!" Fitzwilliam rubbed his arms and looked around. "Did you hear that?"

"The door? Again?" Darcy poked his head into the hall. "No, it cannot be possible."

The front door creaked open. Bingley charged into the foyer.

"Mr. Collins?" Bingley cried. "Do come in."

Fitzwilliam's jaw dropped. "What is he doing here?"

Darcy stormed out, Fitzwilliam on his heels.

"Please forgive my intrusion." Collins mopped water from his face with a soggy handkerchief. "I got caught in this storm whilst walking. Might I take shelter here?"

Darcy skidded in the puddle surrounding Collins. "No, you may not."

"I have never known you to have a sense of humor, Darcy." Bingley laughed. "Of course, you may stay. Consider yourself welcome. We shall be a merry party for dinner tonight as Miss Elizabeth arrived in much the same condition, not so long ago." He waved the housekeeper into action. After she led Collins away, Bingley slapped Darcy's shoulder. "This is quite a bit of oddness, the two of them here in the storm."

"Very odd indeed. Does it not make you wonder—" Darcy said, his eyes fixed on the staircase.

"Do tell me, why ever would you try and turn the sodden fellow out in that tempest? That is most unlike you."

Darcy whirled. "Bingley, you must—"

"That is not how you treat a rival for a woman's affections. Mistreating him will not win you favor in the lady's eyes." Bingley cocked his head, brows raised. "Tell him, Fitzwilliam. Go calm your jealous cousin whilst I see to my newest guest." He snickered and trotted up the stairs.

Darcy growled under his breath, hands working in and out of fists.

"Take a deep breath. Losing your temper now will not serve your purposes." Fitzwilliam led him back to the library.

"Why does Bingley have to be such a generous host? We should have warned him about Collins as soon as we knew his true nature. Miss Elizabeth came here to escape the cad, not be trapped with him." He glanced over his shoulder. "Even though his target has been Miss Elizabeth, you cannot imagine any of her sisters are safe from him, including your Miss Bennet."

Fitzwilliam's jaw hardened, his eyes narrow and cold. "Perhaps this is the best thing," he said through his teeth.

"How is that?"

"We know what he is about. With him in the house, we can keep watch and properly protect our ladies from his designs." Fitzwilliam clasped his hands behind his back and nodded grimly. "Their father has not done an admirable job in protecting them. We shall do better."

Chapter 14

TWO HOURS LATER, in a dress borrowed from Miss Bingley, Elizabeth steeled herself for company and descended the grand staircase. Voices sounded in the drawing room. She paused, eyes closed. Mr. Bradley, Kitty, a laugh—Colonel Fitzwilliam's, Jane must be within as well. Absent was the one voice she most wished to hear—Mr. Darcy's.

Perhaps it was best. What did he think of her now? Few in his station took pity on a woman put upon. After all, she should have fled the room immediately on Mr. Collins's entrance. At least she could rely on Mr. Darcy's discretion, though she would rather rely on his regard.

She summoned her courage, smoothed her skirt, lifted her chin and strode into the room.

"Lizzy!" Kitty met her at the door. "We worried

you might take ill. You look cold." She unwound the shawl from her shoulders and draped it over Elizabeth's.

"I am quite well, thank you." She pulled the wrap tight. Did her smile appear as false as it felt?

"Would you care for some tea?" Miss Bingley asked.

"Yes, thank you." Elizabeth settled next to Jane.

Mr. Bradley's eyes bore into her, the same way Papa's did.

She turned aside. He knew her secret too, but how? Did he read her so easily, or was Mr. Darcy's discretion not to be trusted?

Thunder rattled the windows.

"What a beastly storm!" Kitty dragged another chair to their group and flounced into it. "You chose an awful day to get caught out."

She shrugged and dodged Mr. Bradley's gaze.

"You are courageous, walking in the woods as you do. I would be too frightened to go beyond the gardens by myself." Miss Bingley handed her a teacup.

Elizabeth wrapped her fingers around the warm cup, savoring the mild burn on her palms. "I have traipsed these woods since girlhood and never found anything in them to fear." She swallowed hard.

"Sometimes society is far more frightening than the wilderness." Mr. Bradley lifted an eyebrow.

Kitty cocked her head and blinked. "I cannot imagine why. I enjoy society far more than Papa allows us to engage in it."

Mr. Bingley appeared in the doorway. "You look much improved, Miss Elizabeth. I am glad you arrived on my doorstep before the worst of the storm struck." He smiled his characteristic grin.

Kitty beamed at him with an expression that reminded Elizabeth of Lydia.

Mr. Collins strode in on Mr. Bingley's heels. "How odd both you and I should be caught in the same tempest and still not encounter one another in the wood."

Elizabeth gasped. Her hand shook hard enough to splash tea from her cup. "As vast as the woods are, coming upon each other would be more surprising."

"Tea, sir?" Miss Bingley opened the inlaid tea caddy.

Mr. Collins slid a chair close to Elizabeth. "Thank you, yes."

She inched toward Miss Bingley, face as cold as the window glass.

Mr. Bradley glanced from Mr. Collins to her, questions in his raised eyebrows.

She ducked away, eyes burning. Thunder cracked and a fresh wave of rain pelted against the windowpane. A frigid gust blew through the room. She shivered, though no one else did. Had she imagined it?

Mr. Bradley pressed his hand against the chair's arms. "A letter requires my attention, but this knee of mine troubles me in foul weather." He heaved himself out of his chair. "Miss Elizabeth, would you assist me to the study?"

She jumped to her feet. Anything to be out of *his* presence. "I am happy to."

"Allow me." Mr. Bingley offered his arm.

"It is no trouble." She hurried to Mr. Bradley's side.

"Forgive me, Mr. Bingley. Miss Elizabeth is a much prettier partner." He grasped the crook of her elbow.

Mr. Bingley bowed his head. "How can I argue with a man of such wisdom?"

"Perhaps it is best you escort Mr. Bradley, sir. Propriety demands my cousin should not be alone…" Mr. Collins said.

She stiffened. Total hypocrisy to add to his list of sins? Of course, how fitting. "Mr. Bradley is practically family to me. My father would not regard *his* behavior improper, nor mine."

"I hardly think—" Mr. Bingley tugged his coat straight.

"A man must always consider the delicacy of those under his protection." Mr. Collins glared at her.

Her heart pounded in time with the raindrops on the window pane.

Mr. Bingley snorted and sidled between Mr. Collins and Elizabeth. "Do you imply I am not…"

"Come," Mr. Bradley whispered.

They slipped away, leaving Mr. Bingley to take offense at Mr. Collins.

She held her breath, but no one followed.

"I question the wisdom of insulting the one who offers you shelter from a storm."

"I am not surprised." She peered at him. He did not lean upon her as hard as she expected. "Your knee does not pain you as much as you claim."

They entered the study.

Mr. Bradley patted her hand. "No, though Collins's presence pains you far more than you confess."

Her knees melted, and she clutched his arm. Her throat pinched shut.

He slid a footstool near the worn brocade chair. "Sit." He eased into the seat.

She tittered and perched on the stool. "My mother does not approve of footstools."

"Good for us she is not here. I find them most comfortable." He laced his fingers and tapped his thumbs to his chest. "Now, explain to me what I saw in the drawing room. What happened with Collins?"

Her cheeks tingled. She stared at him, unable to force speech.

His eyes demanded an answer.

"Mr. Darcy told you?"

"He did not betray you when he sought my advice…" He pinched his temples. "My dear, I had a daughter who was imposed upon by such a man. She died in my arms, in childbirth with his babe."

She gasped.

"That is why he told me. I understand as only a father might, I understand."

She pressed a fist to her mouth to contain a strangled sob.

"And I do as well." Mr. Darcy stood in the doorway.

Mr. Bradley waved him in.

He hunkered down on the floor beside them. "My sister, too…I do not condemn you."

She gazed into eyes so tender, so warm she could not blink or even breathe. His good opinion was not lost. Her lips slipped into a smile. Had a sunbeam snuck past the heavy clouds outside?

"Lizzy?" Jane hovered at the door with Colonel Fitzwilliam.

Mr. Bradley nodded, and Jane rushed in and knelt beside her.

"Do not worry, I…I am well." Elizabeth whispered.

Colonel Fitzwilliam pulled a pair of chairs close to Mr. Bradley. Elizabeth scooted over and patted the space for Jane. Mr. Darcy sat next to Colonel Fitzwilliam.

"Better to keep him where you may be able to observe him." Mr. Bradley harrumphed.

"Could it be a misunderstanding?" Jane asked.

Elizabeth exhaled a chuckle. "Oh, Jane, only you. No, his intent was clear."

"The storm will not abate. We must stay the night." Jane shuddered and turned to Fitzwilliam

Elizabeth cringed. "Does Mr. Bingley know?"

"No, and I was unable to persuade him to put Collins back out in the tempest," Mr. Darcy said.

Colonel Fitzwilliam sniggled. "I would be happy to do the honors."

"Bingley might be offended enough now to consider it." Mr. Bradley jerked his head toward the doorway.

"Would that it were so." Mr. Darcy rolled his eyes.

Colonel Fitzwilliam slid off his chair and knelt beside Jane. "Do not fear." He took her hand in both of his. "Collins will not harm you or your sisters."

"No, he will not." Mr. Darcy leaned toward Elizabeth. "Trust me, please."

From the edge of her vision, Mr. Bradley nodded, just barely.

"I will, but you must tell me your plans. I will not be managed like a damsel in distress." She lifted her chin and squared her shoulders.

Mr. Bradley laughed until tears flowed. He rubbed them away with the backs of his hands. "Now that is the Miss Elizabeth I expected. Of course, you shall know all the plans. In fact, you must be part of their design."

Darcy found dinner a pleasant, if somewhat unconventional, affair. The housekeeper predicted extra guests, though not quite early enough for the kitchen to fully prepare. Cold meats, cheese and rolls took their places with vegetables and hot dishes on the table, along with a soup that tasted a tad watered down. Merry talk and toasts to Miss Bennet and Fitzwilliam's engagement covered any remaining awkwardness, despite Collins's attempts to lecture about reaching beyond one's appointed social sphere.

Miss Bingley suggested the ladies withdraw, but her brother insisted cigars and port did not hold the appeal of remaining in their company. So, they all withdrew together. Darcy escorted Miss Elizabeth, much to his satisfaction. Though only a shadow of its usual brilliance, her smile sent warmth coursing through his veins.

A fire blazed in the drawing room, warm and inviting against the still howling winds. Candles glinted off mirrors and glass, filling the chamber with playful flickers. Except for certain company, the setting could not have been more agreeable.

"What about a game of whist?" Bingley rubbed his palms together.

Miss Elizabeth stiffened and looked at the floor.

Darcy cleared his throat. "You will forgive me if I decline."

"Mr. Darcy hates cards and finds pleasure only in reading, for he is a very great reader and does little else." Collins's razor-edged glare belied his light and teasing voice.

"I deserve neither such praise nor such censure. Whilst I am an avid reader, I do find pleasure in many things, though not in cards. My days are quite busy with more than reading, I assure you."

Collins tossed his head and dropped on the settee near the fire. "I suppose you take great interest in the lives of those beneath you."

Darcy turned aside lest he roll his eyes. Collins was quick to occupy the best seat in the room, though Bradley should be the one to have it. "If you refer to my tenants, yes, I am most involved. Their welfare is as dear to me as my own. I cannot succeed save they prosper."

"That explains your singular tastes in—"

Fitzwilliam stepped between Darcy and Collins. "Perhaps the ladies might play for us, unless Bradley brought his instrument."

"An excellent idea." Darcy retrieved the violin from the bookshelf and pressed it into Bradley's hands.

They exchanged a long glance. Bradley rarely exhibited, especially with young ladies present. Darcy lifted his brows and cocked his head. Bradley took the instrument.

Miss Kitty clapped softly. "I did not know you played. How lovely!"

"Do any of you gentlemen sing?" Bradley scanned the room.

"My brother does." Miss Bingley nudged him forward.

"Excellent, come join me. You too, Fitzwilliam."

Fitzwilliam sighed, but obeyed.

Bradley extended an open hand. "What of you, Mr. Collins?"

"If you insist." He pushed up from the settee and joined them.

Bingley brought out a case of sheet music, and they conferred over it. Darcy stationed himself behind Miss Elizabeth and Miss Bennet.

Collins sang surprisingly well, clearly the superior of the three. What a shame his character did not match the beauty of his song.

The ladies displayed next, singing and turning pages for one another as they performed. Though Miss Bingley played most skillfully, Miss Elizabeth's performance entertained him best, particularly the moment she met his gaze and sang solely for him. Pemberley was incomplete without her song. He would not leave Hertfordshire without her promise.

Fitzwilliam joined Miss Bennet in singing a duet, accompanied on the pianoforte by Miss Bingley. Miss Kitty and Bingley came in at the second verse, and by the third, the entire company sang along.

"Shall we play a game now?" Miss Kitty asked.

Miss Bingley looked at Bingley with little girl's eyes. "What a delightful notion!"

"Caroline did not prefer parlor games, so we rarely indulged." Bingley shrugged. "What do you suggest?"

"I know, I know." Kitty clapped softly. "How about Aviary?"

Darcy winced. Hopefully no one noticed. He disliked most games, too.

"What an excellent idea!" Fitzwilliam winked at Darcy. "Mr. Bradley can be our birdman—if, of course, a man in your dignified position will deign to such jocularity."

Bradley laughed. "I believe I might lower myself for the evening."

"Need you a pencil, or will your aging memory suffice?" Fitzwilliam asked.

"Do you wish to discover how much I recall about your boyhood?" Bradley crossed his arms.

Fitzwilliam raised hands in surrender. "Touché."

"If we are to play, you must all tell me your bird. Come now, form a line and tell the old man your choice." Bradley beckoned them close.

For the sake of his companions, Darcy joined them despite his discomfort. Only Miss Elizabeth's comfort and pleasure could have induced him to participate. Each whispered in his ear in turn then formed a circle around him.

"Now my aviary is complete, and one task is left to you all. Answer me these questions and tell me true: To which of my birds will you give your heart? To which will you confide your secret? From which will you pluck a feather? Answer me this and our game will commence." Bradley walked the circle and received whispered answers from each.

"So, tell us, Mr. Bradley, tell us!" Miss Kitty bounced in her chair.

"I have never encountered this result. All of you, save one, chose the peacock from which to take a feather. Mr. Collins, you owe seven forfeits."

Collins jumped to his feet. "Impossible. Utterly impossible. I expected a man of your position to be above cheating."

Darcy gasped. He barely caught his uncharitable words before they escaped.

"Mr. Collins, it is surprising, but these things can happen. In the spirit of the game, will you not play along?" Bradley cocked his head and lifted his brows. "Perhaps your trials in the storm this afternoon taxed you too much for high spirited activities."

Collins brushed his sleeves and muttered something under his breath. "I am sure you are right. I believe I will retire. Good night." He bowed and left.

"What a foul temper!" Miss Kitty sniffed. "I dare say he will wake with a nasty cold in the morning."

In the small hours of the morning, Darcy, Bradley and Fitzwilliam followed the ladies upstairs. Miss Kitty and Miss Bingley whispered and giggled on the stairs.

"It appears you are not quite ready to give up your gay company," Bradley said. "May I suggest you four ladies move to the apartment at the far end of the family wing, the one with the large dressing room? You might comfortably continue your confabulation without fear of disturbing anyone."

Miss Bingley's eyes widened. "Do we dare?"

Miss Kitty tittered behind her hand. "Mama would say we should take every opportunity of enjoying ourselves."

Darcy forced a smile. "Mr. Bradley's advice is always excellent."

Miss Elizabeth glanced at Bradley, then at Darcy. "It is a lovely idea." She wrapped her arm in Miss Bennet's. "We can be Mama's flock of 'titter mice' tonight."

Miss Kitty squealed and clapped softly. "Lydia will be sorry she chose not to come."

"So she shall," Miss Bennet said.

"Oh, this is a delightful plan." Miss Bingley grinned so like her brother, Darcy nearly laughed.

The ladies disappeared into the rooms Bradley had suggested.

Bingley trotted up the stairs behind them. "I assigned footmen to watch the hall as you asked, Mr. Bradley, though I do not understand the need."

"Without a married woman in the house to chaperone our engaged couple, it will ease my mind to have the ladies well-guarded." Bradley lifted his brows at Fitzwilliam.

"Surely you do not accuse me of impropriety?"

"I believe the best remedy of temptation is the assurance of being caught in one's transgression."

"I am wounded."

"Better that than the alternative." Bradley clapped Bingley's shoulder. "Thank you for indulging an old man's whims."

Bingley chuckled. "Any time I may oblige you is a pleasure, sir. Good night." He nodded and edged around them. His steps echoed in the hall, silencing with a shut door.

Darcy, Fitzwilliam and Bradley looked at one another.

"Before you ask, no, I would not station footmen if not for our other concerns." Bradley's eyebrows flashed upward.

"I am glad to hear—"

"I would stay the night in the corridor myself."

Fitzwilliam huffed. "I esteem her too much to dare—"

"I know, else I would have found some way to return them home this night."

Darcy elbowed Fitzwilliam.

Bradley winked. "You will do as we discussed?"

"Yes, we shall both take the room given Miss Elizabeth this afternoon." Darcy glanced toward the guest wing. "You think it is enough?"

"I will not sleep tonight. My door will remain open, and I will watch the hall, too. Even if he should somehow make it to their apartment, they will be safe together." Bradley nodded and trundled toward his room.

"Bradley's plans are sound. Come." Fitzwilliam lead them to the guest room Miss Elizabeth had occupied earlier.

The bed within was still mussed from her presence. Her fichu lay draped over the dressing table. The back of Darcy's neck burned. He ran a finger along the inside of his collar and swallowed hard.

Fitzwilliam dropped down on the bed and yanked off his boots.

"You cannot do it, can you?" Fitzwilliam laughed. "You cannot sleep in her bed."

Darcy harrumphed and untied his cravat.

"You are in a worse way than I thought. I suppose you will survive a night in a chair." He threw a pillow across the room.

Darcy caught it. "Thank you." He turned his back and unbuttoned his waistcoat. Sometimes Fitzwilliam's teasing went too far.

"Darce."

He looked over his shoulder and did not recognize the man who stared at him with haunted eyes and strained jaw.

"Do not mistake my levity. I am entirely cognizant of the seriousness of the situation." Shadows played on Fitzwilliam's face, specters of an officer's life Darcy would never truly understand.

"I had no doubt."

"You do intend to have a conversation with Bennet soon, do you not? Or must I drag you to Longbourn myself?"

"I prefer to speak with Miss Elizabeth first."

"Be sure not to gad about." Fitzwilliam tossed his waistcoat and jacket on the dressing table.

"Just because I do not plunge ahead in haste as you—"

Fitzwilliam lay down, crossed his ankles and threw an arm over his face. "Keep your pronouncements to yourself. Consider which one of us is happily betrothed right now."

Darcy rolled his eyes and blew out the candle. As he expected, the chair was hard and lumpy.

Collins paced his room. The waning candle flame cast uneasy shadows across the walls of the simple chamber—the smallest, shabbiest one in the guest wing. Water dripped from a leaky window onto the sill and overflowed to a puddle on the floor. Occasional flashes of lightning washed out the shadows, bathing the walls in an unearthly, eerie blue.

He strode to the door and pressed his ear against the wood. Finally, silence. Candlestick in hand, he stalked to the servant's door and entered the passage. Wavering flickers painted the plain walls. He paused to acclimate to his new environs. Now, which way? Ah, yes. He clucked his tongue softly and turned to his right. One, two, three doors. This was the one.

He held his breath and cracked the door. The hinges creaked. He cringed and stood rigid. No one stirred. Releasing the air from his lungs, he tiptoed inside.

His candle, a stub now, cast barely enough light to see where his feet fell, but he made his way to the bedside. He sat on the bed and reached for the sleeper's chest.

"What the bloody hell!" Fitzwilliam bolted upright.

Collins dropped the candle. The weak glow touched his shirt. It blossomed into flame.

"Good God!" Fitzwilliam shouted. "Fire! Fire!"

He beat at his blazing night shirt, threw open the door and plunged into the hallway.

Darcy sprang to his feet.

Fitzwilliam rushed towards Collins with a blanket. "Stop! Do not run!"

Collins shrieked as he ran. Bits of flaming cloth fell from his body. Nearby drapes burst into flames.

Darcy scrambled after him. Collins dashed through the guest wing and crashed through the tall window at the end of the hall. Broken glass showered down. His screams blended with those of the wind and rain.

Numbing gusts tore down the corridor, lending their power to the fire. Flames raced up the curtains as charred bits tumbled to the carpet and smoldered. The passageway glowed eerie orange.

"Fire!" Darcy bolted for the family wing, pounding on every door along the way.

Footmen dashed toward him. A loud crash and a scream—Bradley!

Fitzwilliam attacked the flames that threatened the stairway with the blanket. Smoke filled the space.

Miss Elizabeth and the other ladies poured into the hall, coughing and rubbing their eyes. Bingley appeared on their heels. Another blast of cold air whipped the blaze nearer. Miss Bingley screamed, her gown alight.

Darcy tackled her and smothered the flames in the carpet.

"Bradley's hurt! He cannot walk!" Fitzwilliam shouted and waved at the footmen. "You two, get him out."

The two men carried Bradley downstairs.

"Follow them," Fitzwilliam ordered. "Darcy, make sure they get out. I will wake the servants."

Miss Kitty and Miss Bennet hauled Miss Bingley to her feet. They dragged her toward the stairs.

Darcy grabbed Miss Elizabeth's elbow. "You must get out."

"Has everyone been accounted for?"

"We will confirm with the housekeeper." He pulled her along.

Outside, the storm pelted them with stinging, wind driven blows. He and Miss Elizabeth searched for the housekeeper. They found her near the kitchen door, gathering the staff around her.

"Is anyone missing?" Miss Elizabeth asked.

"Where is the nearest water source?" Darcy demanded.

"The cistern, sir, between the garden and the barn." The housekeeper pointed into the sheeting rains. "Miss, there are several…"

He sprinted toward the barn, calling to anyone within earshot. A pile of empty feed sacks lay near the door. He grabbed them and ran for the cistern. Two grooms met him halfway there. He threw bags at them. They soaked them in the cistern and several deep puddles nearby.

Laden with the sodden bags, they met the footmen on the way to the house. The five men charged inside, passing Fitzwilliam as he shepherded two frightened maids outside.

Smoke curtained the staircase, burning his eyes and clogging his lungs. He coughed, but plunged ahead, leading the servants to the fire. They beat the flames with the sopping feed sacks. Fitzwilliam and Bingley joined them with buckets of water kept re-filled by those outside.

Sometime before sunrise, the light from the blaze dimmed and died. Darcy's arms, heavy and numb, hung leaden at his side. "Look for embers." He pushed one groom to his right and another to his left.

Fitzwilliam leaned against the wall and panted. "Bingley, take the footmen and go upstairs."

Bingley nodded and rushed away.

Darcy and Fitzwilliam dragged downstairs and patrolled each room. One blurred into another, until at last, they paced through the final chamber and trudged outside.

The sun peeked through the last of the rainclouds and ignited a brilliant sunrise. The few remaining drops of rain dwindled into nothing.

Darcy's lungs screamed, every muscle protested. He had to find Miss Elizabeth.

A small hand wrapped around his elbow. Elizabeth! The world wavered. She was here and safe. He laid his fingers over hers and squeezed.

"I am relieved to see you." She swallowed hard.

"The fire is out. How many were injured?"

"We believe Mr. Bradley's ankle is broken. Your

quick actions spared Miss Bingley serious burns. One of the maids is burned badly and another sports cuts from broken glass."

"What of Mr. Collins?"

Miss Elizabeth shook her head and led him around the side of the house. "It no longer matters." She pointed to a dark heap lying in a puddle.

Darcy stepped forward. Cold rainwater splashed under his still bare feet. The shape in the mud was a man. He knelt and rolled the body. Collins stared at him with empty, lifeless eyes.

His gut churned. Bile coated his tongue. A heavy hand landed on his shoulder.

Fitzwilliam hunkered down beside him. "I wager he broke his neck in the fall." He picked up a shard of glass. Sunlight glinted off the bloody edge. "After what he did, I cannot say this is not fitting."

"It is not for us to make such judgments." Darcy pushed himself to his feet and rubbed his hands on his breeches. "This sight is not fit for a lady."

"Darcy is correct." Fitzwilliam rose. "Leave him. I will tell the grooms to put the body in the barn. I hope that is agreeable to you, Miss Elizabeth. I understand he is your cousin…"

"Let it be done as you suggest. I cannot thank you both enough." She dabbed her eyes with her sleeve.

Fitzwilliam wiped his hands on his shirt and hurried off.

She held her fist to her mouth. "Forgive me, this is all so…"

Darcy pulled her to his chest. She trembled and clung to him. He pressed his cheek to the top of her head.

"Was it as Mr. Bradley anticipated?" she whispered.

"He dropped the candle on his shirt when he found Fitzwilliam in your place." He rubbed her back. "The material thing is you and your sisters are safe. He cannot harm you further."

She gasped. "Mama—oh, Mama will be devastated and Papa—"

"I shall call for a carriage to take you to Longbourn immediately, before they get news of what happened."

"Yes, yes, but all of you must come with us. Netherfield is not fit for habitation, and Mr. Bradley will need the attentions of the surgeon." She looked up at him with enormous, pleading eyes.

Only those eyes could have induced him to leave with so much work to be done. "I will call for the coaches."

Chapter 15

"MR. BENNET! OH, MR. BENNET!"

Bennet belted his dressing gown and dashed into the hall. Fanny's shriek shattered his nerves. He led the way down the stairs, Lydia and Fanny close on his heels. Hill stood near the front door.

Loud raps echoed against the foyer walls.

"What is this? Are we to be murdered in our beds?" Fanny clutched her chest with one hand and Lydia's arm with the other.

He rolled his eyes and wrenched the door open.

Jane and Lizzy shivered in the doorway. Kitty peeked above their shoulders. Clad in night dresses and wraps, their faces were sooty and hair disheveled.

"What is going on?"

"Please, Papa, may we come in?" Jane pointed behind her. "Mr. Bradley is injured."

He stepped aside. "Injured, how?"

The girls parted. Fitzwilliam and Darcy carried Bradley inside. Hill led them to a chair and shoved a footstool in place.

"We fear his ankle is broken." Lizzy scooted past.

Miss Bingley, Jane, Kitty and Bingley filed in behind her.

"Lydia, call the maids and tell them to heat water." Fanny pointed upstairs. "And fetch a wrap for Miss Bingley. She is shivering so hard I hear her teeth chattering."

Lydia scurried off.

"You smell like smoke." Bennet made his way to Bradley. "I insist you tell me what happened."

Fitzwilliam turned to him. "A fire, this morning at Netherfield."

"Good God." Bennet staggered.

Lizzy pulled a chair close. "Sit down, Papa." She pushed his shoulder gently until he sank into the seat.

Jane encouraged her mother to the settee and held her hands.

"I am sorry to inform you, sir," Darcy glanced at Lizzy, "Mr. Collins has been killed."

Fanny screeched.

Bennet jumped to his feet and dashed to her side. He gathered her into his arms. "Jane, help her to her rooms."

She wrapped her arm around her mother's waist and urged her toward the stairs.

"You should go, too, Kitty." He closed his eyes and shook his head. How long would this shock keep Fanny to her apartments?

"May I take Miss Bingley to my room?" Kitty asked.

"Yes, yes!" Bennet waved them upstairs. "What

happened to Collins?"

"His nightshirt caught fire. He ran and fell through a second floor window." Fitzwilliam looked from Bradley to Darcy.

Their expressions revealed little. Bennet focused on Lizzy. She dodged his gaze and leaned toward Darcy. What had Collins done?

"Was anyone else seriously hurt?" He reached for Lizzy's hand.

"Just a clumsy old man who tripped getting out of bed." Bradley laughed with none of his usual enthusiasm.

"I will send for the surgeon directly." Bennet rubbed his eyes. "Hill, show Mr. Bingley to a guest room and make Mr. Bradley comfortable here. You—" he eyed Darcy, Elizabeth and Fitzwilliam in turn, "join me in the study."

"Yes, sir," Hill squeaked and disappeared upstairs with Bingley.

Lizzy turned to Bradley and pulled a breath.

He lifted his hand. "No, I am fine. You do not need to sit with me. So long as I do not move from my chair, I shall be quite well."

Bennet pointed toward his study. His cold, leaden limbs protested every step.

He stirred the fireplace to life and poured brandy for them all. Lizzy perched on her stool, and he eased into his chair. "I have been on thorns waiting for you to return since I found my study in this state: your mother's journals on my chair, books on the floor, this volume inside your writing desk?" He raised the book Gardiner had given him. "None of this is like you. I can only imagine this is connected to your unexpected visit to Netherfield."

"Papa—" Lizzy bit her lip.

"If you will permit me, sir." Darcy took the book and removed a letter from the pages. "This will answer many of your questions."

Bennet's eyebrows rose very high. The note was addressed to Lizzy. He opened the paper with a snap.

"Please read it. I expect you will find sufficient grounds to forgive my indiscretion."

"Papa—"

He raised his hand for silence and read. Blood drained first from his face, then his fingers. He laid the missive aside and stared at his daughter.

"We had just received word of this by our aunt's steward and—" Fitzwilliam said.

"—determined you should know." Darcy glanced at Lizzy. "I thought it best—"

"—I should tell you." Lizzy laid her hand on Bennet's. "I waited in the study for you to return so I might talk to you, but Mr. Collins…"

"What did he do?" He clutched her cold fingers.

"He came in and insisted I must marry him. I refused and…"

"Collins frightened you, and you fled?" Bennet barely whispered the words. What had he done when he gave Collins permission to offer for her?

She nodded.

"You went to Netherfield, and he followed?" He squeezed his temples. "Has the fire anything to do with this sordid affair?"

Darcy and Fitzwilliam winced.

"Out, both of you. I will speak to my daughter alone." He shooed them out and shut the door.

Bennet sat beside her on the stool. Questions stabbed his heart as they fought for voice. "What happened at Netherfield?"

"What does it matter now? He is gone, and we are not harmed. Do not torture yourself—"

"Who else should feel the sting? It was my responsibility to protect you."

"We are well—"

He glanced at the closed door. "Thanks to the intervention of other men."

"Should we not be grateful for whatever means Providence provided for our protection?"

Her hand trembled under his. He pressed his palm to her cheek. "My dear girl."

"I shall rejoice in our escape and that we need fear him no longer." Her voice broke, and she covered her face with her hands.

He held her tightly. How long since his little girl had wept upon his shoulder? He swallowed hard.

She sniffled and pulled back. "I am well now and will think no more of it. I am determined to remember the past only as it gives me pleasure."

He rubbed tears off her cheeks with his thumbs and kissed the top of her head. "I dearly hope that is all you require." It would not be enough for him.

"I should go and assist Hill with our guests." She stood.

He walked with her and opened the door only to stand toe to toe with Darcy. Doubtless he had stood there this entire time.

Lizzy looked up at Darcy as she passed. Her eyes brightened, and the tiny smile she used to save for her papa, she gave to him. Of all times, why now?

Their eyes met. Bennet's heart pinched. He ushered Darcy in and shut the door.

The next morning, Darcy let himself into the small parlor arranged for Bradley's use. The sunlight danced along the curtains and cast shadows announcing the impending afternoon. A day bed had been moved in from another room for his comfort. Far more pillows and blankets than he needed surrounded him. Bradley seemed to enjoy the attentions and accepted them all graciously.

A breakfast tray with crumb-laden dishes balanced precariously on a small table. His appetite gave hope that his injuries might not be as severe as once feared.

"The surgeon should arrive soon," Darcy said softly.

Bradley jumped and grimaced. "Do not tip-toe around me, boy! You will convince me I am some sort of an invalid, rather than simply a clumsy old man!"

Darcy helped him sit up. "You are not so light on your feet right now."

"I suppose not. Do not worry for me. I will mend soon enough."

"I will see to that."

"Your concern is touching." Bradley studied him, bushy eyebrows lifted. He cocked his head, asking without asking.

Darcy dragged a chair close and sat. "I spoke to Mr. Bennet last night."

"A conversation of a personal nature?" Bradley scooted back, plumping pillows with his elbows.

Darcy ran his fingers along the inside of his cravat. "Yes."

"What did he say?"

"He had reservations."

"You are offended."

"Of course, I am." Darcy raked his hair. "I know you will tell me a wise man overlooks offense, but—"

"He did not voice objections to Fitzwilliam?"

How did Bradley maintain his irritating, implacable calm? "No."

"What was the nature of his complaints?"

"He expressed concerns for my solvency since his daughter's dowry is insufficient to replace Georgiana's fortune."

"And?"

"And he echoed the drivel Collins spouted about his daughter leaving the sphere to which she was born."

"How did you answer?"

"My solicitor can attest to my financial state. As to the other, I am a gentleman, she a gentleman's daughter. We are equals."

"But not in wealth or connection."

Darcy sprang from the chair and paced along the fireplace. "I care not for that! I have found a woman with whom I might find what my father did with my mother. That is the connection I regard."

Bradley nodded slowly. "He denied you?"

"No. He said I am the kind of man to whom he could deny nothing."

"I am bewildered. What is the nature of your distress? We talked of these same concerns ourselves."

Darcy slapped the mantle. "Dash it all! After what happened, the service we rendered his daughters, he of all people, has no right to reservations."

"Ahh, I understand now. Sit, I do not need you

tearing about whilst I try to talk." Bradley pointed.

"I do not—"

"Sit!"

Darcy muttered under his breath and dropped into the chair. "I suppose you are about to tell me—"

"You have no idea of what I am about to tell you, so be still and allow me the privilege." Bradley glowered until he stopped fidgeting. "That is better. Whilst I cannot violate the confidence, I am familiar with a bit of the Bennet family's history. I know enough to realize Bennet feels his failure to protect his daughter most acutely."

"So to acquit himself, he will defend her from the wrong man? He let Collins—"

"Collins is dead. Bennet cannot take action against him. He is trying to soothe his conscience by rising to the occasion with you."

"How absurd! I will not stand for it."

"I agree. It does not make sense. Yet, many times people make little sense. Still, you may choose whether to stand for it or not." Bradley leaned back and gazed at the ceiling. "I suppose you can storm out of here—"

Darcy sputtered.

"Do not argue. I have watched you stalk away enough times. Though, if you do it here, I recommend you do not try to return. Bennet's offense will be far greater than mine."

Darcy dragged his hands down his face and groaned.

"You may opt to set aside your pride and allow Bennet to save face. Grant him permission to be imperfect. After all he gave you leave to ask Miss Elizabeth."

"Without his blessing?"

"If she is pleased, he will approve readily enough. Be patient." Bradley chuckled. "Not what you were raised to expect, is it? Always commended on what a catch you would make; sought by the brightest lights of the *ton*; only to have a grumpy, embarrassed father grumble at you because you rescued his daughter instead of him."

Darcy chewed his lip.

"What is she worth to you?"

What indeed? Could words describe?

The front door opened and muffled voices filtered through the door.

Darcy rose and straightened his coat. "Thank you. I will leave you to the surgeon."

Elizabeth kept company in the parlor, reading, while Jane, Miss Bingley, Colonel Fitzwilliam and Mr. Bingley played cards. Kitty sketched and chatted with the card players, a pencil clutched between her teeth and another in her hand. Lydia sat with Mama and worked on the trim of an old bonnet.

She struggled to focus on the page, but the words kept blurring. The previous day's events played over and over in her mind. So much needed to be done at Netherfield! Her fingers itched for one of Kitty's pencils to start making a list.

Papa appeared in the doorway and beckoned her. She dropped the book on the table and hurried to him. Thrice she had read the same passage, each time to less and less effect. A break would be most welcome.

She followed him to his bookroom. His shoulders sagged, and his eyes were far too solemn.

"Is Mr. Bradley unwell? Did Mr. Whittington—"

Papa rested on the edge of his desk. "No, he is well. The ankle is only badly sprained. If he follows advice, his convalescence should be brief."

"Then what troubles you?"

"Mr. Darcy asked for a private audience with you."

"Oh." Prickles, first cold, then hot, ran across her face.

"You need not meet with him unless you honestly desire to do so. His fortune and consequence are of little account, except you truly like him."

She tried to bite her upper lip to restrain her smile, but it would not be contained. "I do, Papa. I like him very much." She wrung her hands in her lap. "More than like him, I believe I love him, so dearly. He is truly one of the best men I have ever known."

Papa cleared his throat. "He waits for you in the garden." He pointed through the window.

"Yes, Papa." She kissed his cheek and rushed out.

Her feet would not submit to a proper ladylike pace on the path. She stumbled on a stepping stone, barely catching herself from a fall. Two deep breaths steadied her.

"Miss Elizabeth." Mr. Darcy quickly closed the distance between them. A dimpled smile spread across his face.

She gazed up at him, conscious of her heartbeat, like a butterfly in the wind.

"Would you walk with me?"

She took his arm, and they set off along the graveled path through Mama's roses.

The day's warmth already edged out the morning's

freshness. Heady fragrance filled the air as the breeze whispered among the canes.

"My mother loved roses, too. She once had a lovely rose garden, though I do not think it has been maintained since her passing." He glanced at her. "My mother was an unconventional woman. Although born to the highest circles, she cared little for society and treasured her role as Mistress of Pemberley. She loved the estate and its people and disdained women like, forgive my bluntness, Miss Caroline, who only saw their estates as a means to a lifestyle." They walked several steps in silence. "As a result, she was not welcomed among certain circles of the *ton*. Some, I am told, made her the brunt of the little barbs and cruelties exchanged between those with nothing better to take up their time."

"Not everyone has the wherewithal to stand up for their principles in the face of such censure," she whispered.

His fingers tightened delightfully over hers.

"When I return to Pemberley, after Mr. Bradley is sufficiently recovered to travel, of course, I…I do not wish to return alone." He stared at her.

She cocked her head and knit her brow.

"You do not understand my meaning?"

"I am afraid I do not. You just said Mr. Bradley would travel with you. So you will not be traveling alone."

"I believe I detect a small falsehood, Miss Elizabeth." His lips twitched into a mischievous non-smile.

How handsome! His dimples—she had never seen anything like them. Her breath caught in her throat.

"You deserve to hear my intentions declared as clearly as I feel them. I think from the moment I encountered you in the woods, I hoped you might consider a life on an estate somewhat larger than Longbourn."

"You seek to replace your housekeeper? You did not tell me yours was to be leaving you."

He threw his head back and laughed heartily.

Several birds took to wing.

"I shall never have a dull moment with you, though I am not certain I should continue to encourage this penchant of yours to willfully misunderstand me."

"I believe someone must tease you, sir. Has not Mr. Bradley warned that you are too serious for your years?"

"Indeed, though surely you understand my housekeeper has not the privilege of teasing the Master of Pemberley." He stopped before her, his face very close to hers. "Only one much closer to me may claim the license."

Warm breath tickled her forehead and stroked her eyelashes, the air thick with tension. He caressed her cheek with his fingertips.

Could he feel the way she trembled at his touch?

His thumb grazed her temple, but she felt his caress all the way down her spine.

"I have long thought you the handsomest woman of my acquaintance. Allow me to tell you how ardently I admire and love you."

Her heart soared with the birds.

"You are too generous to trifle with me, my dear Miss Elizabeth. My affections and wishes are unchanged from that first moment. But one word from you will silence me on this subject."

She drew breath to speak, but he laid a finger

across her lips.

"Please, allow me to finish." He lifted her hand to his lips, never taking his eyes from hers. "You were as beautiful with soot on your cheek, and the curl at the nape of your neck escaping its pin as you were at the assembly. Yours is a beauty beyond that of other women, penetrating to the very depth of your soul." He dropped to his knee and cradled her hands in his. "Say you will be my wife…Elizabeth."

"Yes, I…I…will."

He stood and pulled her closer still and kissed her, softly at first, then ardently.

Was it wanton that she enjoyed the taste of his lips?

He wrapped her in his arms. His warmth penetrated the core of her being; completing what she did not know had been only half-formed. She leaned in for another kiss and lost herself in the storm of passion.

Little by little, his kisses grew softer, and he relinquished his hold. She laid her head on his shoulder, softly panting in the afterglow.

A deep laugh rumbled through his chest, and he pulled back and looked at her.

What a wonderful sound! His children would always remember him for it. "What do you find so amusing at a moment like this?"

"When I first came to Meryton, finding a wife was the farthest thing from my mind. Indeed, Mr. Bradley and I discussed the unlikelihood."

"It does seem the ways of Providence are not as our ways." She swallowed a giggle and grinned. "To think, I have agreed to marry a trespasser and a thief!"

He stared at her, mouth agape, then dissolved in peals of laughter.

What a fitting beginning!

The next day, after Mr. Darcy, Mr. Bingley and Colonel Fitzwilliam left to attend to matters at Netherfield, Elizabeth escaped to the still room. News of her engagement had sent Mama into a flurry of list writing and Kitty into a sketching frenzy. As much as she enjoyed Mama's unmitigated approval, she longed for a bit of quiet solitude. In the midst of drying flowers and herbs, curing soap and steeping scents, she lost herself in the unmoving air, heavy with fragrance.

"Lizzy?" Lydia peeked in.

She tied off the bundle of lavender and laid it aside with the others. "Yes?"

Lydia bounced in and dropped onto the high wooden stool. "Mama talks of little else than your engagement to Mr. Darcy. She thought you would never marry, and look—you secured such an eligible man! She told Hill to start making plans for a properly grand wedding breakfast and is off to visit Aunt Philips to talk of lace and wedding clothes." She picked at dry buds scattered on the table top.

Elizabeth shoved a stray lock of hair behind her ear. Why had she expected discretion from Mama? "I am pleased to hear Mama's spirits are restored. I feared the events at Netherfield would vex her—"

"La! Lizzy—tell me—is it true?"

"Is what true?"

"That he kissed you after he made you an offer? Was that how you accepted him?"

"No, I did not accept him that way, but yes,

he…I…we…" Her cheeks heated.

Lydia grinned and sucked in a deep breath.

"Please, allow Mr. Darcy and me the privilege of announcing it ourselves, at least to those Mama does not tell today. Give us a few days before you take the news all over town."

Lydia's shoulders fell. "That is not fair! You would deny all my pleasures. It is bad enough you and Jane are both marrying, and so soon after Mary. You know, I should have been the first but for your interference—"

Elizabeth's sigh progressed into a grumble. "Do not begin again. Have you truly learned nothing?"

Lydia's bottom lip extended in her classic pout. She wrapped her arms around her waist and huffed. "No, I learned."

"I am glad." She studied her sister's face.

Lydia's eyes shone. Her lips drooped at the corners with no hint of affectation.

"I learned something, too."

"What did you learn? You already know everything."

A puff of wind rattled the drying herbs overhead. They whispered together, sharing secrets.

"In truth, I know very little." Elizabeth's soft voice hung in the sweet and savory fragrances of the still room. "You knew better about Mr. Collins than I."

Lydia's head snapped up, and her mouth hung open.

"You were entirely right regarding his character. I should have listened to you sooner—"

"It would not have mattered. Papa never attends me." She tucked her chin into her chest.

"I am sorry." Elizabeth edged around the table and

stood near Lydia.

"Oh!" Lydia slumped even further. "That is just the thing! Nothing I do or say or think or anything at all, none of it matters. It is all about Mary and Jane and you. You have done the family proud with the husbands you caught. Why can I not do something that…that…" She collapsed in tears.

She slipped her arm over Lydia's shuddering shoulders. "I am sorry for ignoring you. I was wrong. You were very sensible about Mr. Collins, and I am proud of you."

"But no one paid me any mind then, and no one ever will. No one pays attention to me at all."

"It can be difficult to be the youngest among so many sisters."

"You have no idea." Lydia laid her head on Elizabeth's shoulder.

"Have you considered that once Jane and I are married only you and Kitty will be here for Mama to fuss over?"

Lydia looked up, eyes wide.

"And until then, we shall make every effort to see you are part of all our preparations."

Lydia flung her arms around Elizabeth. "Oh, thank you!"

"Just promise to forgive me and that you will continue to spend at least five minutes of every day in a sensible fashion."

Lydia giggled.

Bennet picked his way around the trunks and boxes piled in the hallway. Just this morning, Mrs. Bennet demanded they be removed, lest the guests for the wedding breakfast see them. Thankfully, Bingley had offered space at Netherfield.

Five weeks had passed in a flurry. Banns were read, wedding clothes—so many clothes—ordered, wedding dresses sewn, trunks packed and repacked. Everything in his life seemed in a whirlwind.

He slipped into the study and fell into his favorite chair. All the lumps and bumps in the seat matched his own. At least some things would not change.

Bennet was not by his nature a reflective man. Reflection tended to bring on discomfort and discontent. But his house—and his life—were already in disarray on the cusp of his daughters' weddings. A little reflection would hardly worsen his discomfiture. Everything around him was changing. Change brought disorder and discomfort. Change took away…

A lump rose in his throat. He stood and locked the door. A visit to the brandy decanter, and he returned to his chair.

Many believed daughters held little consequence to a father. He sipped his brandy and leaned back. Society told him he should want fine, strapping sons—an heir and a spare to inherit his estate and carry on his name. But he did not.

Oh, he had intended to father a son, to be sure, but his heart had not been in it. Perhaps that was why Fanny only conceived daughters. So his father had argued when he scolded Bennet for not producing the required heir. As if a father's will could influence the choices of Providence. He shook his head and closed his eyes.

Though he would never say the words aloud, it

was best this way. After living with his father and a brother who just was like his sire, he did not trust himself with sons. A son might be like his grandfather or like Collins's father. He shuddered. No, far better to have daughters.

Upon daughters, a man might dote and delight, rather than try to shape them into his image. He laced his fingers and rubbed his thumbs together. His daughters satisfied all his domestic desires, except for one thing. They were leaving.

True, he hardly missed Mary, but Jane and especially Lizzy were his girls. Jane read to him. She had the most delightful reading voice. Lizzy played chess with him and was the one with whom he discussed and debated. Only yesterday, he had bounced them on his knees, taught them to love the classics and to reason.

He pulled his top lip down over his teeth. Emptiness seized his belly. What he would give to turn back time and be with his little girls again! He stroked his chin.

On the other hand, even now, he tolerated Fitzwilliam's company well enough. Though he would not admit it aloud, even Darcy's presence grew more and more tolerable as well. Perhaps he might be welcome wherever Jane and Fitzwilliam settled or perhaps even at Pemberley. Then, if…no…*when* children came, his grandchildren, he would be the grandfather his girls never had. Surely one among them would have Jane's disposition and another Lizzy's. He might be able to recapture those days after all.

A week later, on a bright Saturday morning, Bradley waited in a small room at the back of the Meryton church with Darcy and Fitzwilliam.

"The Gardiners just arrived." Bradley slapped their backs. "Whoever would have thought Miss Maddie's nieces would be your wives or that you would have gotten yourselves wives here? How mysterious are the ways of Providence."

Darcy shook his head and adjusted his collar.

"Do stop, or you shall ruin the fine knot your valet tied for you." Fitzwilliam elbowed him in the ribs.

"I am far more interested in the one my vicar shall tie."

Bradley cleared his throat. "You both are richly blessed with your young ladies."

"You have never spoken truer words, sir." Fitzwilliam grinned.

"I could tell you many things right now, but I shall limit myself to one." He leaned on his cane and peered at them. "Men often make much of the Good Book's injunction for the wife to obey her husband. I would remind you of the similar command upon you. Husbands love your wives, even as Christ also loved the church, and gave Himself for it. As our Savior laid Himself down as a servant to His church and sacrificed Himself for her, so too, are you to offer yourselves to your wives. If you remember this, it will go well for you."

"You said something similar to my father, did you not?" Darcy lifted an eyebrow.

"How do you know?"

"His journals. He called it a lesson hard learnt, but most worthwhile."

"See you do not take as long as he did to understand. Take it to heart, and I believe you will enjoy the same felicity in marriage he did. Come now, it is time."

They followed him to the front.

Darcy cast a sidelong glance at the pews. Lord and Lady Matlock, the Viscount, his wife and Fitzwilliam's sister filled the first row. Georgiana caught his eye and smiled, an excited tremor in her shoulders. She had always longed for a sister.

Bingley and Miss Bingley sat beside Georgiana. They had made a special journey back to Meryton from London, where they had withdrawn following the fire at Netherfield. The two youngest Bennet sisters sat nearby, and the Pierces sat just behind them. Marriage clearly agreed with them both.

The Gardiners sat near the front with Mrs. Bennet. Her eldest daughters married and the opportunity to entertain peers in her home—if a woman could have been happier, he could not imagine it.

Bradley called them to order and a hush filled the room.

Mr. Bennet walked down the center of the church, a daughter on each arm.

Darcy was certain Miss Bennet was lovely, but he saw only his Elizabeth.

Bradley's strong voice filled the sanctuary. "Dearly beloved, we are gathered together here in the sight of God, and in the face of this congregation, to join together this Man and this Woman, Richard and Jane, and this Man and this Woman, Fitzwilliam and Elizabeth, in holy Matrimony; which is an honorable estate, instituted of God in the time of man's innocency, signifying unto us the mystical union that is betwixt Christ and His Church..."

Darcy had heard these words before, yet they never had meant what they meant now.

"...not by any to be enterprised, nor taken in hand, unadvisedly, lightly, or wantonly, to satisfy men's carnal lusts and appetites, like brute beasts that have no understanding; but reverently, discreetly, advisedly, soberly, and in the fear of God; duly considering the causes for which Matrimony was ordained."

Darcy glanced at Fitzwilliam. Serenity bathed his countenance, melting years and troubles away.

"First, it was ordained for the procreation of children, to be brought up in the fear and nurture of the Lord, and to the praise of His holy Name.

"Secondly, it was ordained for a remedy against sin, and to avoid fornication; that such persons as have not the gift of continency might marry, and keep themselves undefiled members of Christ's body

"Thirdly, it was ordained for the mutual society, help, and comfort, that the one ought to have of the other, both in prosperity and adversity. Into which holy estate these two couples here present come now to be joined."

Darcy turned to Elizabeth, his dearest, loveliest Elizabeth. His completion, his helpmeet, his comfort, his love. She blinked slowly and nodded. She loved him, too!

"Wilt thou have this Woman to thy wedded Wife, to live together after God's ordinance in the holy estate of Matrimony? Wilt thou love her, comfort her, honor, and keep her in sickness and in health; and, forsaking all others, keep thee only unto her, so long as ye both shall live?"

Together Fitzwilliam and Darcy replied, "I will."

Bradley's eyes shimmered. "Wilt thou have this Man to thy wedded Husband, to live together after God's ordinance in the holy estate of Matrimony? Wilt thou obey him, and serve him, love, honor, and keep him in sickness and in health; and, forsaking all others, keep thee only unto him, so long as ye both shall live?"

"I will."

Those words, the sweetest she ever uttered, would surely echo in his memory all of his days.

The next few moments blurred past until someone pressed the cold, golden band into his hand.

"With this Ring I thee wed, with my Body I thee worship, and with all my worldly Goods I thee endow: In the Name of the Father, and of the Son, and of the Holy Ghost. Amen."

He slipped it on her finger and helped her kneel beside him.

"Let us pray.

"Eternal God, Creator and Preserver of all mankind, Giver of all spiritual grace, the Author of everlasting life, send thy blessing upon these thy servants, this Man and this Woman and this Man and this Woman, whom we bless in thy Name; and may they ever remain in perfect love and peace together, and live according to thy laws, through Jesus Christ our Lord. Those whom God hath joined together let no man put asunder.

"Forasmuch as they have consented together in holy Wedlock, and witnessed the same before God and this company, and thereto given and pledged their troth either to the other, and declared the same by giving and receiving of a Ring, and by joining of hands; I pronounce that they be Man and Wife together, In the Name of the Father, and of the Son, and of the Holy Ghost. Amen."

He helped her to her feet, and they turned to face their friends, their family and the rest of their lives, man and wife.

Acknowledgments

So many people have helped me along the journey taking this from an idea to a reality.

.Barb, Audrey, and Matt thank you so much for cold reading and being honest!, Jan, Kathryn, Debra Anne, and Gayle your proofreading is worth your weight in gold!

My dear friend Cathy, my biggest cheerleader, you have kept me from chickening out more than once!

And my sweet sister Gerri who believed in even those first attempts that now live in the file drawer!

Other Books by Maria Grace

Given Good Principles Series:
Darcy's Decision
The Future Mrs. Darcy
All the Appearance of Goodness
Twelfth Night at Longbourn

Given Good Principles Series:
Mistaking Her Character
The Trouble to Check Her

Remember the Past
The Darcy Brothers
The Darcys' First Christmas
A Jane Austen Christmas: Regency Christmas Traditions (non-fiction)
A Spot of Sweet Tea: Hopes and Beginnings (short story collection)

Short Stories:
Four Days in April
Sweet Ginger
Last Dance
Not Romantic
To Forget

Available in paperback, e-book, and audiobook format at all online bookstores.

On Line Exclusives at:

www.http//RandomBitsofFascination.com

Bonus and deleted scenes
Regency Life Series

Free e-books:

Bits of Bobbin Lace
The Scenes Jane Austen Never Wrote: First Anniversaries
Half Agony, Half Hope: New Reflections on Persuasion
Four Days in April
Jane Bennet in January
February Aniversaries

About the Author

Though Maria Grace has been writing fiction since she was ten years old, those early efforts happily reside in a file drawer and are unlikely to see the light of day again, for which many are grateful. After penning five file-drawer novels in high school, she took a break from writing to pursue college and earn her doctorate in Educational Psychology. After 16 years of university teaching, she returned to her first love, fiction writing.

She has one husband, two graduate degrees and two black belts, three sons, four undergraduate majors, five nieces, six new novels in the works, attended seven period balls, sewn eight Regency era costumes, shared her life with nine cats through the years and published her tenth book in 2015.

She can be contacted at:

author.MariaGrace@gmail.com

Facebook:
http://facebook.com/AuthorMariaGrace

On Amazon.com:
http://amazon.com/author/mariagrace

Random Bits of Fascination
(http://RandomBitsofFascination.com)

Austen Variations (http://AustenVariations.com)

English Historical Fiction Authors
(http://EnglshHistoryAuthors.blogspot.com)

White Soup Press (http://whitesouppress.com/)

On Twitter @WriteMariaGrace

On Pinterest: http://pinterest.com/mariagrace423/

Printed in Great Britain
by Amazon